INFILTRATION

Infiltration Series (Book 1)

SUSANNA ROGERS

Bucher & Reid

Bucher & Reid

Cover by Amygdala Book Design

978-0-6481868-1-6

DEDICATION

To my buddy, James,
because you're the best

.

ALSO BY SUSANNA ROGERS

Regeneration (Book 2) – out soon
Validation (Book 3) – out soon

ACKNOWLEDGMENTS

I have too many people to thank and can't possibly do this in any particular order. I'm also very nervous I may have left someone out. A big thanks to James Rogers, Louis Rogers, Chris Kunz, Michael Cain, Lotte Plumb, Josie Kelly, Sacha Pulsford, Sophia Robbins, Annie Sommer, Stephanie Swain and a special mention to Taya Lunn because I made you cry and that made me very happy.

The list goes on – thanks to Claire Boston, Lorraine Mauvais, Juanita Kees, Teena Raffa-Mulligan and Anna Jacobs. Also to my technical and medical experts Tessa Plumb, Nick Stott, Tony Rogers, Andrew Tran, Jo Taylor and Brendan Murphy.

INFILTRATION

It wasn't supposed to happen this way. I was lying on something soft but prickly, something that felt a lot like grass. Smelled like grass too. Propping my head up, I looked around and saw trees, garden beds, a bench and a small playground. This was all wrong. I wasn't in bed…and I was naked.

The sun was low, the air crisp, almost as if it was an ordinary morning. I'd been told that between the distance and the time, the trip would take it out of me and it had, but I couldn't let that hold me back.

Sucking in deep breaths, I surveyed my surroundings and took stock of the situation. The distinct lack of clothing was a problem and I still had to work out where I was and make my way to my new home, hopefully not too many obstacles.

Then I noticed a newspaper on the bench. An actual newspaper. I stumbled to my feet, my eyes riveted to the paper as I walked across and picked it up. *I'd made it!*

Things were going my way after all. The park looked familiar now that I'd had a chance to get my bearings. Having already checked out the general area using satellite footage, I was reasonably sure this place wasn't far from my new home.

And sheets of newspaper could double as clothing or provide some sort of coverage or I'd be spotted in an instant. I screwed up a sheet in each hand, trying to cover the front of my body as best I could. It was better than nothing. Or maybe not.

A high-pitched yelp cut through the air. Made me jump. I'd let my guard down. Then I saw him approaching, coming closer, scampering toward me. Sure, he looked like a white terrier puppy chasing a ball onto the grass but he might actually be an enemy scout. At the very least, he had an owner who might see me and that was bad, very bad.

I had to get out of there, and quick, so I dropped the newspaper and ran to hide in some bushes. Strange organic smells wafted to my nostrils, like those of mulch and greenery, or perhaps that wasn't so strange given my location. Meanwhile the puppy picked up the tennis ball in his mouth and raced toward me, dropping the ball at my feet. He barked again.

"Ssshhh, little fella," I whispered, ruffling his silky fur. I picked up the ball and threw it across the front of the park so it landed further down the road, then hid back in the bushes.

The terrier scooted on down the street, closely followed by his owner, a middle-aged man wearing headphones. Crouched in position, I breathed a sigh of relief and waited until they passed. I hadn't been seen, after all. Time for my getaway. I eyed the crumpled newspaper on the bench, wondering if I should I cover myself or run. *Run.*

I sprinted in the other direction – past houses with

front gardens and cars parked on the street, past all these things that looked normal, only none of this was normal.

My new house finally in sight, I ran faster than I'd ever run before, across the front yard and down the side path. By the time I reached the back door, my lungs were burning from exertion. I doubled over and caught my breath.

When I tried the door, I found it was locked – something else that wasn't supposed to happen. I couldn't even kick the stupid thing in for fear of making too much noise, so I tiptoed back down the side path and climbed the tree that was wedged between the house and the neighbor's. Hopefully it would get me to my bedroom. Talk about undignified. Naked tree climbing was definitely not a good start to the day.

The window was open and a second after I jumped inside, there was a knock at my bedroom door.

Things were about to get more complicated.

CHAPTER ONE

"You're running late, Nicola honey."

Honey? Did people really say that around here?

As if waking up naked in the park wasn't bad enough, now I was going to be late for my first day. I was organized. I was used to military precision. Hey, I *liked* military precision.

Opening the door a few inches, I stuck my head around the edge. "I'll get dressed now, Mother."

"Mother? Since when did you become so formal?" Her brow furrowed. "You haven't even had a shower yet. And don't forget your robe."

How did she know? I closed the door and grabbed the pink toweling robe hanging on a hook. Pink? I was definitely not the sort of delicate feminine creature who liked pink. Someone had got that part wrong.

After taking the world's quickest shower in the bathroom down the hallway, I threw on my school uniform, a blue skirt and white top that were the perfect camouflage for the day. Fumbling through the shoes piled at the bottom of the closet, I had trouble finding anything decent until I noticed a pair of functional black leather lace-ups. They'd do.

Downstairs, Mother was fussing in the kitchen while a man sat at the table, his head over a newspaper, a cup of coffee in his hand. *Father*. He was slightly overweight, hairline receding, his brown hair cropped short. Lifting his gaze, a smile lit up his face and his blue eyes sparkled.

"Don't I get a good morning from my girl?" he asked.

"Morning," I said in the brightest voice I could muster, adding heartily, "Dad."

He took a sip of his coffee. "That wasn't too hard now, was it?"

He had no idea.

I glanced at the clock on the wall. "I've got to get going."

Getting to his feet, he leaned over and kissed me on the cheek. Stunned, I wasn't sure what to do so I thought about everything I'd been taught and returned his kiss. I had to be careful. Little things like this could give me away.

Mother swept the car keys from the table. "I'll drive you."

"Really?"

"Come on," she said over her shoulder, walking out of the door.

"Hey!" Father called out as I followed.

He tossed a granola bar to me. Breakfast. I couldn't believe it. These people were really taking care of me.

In the car, I glanced at my 'mother' while I chewed on the bar. She had a friendly face with a warm smile, pale eyes and shoulder-length brown hair several shades darker than mine, which made her a good match for me with my blue eyes and light brown hair.

The drive to school felt surreal. The houses were mostly bungalows, hardly surprising since this was California. Some were Spanish style, some more contemporary, though to me they all looked dated. I'd seen photos of the area before my arrival, yet they didn't come close to capturing the atmosphere and quaintness of the neighborhood. The quality of light was so different here, so crisp and clear it made the world seem brighter.

"You're very quiet," Mother said.

"Could you drop me off around the corner?" That'd give me time to observe what was going on before the start of the school day.

"Sure, honey." She pulled over. "Don't worry, you'll make friends and fit in just fine."

They were two things I had to do.

Then there was number three.

Raising her hands as if in a truce, she added, "I won't try to kiss you while it's humanly possible anyone might see."

I smiled wanly and got out of the car, closing the door behind me. It wasn't her words that got to me so much as the tone of familiarity and the way she looked at me, the affection in her eyes. I wasn't used to all this warmth and encouragement, and it threw me.

Altabena High School lay ahead. A group of girls slightly younger than me walked past, giggling and staring. More specifically, they were laughing *at me*, though at what, I didn't know.

As I looked at them, I noticed they all wore their navy skirts much shorter than mine, just under their butts, in fact. Uniforms had been introduced across the country by the Bartley government to give a sense of unity, yet these young women were trying to bend the rules. How strange.

Still, if that was the case, then I had to do the same in order to fit in. I stopped and hitched my skirt up by folding it over at the waist, left my white shirt untucked the way the other girls had, and got on my way.

Opposite the school, I stopped at the edge of a large group of students waiting to cross the road. They wore various sorts of sneakers: Converse, Nike, Adidas. I'd read about those brands and would have to wear something similar tomorrow but for now I was stuck with sensible black leather school shoes.

The students appeared to be making their way to school except for two young men ahead of me who were having an argument. One of them had curly hair that had obviously been bleached, the dark roots obvious, all of which made a mockery of his school uniform. The other was a little older, probably not a student at Altabena High, and he wore a leather jacket and jeans. This was exactly the reason I had to be careful.

A girl with blond stripes in her brown hair came closer as we crossed the road. I wasn't sure what the style was called – foils, perhaps – whereas I knew what my hairstyle was called. A ponytail.

She screwed up her nose. "Are you new or something?"

I nodded. "Very. This is my first day."

"Well, with those shoes it looks like it's your first day on the planet."

An astute observation. She wasn't far from wrong.

"Are you a senior?" she asked.

"Yes."

She tilted her head and frowned. "Because you look

really familiar. Have we…?"

"We have definitely not met before." I extended my arm to shake her hand. "Nice to meet you, I'm Nicola Gray."

She looked down at my hand as though it were poisoned, so I pulled it back. Maybe teenagers didn't shake hands here.

"I'm Lauren Wilson." She pointed at my feet as we walked. "You'll definitely have to lose the shoes."

Lose the shoes? It didn't make sense. If I lost something on purpose, it wouldn't be lost. It'd be thrown away. Then it came to me. "They're too square, aren't they?"

"Square?" Lauren stared at me as if I was a moron. What had I said?

Suddenly, the young man with curly bleached hair and ridiculous dark roots careered into the side of me. He'd been pushed and I'd let myself get distracted. My first mistake. I wasn't making another.

I dropped my bag, glancing across at the guy in the leather jacket. He was sneering, his eyes on the other fellow, ready to throw a big punch, a haymaker. Such an amateur.

I stepped between the two of them, blocked the punch and scooped it away. Too easy. The hard part was stopping myself from hitting him back.

He stared, took a step back. "What the…?"

I looked him in the eye. "That wasn't a good idea."

He laughed. "Lucky for you I don't hit girls. You are a girl, aren't you?"

Before I could answer, he stabbed his finger in the air at bleached-hair-boy. "You'll get yours, pal." Then he turned and left.

The fellow with the terrible dark roots put his hands out and announced to the crowd who'd been watching, "Show's over."

The students moved on. Meanwhile he couldn't stop grinning as he gave me a friendly whack on the shoulder before leaving and said, "That was wild. Thanks heaps."

Lauren handed me my bag. "Where'd you learn to do that?"

My mouth dropped open. I should've had a good answer but couldn't think of anything.

"Forget it." In a complete mood change, her eyes widened. "What the hell were you thinking? You don't mess with dudes like that. The guy with the leather jacket isn't exactly Snow White. He's the local dealer."

I wondered if she meant firearms, weapons or artillery. "An arms dealer? Here at school?"

"No, stupid, a drug dealer!" She shook her head. "You've got to be kidding me."

"That's it, I was kidding." After some consideration, I asked, "Shouldn't we call the police?"

"What? And snitch?" Exasperated, Lauren threw her hands up. "We should get to class."

I nodded. "Yes, that was a heavy scene."

She screwed up her face. "Are you shitting me? Where'd you learn to talk like that?"

I couldn't tell her the answer and even if I could, she wouldn't believe me. I'd watched lots of old movies in an effort to gauge the language of the time but maybe I hadn't nailed the right era.

"I'd better report to the office," I said in a small voice.

"Yeah, you do that. See you later." She turned to leave.

"See you," I said, emulating her speech pattern.

Lauren stopped and hesitated, then pulled a cell phone from her pocket. "Look, if you need anything, call me."

I fumbled in my bag for my phone, then had trouble navigating the icons and working out what to do.

Lauren frowned. "What now?"

"It's an old phone," I said by way of explanation.

"No way." She leaned over to look at the item in my hand. "That's the latest G-Phone. They're so cool."

Cool. That was a word I recognized from my research. At least my phone was cool, even if I wasn't.

"I mean, it's new," I said. "And I've barely had a chance to use it yet."

"Those new models are fab. So intuitive to use."

I stopped myself from saying anything. The technology was ancient by my standards.

"Look," she said. "Give me your number and I'll text you so you've got my details."

I reeled it off. Luckily, I was good with numbers. It was people who were harder to work out. For one thing, Lauren was going out of her way to be kind when she didn't have to, especially since she seemed to think I was a bit weird. I wasn't used to all this…kindness.

At the front office, I spoke to the receptionist who scanned her computer, looking for the necessary information.

"What was your name again?" she asked.

"Nicola Gray."

I'd kept my first name and taken on the surname of my new family. This had all been organized well in advance so my name had to be on the school system. I felt a pinch of discomfort nonetheless.

"Nicola Gray…seventeen years old…we've already sighted your birth certificate." She read the words off the screen, then told me to take a seat.

While I waited, she shuffled through papers, checked out something on her computer and printed off a timetable for me.

As it turned out, I only caught the final ten minutes of my first class and I'd never been so grateful to be late. Home economics. Sewing, no less. Such a frivolous and feminine class was not for me and I couldn't get out of there fast enough.

During the break that followed, I placed some books in my locker and wandered around trying to get my bearings and learn the lay of the land. I also took careful note of my fellow students, listening to the way they talked and observing their gestures and mannerisms.

There were hundreds of students at Altabena High School so that was a lot of people to get through to find my target. Information about him was scant. Though the year of his birth had been confirmed, I wasn't certain I was at the right school, or even the right town for that matter.

Science was next, human biology to be precise. Hopefully this would be more stimulating than sewing and I'd fit in better. I was scanning the students heading into the classroom when I spotted Lauren.

"Over here," she yelled.

Another act of kindness. I sat next to her while the teacher set us the task of reading a chapter from an E-textbook on our laptops.

The G-Top was a classic in design and technology, though to my eyes it was a heavy clunky thing, probably because plithium hadn't been invented yet. At least it was largely intuitive, as Lauren had put it.

Meanwhile the teacher, Mr. Rodriguez, sat at his desk. He'd trimmed his beard into a goatee with a fine chin strap of hair along his jawline. I'd seen similar styles in the old movies I'd snuck off to watch whenever I had the chance. I loved finding out about other eras and getting a glimpse into different worlds, maybe a little too much.

"What's he doing?" I asked Lauren.

"Going through the roll," she replied. "If you miss a single lesson, the school sends a text message to your parents."

The teacher wasn't saying the names out loud which meant I was missing my big chance to find out who else was in the class. At this rate it could take days or even weeks to locate the person I was after. I could ask around, of course, as long as I didn't make myself conspicuous.

A couple of boys at the back of the class were playing up, causing two girls to cover their mouths and giggle. I turned to look, amazed that this sort of behavior seemed normal here.

The teacher stood and made his way to the rear of the classroom. He closed the laptop in front of one of the disruptive boys and stared at him. So did I. The young man was good looking if you liked that sort of thing. His dark hair was wavy and a little too long, cut into no particular style but it didn't seem to matter because he had a style of his own. His green eyes were striking, his smile disarming, and though he seemed to have impressed the two girls, the same couldn't be said for me.

"Okay, Benny Boy, what can you tell us about the cardiovascular system?" Mr. Rodriguez asked.

My heart jumped to my throat. Ben? Was it possible?

I should've recognized him at first glance. He was much younger here than in the picture I'd seen and that must've thrown me. This wasn't something I could take a chance on. I had to be certain.

"You need a strong cardiovascular system to keep up your fitness for sports and football," he replied.

The teacher leaned across the desk. "A doctor or a football player – which will it be?"

Benny Boy shrugged. "Who says I have to choose? I might be a Nobel Prize- winning medical specialist by day and an NFL player by night."

"A gigolo by night, more like it," someone called out.

The class laughed.

I smiled, trying to appear amused to fit in. Ben didn't look like a mass murderer but then, no one ever did. Serial killers looked like everyone else.

"Besides, he doesn't play football any more," another person yelled.

"You'd better have a good definition of systemic circulation if you want to avoid a detention," Mr. Rodriguez said to Ben.

"Systemic circulation is the portion of the cardiovascular system which transports oxygenated blood away from the heart to the rest of the body, and returns oxygen-depleted blood back to the heart," Ben stated without hesitation.

"Okay, how much blood is in the human body?" the teacher asked.

"A rough guide might be about five liters or more for a grown man, perhaps as little as 3.3 liters for a 50 kilogram female such as one of these two."

He gestured to the two girls opposite him. They

whispered and giggled, no doubt more impressed by his good looks than his knowledge.

I weighed somewhere over 50 kilos. Thankfully, the US had moved away from imperial measurements as part of the government revamp, so at least I didn't have to bother with quarts and pints.

"I'm glad you've got that covered," the teacher said.

Ben shrugged. "That's just rote learning. It's not creating cures for diseases or doing anything important."

"However, you're still disturbing the rest of the class," Mr. Rodriguez said in a stern voice.

Ben nodded and put his head down. The teacher walked away.

Eventually the bell rang and we gathered our books, preparing to leave the room.

I was almost too nervous to ask Lauren the question. "Who was that?"

"Ben Tanner," she said.

It was him.

Her lips curled to a sly smile. "Why? Do you think he's cute?"

"Actually, I thought he seemed smart."

She nodded. "He is. But do you think he's cute?"

"Sure, there are lots of cute guys here."

Hopefully I was starting to sound like the other teenagers around me. I'd thought the most difficult part of my mission would be locating my target, Ben Tanner, but I was wrong. The hardest part was yet to come. I had limited time to ingratiate myself into the school and the community, gather intelligence, and report back to my superiors. It'd compromise my mission to eliminate him too soon.

But that was exactly what I had to do.
Kill Ben Tanner.

CHAPTER TWO

Only a matter of hours into the mission and already I was ahead of schedule. After the shaky start I'd made, that had to be a good thing.

I'd been chosen for this job because I was the top student at New Nation Military College. There was another reason too that had nothing to do with my skills and talent. In the one existing photo of Ben Tanner, he was with his wife who bore an uncanny resemblance to me. My superiors thought that if Ben was attracted to certain females or went for a particular 'type', that put me ahead of the other candidates for this role.

I'd also been chosen because I was a hero. Except I wasn't. I definitely wasn't the killing machine the authorities thought I was. Nowhere near it.

But I was a good soldier and I had to do this.

Meanwhile I was also supposed to be a high school student and it was part of my job to fit in. This was going to be harder than I thought.

Lauren slammed her locker door shut. "Have you got physical education next too?"

"Yes," I said.

"You wouldn't believe the stuff they get us to do at this school."

"What stuff?"

"Today we've got specialist training. Honestly, it's torture."

Now she had my attention. "Really? What's involved?"

"Everything from sprints and running mini-marathons to weights and even boxing. It's like we're in the army."

"Is there a problem with that?"

As soon as the words slipped out, I knew it was the wrong thing to say. Lauren looked at me as if I was an idiot. With so much to learn in this new environment, I was beginning to wonder if I was.

She threw her hands up. "You're not going to go all weird on me again, are you?"

I shrugged. "I hope not."

The PE program she described sounded familiar to me. It must be the beginning of government programs to strengthen young people and help them build moral fiber and physical endurance. Where I was from, we took it for granted that everyone had to go through the same grueling schedule designed to separate the weak from the strong.

Lauren's reaction was harder to work out, though. Schools and young people had welcomed the initiatives. Everyone knew that.

"Just warning you," she said. "Mr. Matthews is a slave driver. You're not going to like this."

I figured I'd start off easy when the physical education session began, try to fit in with the other kids and do what the teacher told us to. Thousands of other teenagers did this every day, so how hard could it be?

Lauren picked up the bag with her gym gear in it. "Let's get a move on."

Okay, time to get changed. I reached into my bag, dug out a pair of navy shorts and a dark green sports shirt, leaving them on top of my bag in readiness.

Lauren looked puzzled as she motioned for me to get going. "We're late already."

I could hurry if that's what she wanted, so I pulled my school shirt off over my head, ready to get changed.

Her mouth fell open. Other students pointed and giggled. If only I had a clue what I'd done wrong. It wasn't as though I was naked. I was wearing a bra, after all.

A boy with long wavy blond hair stopped and wolf whistled, his eyes riveted to me. A whistle? Even for a teenage male, that was immature, not to mention unnecessary.

Lauren stepped between me and the passers-by, panic in her eyes. "Are you crazy? Get some clothes back on. Quick, before anyone else sees."

I reached for my sports shirt and slipped it over my head, which is what I'd planned to do in the first place.

Behind Lauren, I caught a glimpse of Ben Tanner, a smile on his face. *He'd seen.* But what had he seen? Why was this such a big deal?

"You said we were late." I looked behind Lauren and saw people were moving on, Ben included. "I thought we were getting changed into our sports uniform."

"*Not here*," she said, clearly exasperated. "In the locker rooms. What is with you?"

"I…I'm…"

Lauren's eyes narrowed. "I'll show you where we're going, then that's it. After that, you're on your own."

She grabbed my arm and we walked down the hall to the locker rooms, the *girls'*, I noticed. Inside, we got dressed into the rest of our physical education uniform.

Lauren shot me a sideways glance. "Were you trying it on back there?"

"I'm not from around here," I said.

"You can say that again. Come on." Her voice was sympathetic as she motioned toward the door and we headed for the oval along with the other girls. "By the way, how'd you get the six pack?"

I had strong abdominal and core muscles from years of military and martial arts training. I wasn't bulked up because I didn't have the frame for that, however I was strong and toned and had earned every ounce of muscle mass. Maybe it was vanity on my part but I was also flattered she'd noticed, not to mention grateful she was still talking to me.

"Long story," I said. "I've done some fairly rigorous training."

"Maybe you'll like Mr. Matthews, after all." She rolled her eyes. "He's the king of rigorous training."

He was a little taller than me with broad shoulders, a strong chest and muscular legs beneath his running shorts. With tanned olive skin, he looked like he spent a lot of time outdoors. Lucky him. On a sunny day like this I was glad to be out here too. It seemed too much of a treat to be part of the curriculum.

On the oval, the students in our group followed Mr. Matthews' instructions and limbered up slowly before launching into a workout similar to the one Lauren had described earlier.

It was nothing too demanding, a combination of

strength exercises such as push-ups and squats, interspersed with cardio which mostly consisted of running. I forced myself to hang back but it was difficult when I finished each exercise before the others and then had to waste time to allow them to catch up.

"For the next drill, we're going to alternate rounds of boxing with sprints," Mr. Matthews said.

The students around me moaned so I added a small groan of disapproval myself.

"Nicola, you're with me," the teacher instructed.

All eyes were on me. Maybe I wasn't doing such a convincing job of 'hanging back'.

"Do I have to?" I asked.

He picked up a pair of hand mitts and tossed me a pair of boxing gloves. "Yes, now get over here."

I joined him, but only after letting out a long sigh as if annoyed. This wasn't so bad. I was finally starting to get the hang of being a teenager.

"Okay, guys, you know the drill," Mr. Matthews yelled. To me he said, "I want twenty strong, hard punches, then you sprint to the tree and back. After that, we do it all over again."

I nodded and sent in twenty punches. Mr. Matthews looked shaken as I drove him back with my strikes and he struggled to keep the pads in place.

When I came back from my sprint, he asked, "Where'd you learn to do that?"

"Um, I've done this before," I mumbled.

"Then do it again."

After several rounds, the punchers and pad-holders switched roles, however I didn't have to swap with Mr. Matthews so I got to do extra training. Just lucky, I guess.

This was nothing compared to the program I'd been through in New Nation where physical exercises were only one side of our training. It didn't compare with being locked in complete darkness to test my mental resilience or some of the simulation exercises. Then there were fear exercises that were definitely not simulated, exercises involving deadly spiders, snakes and even alligators.

I always did well, mostly because I was skilled at appearing calm on the outside, and the tests didn't measure what was going on inside. I was good, just not as good as I wanted to be or as good as anyone else thought I was.

At the end of the final round, I doubled over to catch my breath, and glanced up to see a smug smile on the teacher's face.

"I knew I'd break you," he said under his breath.

I straightened, my gaze riveted to his.

He reached for a kick-shield from the pile of sports equipment and said, "We're not finished yet. Do you know how to do round kicks?"

"Yes," I replied.

He held the shield in place for leg kicks. "I want you to kick," he added under his breath, "until you drop."

I was up for the challenge, so I round kicked the shield, ten kicks left, ten kicks right, over and over again. I was like a machine as I sent in kick after kick, pushing Mr. Matthews back with each strike. The drill was clearly meant to wear me out – and it was – but I knew what he didn't. I would never give up.

"Excuse me, Mr. Matthews," called a man coming up behind him.

The teacher looked toward the sound, his eyes off the

shield and the kicker. Big mistake. The first rule of pad holding is to keep your eyes on the striker.

Too late. I'd already launched my kick and there was no stopping it. Mr. Matthews' leg slipped out from under him as I swept it away and he landed on the ground on his butt.

"Oh no," I yelled, leaning over him. "Are you okay?"

"Fine," he said.

He wasn't seriously hurt because the shield had done its job, but he didn't look fine either. He looked embarrassed, not to mention extremely annoyed. And it didn't help that the kids were all laughing. I'd messed up. Again.

The male teacher who'd been headed our way and I helped Mr. Matthews up.

"Dismissed," he said. "Show's over."

That was the second time I'd heard those words today. I wasn't trying to put on a show. I was supposed to be blending in and gathering information, an important part of my mission.

It was also the reason I couldn't eliminate my target right away. Because if I was thrown into jail on a murder charge, I wouldn't be able to document my surroundings. And now I was about to be blasted by the teacher.

Mr. Matthews shook his finger at me. "We start a new martial arts program next week. I expect you to be there on the first day."

"Is that an order?" I asked.

"Absolutely. You will be there or else."

Lauren put her arm around me as we walked toward the change rooms, a grin on her face. "What a hero!"

I looked around. "Who?"

"You, silly," she said. "We've been dying for someone to teach that dude a lesson."

Great, I was a hero again, except I didn't think I'd behaved heroically. Far from it. I'd stuffed up and the only good thing was that the teacher wasn't badly hurt.

"I didn't mean for any of that to happen," I said.

"I know. Ain't it sweet!" She put her hand up as we walked and I stared at it blankly.

"High five," she said.

Luckily I knew what that was and slapped her palm. Back at the academy, no one had celebrated and supported me like Lauren. And we'd only just met.

The two girls who'd giggled at Ben Tanner in science class joined us briefly to give me high fives as they passed, still laughing. They were both very attractive, one of them blond, the other African-American, both of them professional gigglers if past experience was anything to go by.

Lauren's gaze was riveted to the girls ahead of us, a look of admiration on her face. "Simone and Taylor are so cool."

"Are they?"

"By the way, Mr. Matthews can't force you to do that additional training. It's optional, like joining the band or the rowing or basketball team."

Optional? These kids had the *option* of joining a team, or playing some other sport or activity – was that what she was saying?

At the academy in New Nation, we had a military band which performed at formal events. Students with musical aptitude joined the band. There was no choice, and you certainly couldn't *choose* to do something as futile and impractical as basketball.

Anyway, it sounded like the teacher couldn't force me to go to the martial arts arena after school when I had other things to do and that suited me fine.

I nodded. "Mr. Matthews is one mean dude."

Lauren stopped, her hands on her hips. "Nicola, can't you talk like a normal person?"

"But you said 'dude' not two minutes ago."

She shook her head. "Just be yourself."

We kept walking. Be myself? That was not a good idea.

I had to be someone else altogether or I wasn't going to survive.

CHAPTER THREE

"'Tis better to have loved and lost than never to have loved at all." The English teacher, Ms. Swann, leaned against the front of her desk, looking across the classroom. "Can anyone tell me who wrote that?"

"Shakespeare," someone piped up.

"Guess again," the teacher said.

Beside me, Lauren Wilson looked around the class as if she didn't want to answer, then said, "Lord Alfred Tennyson."

"Thank you, Lauren." The teacher's shoulders relaxed with relief, and she added, "Sometimes I wonder what I'm going to do with the rest of you. Tennyson is saying that if you loved and it ended badly, it was still worth the pain. That to love and be hurt is better than to never have experienced love at all. Such is the power of love." She added with a smile, "He didn't say that last bit. You can put that quote down to Lisa Swann."

The starry look in her eyes told me she was trying to connect with the students, to pass on her enjoyment of literature, to make us appreciate it. Her sentiments may have been noble but as I looked around at the bored faces in the class, I didn't fancy her chances.

Lauren leaned across and whispered, "Tennyson's words are so moving."

I raised my eyebrows. "Really?"

"I only wish I could come up with stuff like that."

Just as I was wondering why, the bell rang and Ms. Swann asked Lauren to stay behind for a few moments. Meanwhile I was out of there along with everyone else in the class. In the hallway I caught up with Simone and Taylor who'd been sitting behind us in English.

They said hello, then promptly ignored me, having an in-depth gossip about people I didn't know. Even though people-I-didn't-know was a large group, I thought they could've been a bit friendlier. Was this what happened when people were 'cool'?

Someone sidled up to me. The wolf whistler. He was grinning, so I smiled back because I needed all the friends I could get. Besides, he might know Ben Tanner well or have expertise and information in another area that could help me.

"Nicola Gray," I said.

"I know," he replied as we walked. "The bit where the English teacher said, 'Would you please welcome the new girl, Nicola Gray' was a bit of a giveaway. I'm Rex Anderson."

"Nice to meet you, Rex."

There was a sparkle in his eye. "You don't know that yet, whereas I've seen a lot more of you than you have of me."

I was never going to live this down. I decided not to

give him a hard time about wolf whistling. Better to change the subject.

"Well, you're talking to me which is something, I guess," I said.

"And it's not so bad."

"So far, so good."

I stopped in front of my locker and shoved my books inside. No sign of Lauren. Rex was still hanging around.

He sidled up close to me, his hand on my shoulder. "I'd like to see *more of you*."

His lips had parted as if he was about to start drooling. Not a good look. My eyes narrowed. Something told me this wasn't going to go well.

"There's a lot more you could show me," he said.

His hand dropped to my breast. I lowered my gaze to my chest. What did he think he was doing?

My training cut in. *Don't hurt him.* Not too much, anyway. I stepped in, wrapped my arm around the front of his neck, nudged my leg to the back of his knee and threw him to the ground.

He landed on his butt, his books dropping to the floor though luckily his laptop made a soft landing on top of them.

"Are you crazy?" he muttered.

"Is there anything else you'd like me to show you?" I asked.

He lifted a hand, his face contorting to a scowl. "No, I'm sorry. I thought you were up for it."

"You thought wrong." I raised my eyebrows. "Is there anything else that's *up*?"

He scuttled back. "No, it's down. Everything's down."

A small crowd had gathered. A boy to one side

laughed while two girls clapped. Ben Tanner stood beside them, a bemused smile on his face. This was definitely not going to plan. I didn't want to create another spectacle or hurt Rex but I didn't know what I was supposed to do. Talk about useless.

Rex was already getting to his feet. Head down, I stepped out of his way, picked up his books and laptop, and passed them to him. He brushed down the front of his pants and begrudgingly took his belongings.

"Look, let's just forget about this," I said quietly.

"Whatever. I'm outta here."

I saw the other kids moving on too but was too shy to check what Ben was doing. Since when had I become timid? This wasn't like me at all.

Shoving a folder into my bag, I closed the locker.

Deep breaths. The hardest part of the day was over. I could leave these errors behind me. All I had to do now was get home and deal with my family, except judging by the mistakes I'd made already, that could potentially be extremely difficult. I had to keep my wits about me.

I turned to see Ben Tanner standing in front of me, his backpack over his shoulders, hands on his hips, his eyes on mine.

He was looking at me.

The book I was holding flew out of my hand, my phone slipped from my fingers and my bag dropped to the floor.

"Hold on," he said. "I'll help."

One thing I'd never been was a helpless female, but I just stood there with my mouth open while Ben handed me my things. I put the loose items into my backpack, slung it over my shoulders and pushed a few stray strands of hair behind my ears.

He gestured toward the door. "Are you heading off now, Nicola?"

"Yes," I said as we walked down the hall.

He knew my name. Had he asked around? No, most likely the science teacher had said it in class and Ben remembered. Not that it was important, far from it.

"You've made a big bang on your first day." He smiled, probably to put me at ease. It was the sort of smile people described as disarming, one that'd have other girls eating out of the palm of his hand. Not me, though.

"It's not like you think," I said. "What happened with Mr. Matthews was just a mix-up and it was mostly his fault. I was only doing what I was told."

"Whoa, I haven't heard about this. What happened with Mr. Matthews?"

I looked straight ahead. "Nothing."

A group of kids barged in front of us, causing a distraction, and we edged our way out of the front gates.

Ben pointed up the street. "You heading this way?"

"Yep." Maybe I was getting better at sounding like everyone else, after all.

"Good, then we can walk together," he said.

"Sure."

Ben's brow furrowed. "So, that striptease in the hallway earlier, what was that all about?"

"Well, it was…a dare," I said.

"A dare?" He didn't sound convinced.

"Sure. It earned me twenty bucks."

"Sorry about Rex. The guy's an idiot. We're not all like him. Some of us have a brain."

"I'm sure Rex has a brain," I said. "He just let himself

get ruled by his emotions and base urges."

Ben stopped, raised his eyebrows. "You sound like a human biology textbook."

How did he know where I'd got the information?

"I just meant he shouldn't have done that," I said. "He shouldn't have grabbed my breast."

"You're absolutely right." Ben put his hands up. "And I am absolutely not going to grope you."

"No, I didn't think you would."

Ben was certainly a healthy specimen. I'd already gathered in science class that he was into sport. I could tell from the way his shirt hung from his shoulders that he'd built up his pectorals and carried a fair amount of muscle. These were observations only. I wasn't like Rex with his 'base urges'.

"Good," Ben said. "Glad we've got that clear."

Nothing was clear. I couldn't even remember what we were talking about.

In New Nation, I'd been extremely focused when it came to the mission, my role, my purpose in life. Now I'd arrived in Altabena, my brain was turning to mush and I was having difficulty working out the simplest things. What's more, no one else seemed to be having the same trouble.

"And if I ever need anyone to beat up Rex Anderson, you'll be the first person I'll call," Ben added.

"I wouldn't want to beat him up," I said. "I don't believe in unprovoked violence."

He stared at me. "I was joking."

I stared right back. "So was I."

The look on his face told me he didn't believe me. "By the way, that stuff the other kids came up with about me being a gigolo, that's not really me."

"Really? Then what's *you*?"

He spread his hands. "I'm just a regular guy."

"I don't believe that for a minute!"

The words tumbled out before I could stop them. Ben laughed. At least he wasn't insulted.

I cleared my throat. "I mean, usually when someone gets teased, there's a grain of truth behind it."

"Nah, I don't think that's it." He stopped at the corner, holding my gaze as he spoke. "You do things your own way. You don't mind being different."

But I did mind. A lot.

Ben's fingers brushed the bare skin of my arm as he turned and left to join a group of boys ahead. It made me strangely warm inside, only for a moment, though that was a moment too long. I thought about following him home but decided it could wait. There were other ways to obtain more information and his address.

Meeting my target was much more nerve-wracking than I'd expected. People here seemed to make decisions based on their feelings but that kind of thing didn't happen any more.

I was from the future. We knew better.

Where I came from in New Nation in 2120, everyone knew emotions were base urges to be overridden. The country was dotted with Badlands where those who'd been struck with the killer virus and survived still lived. These unfortunate forms of life were still human only with mutations, one of which was strange telepathic powers they used to impose feelings on the rest of us.

We all had some level of emotion within us, however the folk in the Badlands worked on this weakness, intensifying these feelings and skewing our judgment. Emotions couldn't be trusted, unlike the power of the mind.

I kept walking home, watching as Ben and his friends ahead of me turned a corner so they were out of view.

In the future, Ben Tanner was going to create a deadly virus that would devastate the Earth's population. Billions of lives would be lost, and I could save them. That was why I'd been sent here.

All I had to do was dispose of Ben Tanner.

Before I'd arrived, I had experienced subtle feelings. I was human and could be imperfect. Still, I'd always managed to keep my emotions in check and had certainly never let them take over, but these latest feelings were much stronger than anything I'd encountered before.

My mission was suddenly more complicated. It was one thing to consider eliminating someone who was going to be a mass murderer in the future, and it was another when the guy came across as a good person.

I liked him. How had that happened?

It made my task harder.

Harder but not impossible.

I couldn't fail when so many lives depended on it.

CHAPTER FOUR

The back door was unlocked so I walked straight in. I'd never had a family before, or a home for that matter, and wasn't sure what to expect after this morning.

"I'm in here, honey," someone called out from the kitchen.

I dropped my bag by the door and slumped onto one of the chairs at the table. Who would've thought a day at school would be this exhausting?

Mother turned from the kitchen bench. "Waiting for me to serve you, as usual?"

"Is that okay?" I hoped I didn't sound rude but was uncertain what to do.

"It's lucky for you I've just put the coffee on."

"Lucky for me there are muffins too."

I reached for one from a platter on the center of the table, and took a bite. Still warm from the oven, they were chocolate with white chocolate chips. How decadent. It made me wonder if these muffins had been baked especially for me, a thought that only made me nervous.

By the sink, Mother poured coffee from a French

press into two mugs and added milk. While she rinsed the plunger, I got up and placed the mugs on the table, earning a smile for my efforts.

She joined me at the table. "How was school today?"

"It was okay, pretty boring really." I'd been fairly sure that was the sort of thing a parent would ask so I'd rehearsed the lines already.

"Did you meet anyone?"

"A girl called Lauren, a couple of others."

"That's a good start," she said. "You can't expect things to fall into place immediately. This is a new town for Dad and me too. We're both starting new jobs. All three of us are in the same boat."

I could see why the Grays had been chosen as my 'parents'. The timing was perfect. No one knew them here, so the sudden appearance of a teenage daughter wouldn't seem odd.

My superiors had arranged for computer chips to be implanted in their brains, creating my presence in their lives and giving them memories of raising a child to the age of seventeen. I hadn't been given the same chip because my mind had to be on the mission, not on this imaginary family.

Other items had been planted for me here too, from clothing to paperwork and a birth certificate so I could be officially enrolled at school, though the authorities had forgotten to send the vitamin supplements we all took. An oversight.

It amazed me that they could plant computer chips into the past with such precision, yet they'd used the wrong coordinates for my landing this morning so I ended up in the park.

Apparently smaller items were easier to transport, and the transfer of organic matter – such as human beings – was infinitely more complex. What's more, it was even more difficult to bring things back so the authorities were still finalizing the program for my return trip. I had to wait for confirmation that they could do so and then I'd have to eliminate my target as soon as they gave the go-ahead.

"Is that a newspaper?" I asked, reaching across.

In New Nation, information was distributed electronically by government agencies. This morning was the first time I'd seen a hard copy newspaper.

"Looks that way," Mother said. "It's the local suburban paper."

The headline read, *No High Rise for Altabena*. It appeared that local residents were objecting to dual high rise towers planned for the site of an existing community center on the basis that the project was unnecessary and out of character with the surroundings. The township authorities had knocked back the development, however State Ruler Harrison Bartley recently rescinded the decision, giving approval for the project to go ahead.

I frowned. "It states that local residents object to Bartley's decision."

"Yes." Mother pointed to the newspaper. "There are plenty of letters to the editor about it and a protest rally is being planned."

"But that can't be right. How can these people say they don't want something when the State Ruler has sanctioned it?"

Mother gave me the same stare Lauren had earlier today when she'd looked at me as if I was an idiot. "Nicola, have you seen any other thirty story office blocks in Altabena?"

"No."

"Well, maybe the proposed development *is* out of character." She shook her head knowingly. "This sort of thing has been going on for a while and in other towns too."

"Really?"

"Last year, they changed the law so that State Ruler Bartley and the government has the legal right to do almost anything they want."

"Is that so bad?" I asked. "Isn't it the government's job to get things done?"

"They're supposed *to serve the people*." She stopped, a puzzled look on her face. "When did you become so interested in current affairs?"

This wasn't current affairs. It was history, though certainly not the history I'd been taught at school.

In New Nation, humanity had endured a deadly virus, increasingly erratic weather and a series of disasters, few of which had been natural. But people had survived. Thrived, in fact, thanks to the Bartley government, its strict regime and thorough overhaul of society. New Nation wouldn't have survived without the government. And society – or what was left of it – had welcomed the rules and changes.

These people around me had no idea what was coming. No idea at all.

"I was only asking," I said.

Mother was warm and encouraging as we finished our coffee and muffins, which only reminded me I didn't belong here. This wasn't like the military college where I'd been raised, where they knew me, where Lucien was waiting. He was special, much more than just my captain.

He was my reason for being here and I couldn't possibly let him down.

Mother stood. "I'm just popping out to the store, honey. Can you please tidy the kitchen?"

I raised my eyebrows. "Tidy up? Because I'm a girl?"

She waited a moment. "No, because you live here."

"Oh. I've got homework."

Mother put her hands on her hips. "The two things aren't mutually exclusive, you know. You can clean up first, then do your homework."

"But…" I began.

"No buts. It's time you did more around the house and became a bit more capable. I start my new job in a month and you'll need to help out by cooking dinner from time to time."

"Me?"

"Perhaps something along the lines of spaghetti bolognaise."

Never show fear. It was one of the first principles I'd been taught in combat training.

"I should be able to manage that," I said with great confidence though I'd never cooked anything so complex. I could hunt small animals and even larger game. Once, I'd even shot a wild boar that had fed the entire regiment, and I could start a fire in nearly any conditions.

I glanced at the kitchen stove. I'd choose wild boar over that any day. To me, that strange item of domestic equipment looked scarier.

"Is there anything else you'd like me to do in the meantime, Mom?" I asked.

"No, I wouldn't want to stand between you and your homework."

I carried the empty mugs and plates to the sink. Mother left, which was just as well because it was better she didn't witness my ineptitude in the kitchen.

Afterwards, I made a detour on the way to my room. An important one. My superior officers had told me that Philip Gray, my supposed father, had a Glock 17 in his nightstand.

In my parents' bedroom, I opened the drawer of the nightstand. The 9mm automatic was exactly where my superiors said it would be. The first thing I did was eject the magazine and rack the slide. I caught a bullet as it was ejected from the chamber. Yep. Loaded. I racked the slide to load the gun again and put it back where I'd found it. For now.

Strangely, guns had barely changed in the last 100 years. In New Nation, we had other weapons but still used guns because they were highly efficient.

Back in my bedroom, I sat at my desk, pulled out my notes and laptop, and stared at the computer – yet another example of how well the government took care of the people. They made sure every student was issued with a laptop for study purposes. Mother was wrong about the government. She had to be.

I heard a musical tone, looked around, then dug around inside my bag to find my phone flashing with a text from Lauren. Text messages were so primitive it made me smile. I'd better get used to it.

The message read:

I heard you punched Rex out. Way to go, girl!

Lauren hadn't been there so how did she know? I found her name in the address book of my phone, which wasn't hard since she was the only person listed, and called her. When she picked up, I explained what had happened earlier that afternoon.

"So Rex doesn't have a black eye?" she asked.

"No," I replied.

"That's kind of disappointing."

"Not if you're Rex, it's not."

"True, but the version I heard was funnier."

"So where did you hear about my incident with Rex anyway?" I asked.

"On PeoplePlace."

Of course. They used a primitive form of social networking here, one that would be a potential source of information on Ben Tanner. I should've thought of that sooner.

"Thanks, Lauren," I said. "I'm going to sign up right now."

"You mean you're not on PeoplePlace?" The surprise in her voice bordered on disgust. "Wow, I've heard about people like you."

"I was barred from it." I had to think quickly. "Strict parents. That's all behind me now. Please don't tell anyone."

"Okay," she said.

We hung up and I got to work on the laptop. The system was so slow I wondered if it had timed out. It hadn't. Nothing was instant in this place.

That would all change with the introduction of bono technology, however in the meantime people were stuck in a technological plateau that went on for decades. And I was stuck with them.

Finally the system loaded and I sent requests to become PeoplePlace friends with everyone I'd met at school that day. Most important of all, I became Ben Tanner's friend.

I scrolled down his personal landing page covered in photographs, mostly of him and his friends goofing around and grinning for the camera. Digging deeper, I found some pictures of Ben with his family. Of course, like everyone else in Altabena, he had a family – a cute little sister, handsome older brother and a father, though there was no sign of a mother.

In one photo, Ben's father was staring at his son as if he was the brightest star in the heavens, pride and love emanating from his features. For a moment, just a moment, a small pang shot through me as I realized no one had ever looked at me that way.

But the picture was all wrong. Did this man have any idea what Ben was going to do one day? Probably not. Would that override his good opinion of his son? The answer was no doubt the same.

That was one of the problems with families. The emotions they entailed overrode common sense, good judgment and the greater good of mankind. By their very definition, families were selfish entities.

I had to be better than that. My job was more important.

Leaning back, I rolled down my skirt, pulled a thin layer of matter from the top of my hip, and laid my PR device on the desk. *This* was the future.

My Personal Recorder was roughly the size of a cell phone, only paper thin and made of plithium. It was a mobile device with immense capacity that made my school laptop look like a toy. Security wasn't an issue as it would respond only to my fingerprints and voice commands.

"Collate all information on Ben Tanner," I said.

The device lit up as it located my laptop and infiltrated the data. Technically, it didn't download information because the PR didn't rely on other devices to release information.

What about academic records? I located the relevant information on the school mainframe. Ben Tanner seemed to be an excellent student, good both at sports and academically, and also a valued member of the school community.

This was a lot more information than we had on him in New Nation. At some point, he'd done an excellent job of removing nearly all the identifying data about himself so he was practically untraceable.

I gave the voice command to my PR, then sent a quick message to Lucien saying I'd located the target and had begun collecting information. I stared, waiting for a reply but none came.

It was a worry, something I'd have to check on later. I slapped the PR device back onto my hip where it melded with my skin so it was invisible unless you knew where to look for it.

A knock at the door made me jump, reminding me I should never allow myself to get complacent, not even for a moment.

So polite, Mother waited until I told her to come in, then popped her head around the door.

"By the way, I forgot to tell you," she said. "The Everills emailed me. They're coming to town."

"The who?"

"Angelo and Lydia, our old neighbors. I know you think they're boring but I'm sure you can find some time for them. They did watch you grow up, after all."

No, they hadn't. What was I going to do when these people turned up and my parents suddenly had a seventeen-year-old daughter? How on earth was I going to explain that?

What's more I couldn't even ask my mother for more information about them because I was supposed to already know who they were and what they did.

If only the Everills would stay on the other side of the country where they belonged.

I had enough on my plate without having to deal with this too.

CHAPTER FIVE

It was one week down in Altabena. So far, so good. I wasn't creating too many waves at school and I'd met lots of people, all of whom were contributing to my knowledge about society. Also, Mother hadn't mentioned our 'old neighbors' again so I hoped they might've changed their plans.

After school, I went to the girls' locker room to get into my gym gear. Mr. Matthews had tracked me down and insisted I participate in the martial arts program. I was about to leave when I felt a pinprick on my hip. My PR device. I looked around, then moved into a toilet cubicle, peeled the device from my hip and checked the message. It was brief.

Send an update on the status of your mission immediately.

Hadn't they received my previous messages? And this might be the least of my problems if they had some sort of technical failure in bringing me back. I shuddered at the thought, then sent a message and hoped for the best.

Down the hall, I pushed open a door marked 'Arena' and stepped inside. I needed a distraction and this was definitely the best place for that. The aroma of vinyl and leather equipment mixed with the stale odor of bacteria and fresh sweat. My kind of smell.

Though it was fair to call this an 'Arena', that was really a fancy word for a large room with padded blue mats on the floor for wrestling, a ring in one corner, and punching bags hanging along two walls.

Mr. Matthews stood at the far end of the room with a small group of wrestlers while some other guys were punching the pads on the mat. Ben Tanner spotted me and waved.

Several girls who were were training called me over and introduced themselves. They'd heard how I knocked Mr. Matthews over and wanted to find out more.

People were so friendly here. There was a certain camaraderie in New Nation but it wasn't like this. It wasn't warm and it certainly didn't feel personal.

After warming up, I grabbed a pair of boxing gloves from a large equipment crate and started punching the bag, working in short rounds. Now I was in my element. Just me and the bag. Truth was, I loved smashing the bag. Punching and kicking made me feel powerful and strong and healthy. Made me feel alive.

Between rounds, I spoke to some of the girls while catching my breath. They seemed impressed with my work rate, while I figured that was the reason I was here. To work.

"Oh no," said one of the girls.

The principal, Ms. Di Giorgio, stood at the edge of the mat looking extremely out of place in full make-up, a tight gray skirt and short blazer, her bleached hair piled on top of her head. She stepped out of her patent heels, thereby losing several inches in height, and strutted across the mat to meet Mr. Matthews.

They had a short discussion, then she said in a loud voice, "These children need more discipline. I'm glad we've got you here for that." Looking around the room, she added, "You have a fine teacher here in Mr. Matthews and you should always obey his instructions and follow his example."

Lecture over, she left, while I wondered what that was supposed to be about.

Mr. Matthews approached me. "You look like you're in good shape, Nicola."

"Thanks," I said, though it didn't sound like a compliment.

"Would you like to do some sparring?"

"I'd rather not, since it's my first time here and all."

He planted his hands on his hips, looking down on me. "It's understandable if you're scared. If you're afraid of getting hurt, perhaps you can do something easier."

I was a lot of things and scared wasn't one of them. I certainly wasn't worried about getting hurt. Getting used to pain was part of training, part of military college, part of life.

And I was not afraid.

"Sure," I said. "No problem."

The teacher stepped to one side so I could see behind him to the ring. "Because Roger over there would like to spar with you."

I presumed the fellow leaning against the ropes with his mouth open, drooling, was Roger. Though not much taller than me, he was powerfully built with muscles on top of his muscles. Sweat dripped from his short, glossy black hair, his face red with exertion.

"Could you have picked someone bigger?" I asked.

"I hope that wasn't sarcasm, young lady."

"Just an observation."

"We don't have all day." He pointed to the ring. "Get over there."

I walked across, held the ropes apart and stepped in to greet Roger.

"They call me Moose," he said.

I shrugged. "They call me Nicola."

He made a strange sound half-way between a laugh and a groan, which was a bit of a worry. Perhaps he was purposely trying to sound dumb to put me off my game.

"These rounds will be boxing," Mr. Matthews said, his hand on the corner post outside the ring. "No kicks, knees or elbows. Time starts now."

I was about to complain because they were some of my favorite weapons but stopped myself. I wasn't here to display my skills and that probably wouldn't happen against such a large opponent anyway. I just had to get by.

As soon as Moose and I touched gloves, he launched into a barrage of punches. I slipped and shuffled away. The smell of stale bacteria from his gloves hung in front of my face.

More punches. I ducked and stepped off to the side so I wasn't standing straight in front of him. He looked around as if wondering where I'd gone. I was faster than him, my main advantage.

He came at me again. His punches were hard, too hard for sparring, but this wasn't the time to speak up. I'd wear it and hope for the best. I pawed at him with jabs to keep him at bay, but they weren't knockout punches, and I didn't think the plan was to knock each other out.

My guard was up, but Moose's big right hand slipped between my gloves and landed smack on the middle of my face. My nose stung, though the pain quickly dissipated. Nothing to worry about. Still, I didn't like the way this was headed.

"That's too hard," I yelled.

He grinned and made that weird laughing sound. Through the corner of my eye, I saw Mr. Matthews' lips curl to a smile. He wasn't exactly jumping up and down in agreement with me.

Moose came at me again. I covered. He stepped in closer. Wound up for something big. Shit, there was a head butt coming my way. An illegal move.

I ducked. Every nerve in my body was on edge. I came back with a hook. Landed it on his jaw. His mouth dropped open.

Enough was enough. I wrapped my hands around the back of his neck and yanked him down. I had him in the clinch. Had control of his head. Moose was in the perfect position for me to send in the knees and smash him.

But I didn't.

"Noooo!" Mr. Matthews yelled.

I shunted Moose away, held my hands out. "No more."

Moose straightened, his face contorted into a scowl, and he lunged at me again. No way was I going to cop another pummeling. I sent in a big right hand just as he was coming toward me.

He walked straight into my fist, reeled momentarily, and dropped to the ground on his knees. Crumpled into a giant concertina, which wasn't what I wanted either.

"Oh no, are you okay?" I asked.

Mr. Matthews was inside the ring in a flash, crouching down with his arm around Moose. I was glad someone was helping him, yet this whole situation was way out of line.

And I was on my own.

I glanced around the room. People everywhere. So why did I feel so alone? I shouldn't be feeling anything, yet my senses were overloaded and I was aware of everything around me.

Most of all, I was aware how different I was from these people. I wasn't practicing or training or play-acting. I'd been sent here to kill someone.

I took a deep breath. There was still time for me to gather more information on society and on Ben, and to find out more about how he operated and decide the best way to take him out. I had a job to do.

When the time came I'd be on my own and that was how it had to be. No sergeant above me, no regiment alongside me, no fellow soldier or team members.

This was how it'd be in the end.

Just me.

Finishing the job.

CHAPTER SIX

No point hanging around in the ring when I wasn't needed, so I stepped out and took off my gloves.

Mr. Matthews helped Moose to a bench, then came over to where I was waiting by the side of the ring.

"No clinching," he said.

"I'm sorry," I said though I didn't mean it. I'd been under fire and my training had cut in. In truth, it was lucky something much worse hadn't happened.

"Clinching was not allowed," he repeated.

My chest heaving with deep breaths, I was ready to explode. As if I was the bad guy? As if I was the one who'd tried to heat butt someone half my size.

Anger swelled in my stomach. I'd never argued with a teacher before. There was always a first time.

"Head butting is not allowed either but that didn't stop Moose," I said. "And you didn't pick him up for it."

He shook his finger at me. "You knocked out my best fighter."

"He walked into my fist," I said. "What was I supposed to do?"

"Enough!" Mr. Matthews' face reddened. "I'll deal with you later."

He got no argument from me. I stepped back, only to see Ben Tanner heading in our direction, his stride purposeful. I'd only ever seen him looking friendly and relaxed whereas now he seemed intense, his expression serious.

"Excuse me, Mr. Matthews," he said, as the teacher was turning away.

The man stopped, hands on his hips. "What?"

"Do you have any idea what you just did? That was way out of line, downright dangerous. You shouldn't have put Nicola and Moose in the ring together." Ben's upper lip curled to a sneer as he added, "*Sir.*"

I'd never heard the word sound so insulting.

The teacher's face contorted to a scowl. "Excuse me?"

"You can't put a featherweight in with a heavyweight like Moose."

"I just did." ·

"And it wasn't fair," Ben said, insistent. "That's my point."

"You're right. Turns out it wasn't very fair at all. Moose has never been knocked out before."

"That's not what I meant and you know it."

The teacher pointed at Ben, then me. "You're forgetting something. I'm the teacher and you're the students. You should know your place by now. I can make life very difficult for you, both of you."

He walked off, leaving me in a state of mild shock. No one had ever stuck up for me the way Ben had before, not that I could remember. It took my breath away.

Mind you, I'd never seen a teacher behave like Mr.

Matthews either. He seemed to have had something akin to a tantrum. What was going on around here? This country had serious problems.

Ben's shoulders dropped, his stance more relaxed, a cool grin on his face now the teacher had left.

Only a few minutes ago, I'd felt alone, and that was as it should be. This was all wrong. Ben was the last person who should be on my side. If only he knew.

"I'm only sorry I didn't say something sooner," he said. "I didn't like seeing you head into the ring with Moose."

"I'm sure he's fine," I replied.

"He's not the one I was worried about."

"Oh." Now I was reduced to single syllable words. I had to do better than this, so I added, "Thanks for sticking up for me."

"No problem." He grinned again. I wished he wouldn't do that. "We're not all bad here. Do you ever do any grappling or wrestling?"

"Sure."

"Do you want to have a roll?"

My throat constricted and words wouldn't come out. *Did I want to have a roll?*

In these surroundings it was a perfectly reasonable question. It was simply how someone asked if you'd like to join them on the mat for a wrestle, but there was nothing normal about any of this. For one thing, my heart was racing and we hadn't even started yet.

At this rate soon I'd be giggling and fluttering my eyelashes. Well, I was not a flutterer. I'd never fluttered in my life and wasn't about to start now. I had to fight this every step of the way and knew exactly how to get myself back on track.

"Sure," I said.

Wrestling and grappling was much more technical than it looked. I'd done my fair share with other girls at the academy as well as men who were much bigger than me, and could hold my own.

Ben lay on his back on the mat and motioned for me to join him. I kneeled between his legs which he wrapped around me in the guard position. This was a common position in Brazilian *Jiu Jitsu*, yet nothing about this was standard.

We were on the ground together and I felt the heat of his body, the rise and fall of his breaths, the strength of his muscles.

I felt a lot more than I was supposed to.

He rolled me over so he was on top. Ben was considerate and didn't put his full weight on me. He was strong and manly too, much more so than your average teenager.

No, I should never have let him get the upper hand. This was a technical sport. *Stay technical.* The whole point of this martial art was that a smaller, weaker person could successfully defend against a bigger opponent by using leverage and proper technique.

Leverage. I angled for position, swept him over and got him in an arm bar, a submission hold. He tapped out, the signal for me to release him.

"You're full of surprises," he said.

While he was distracted I got him in side control, my body on top of his, my full weight on top of him. As I landed with a thump, the air left his body.

Now it was down to business. We took turns grappling

for position, playing off each other, and taking turns practicing holds and submissions.

This was what I was good at. I knew what to do and where I stood. This was my world and I was not some stupid giggling female going weak at the sight of a male.

I was getting a feel for Ben's strengths and weaknesses. Not that I'd eliminate him with my bare hands. Too many things could go wrong with hand-to-hand combat. For one thing, twisting someone's neck was harder than it looked. Muscles, tendons, neck bones, all these things provided resistance. And a broken neck didn't mean instant death. There were way too many variables. I could get badly injured, for one thing.

And it was too close, too intimate. Still, I had to be prepared.

We upped the pace. That was one of the things I liked about grappling and *Jiu Jitsu*. You were always fighting, jostling for position, and it never stopped. My heart rate increased for all the right reasons. Because of the strength involved, the physical exertion, the need to stay alert.

Ben made a tactical error and I had his back. A big mistake. From here, he could only defend, while I had plenty of opportunities to attack or submit him. I slid one arm beneath his chin, inching my arm around, his body already locked into position with my legs.

There was nowhere for him to go but still he struggled. So did I until the bent V of my arm was under his chin. I secured my hand to my shoulder to hold the choke in place. I'd never give up my position.

This was what I was supposed to do to him eventually. Finish him. Not now, but later. It was why I'd been sent to Altabena.

I'd killed before. My superior officers wouldn't have sent me on the mission if I hadn't. It had been so much easier then.

I squeezed my arm tighter. Ben tapped. And I let go.

He rolled away. I sat with my arms resting on my bent knees, my breaths ragged.

You won't be able to do this.

It's all wrong.

"You don't like to lose, do you, Nicola?" Ben looked up at me through the messed-up, dark, wavy hair that fell over his forehead.

"Winning is so much better," I said.

So why didn't I feel good? Why wasn't I celebrating?

His eyes narrowed. "I can't work you out. Where do you get that competitive streak?"

"M-me?" I placed a hand on my chest. "I'm not competitive. I just like to win all the time."

Ben leaned back on his hands, staring at me as if I were a moron, a look I was getting used to.

I took a deep breath. "Okay, I can't help myself. It's the way I've been raised. I like to compete and, more than that, I like to win."

"So, are your parents highly competitive?" he asked. "Is that where it comes from?"

"Not at all."

He meant my parents in Altabena. I couldn't tell him the truth, that the schools in which I'd been raised had extremely high standards, that it was an honor to have made it into military college, that I'd been reared to be the best at what I do.

"No, they're..." I began. "That's different..."

"So your competitiveness came out of thin air?"

I shrugged. "I'm not sure exactly where it comes from. What about you?"

"I've got an older brother," he said as if that were an explanation.

"And?"

"You know what it's like with siblings."

"Not really."

"So you're an only child, I didn't realize."

I nodded though that wasn't quite true. I had an older brother in New Nation who I hadn't seen for years. He worked for the military too, patrolling the Badlands, a highly dangerous job.

We hadn't grown up together so I barely knew him. Several years ago, I'd thought we might have something in common since we were both at military school and had tried to initiate a friendship, however he'd told me he was too busy.

His answer had niggled at me back then – more than niggled if I was going to be honest. There hadn't even been anyone I could to talk to about it because the fact I was nothing to him wasn't something to get upset about, not in New Nation.

Ben said, "My brother and I were always wrestling and getting into scuffles. Josh is away at college now. When we were kids, he was always bigger. I had to learn to hold my own or I'd get flattened."

I raised my eyebrows. "You didn't like being downtrodden?"

"You've got it wrong. We were kids, mucking around, having a good time."

The idea was so foreign to me that it made me wonder what that would've been like. I nodded.

"There's another thing I learnt from my brother," he said. "That it's better to talk your way out of situations than fight your way out."

"Not always. Not if you're dealing with a dangerous opponent. Sometimes attack is the best defense. Sometimes it's the only way."

"Not for me."

"So you're a martial artist and a pacifist?" I asked.

"Yep."

"Then why do martial arts at all?"

"It's about control. Controlling aggression, to be precise. Believe it or not, I used to be an angry young guy."

Intrigued, I edged closer to Ben. "How angry?"

"I used to get into fights, lash out, make trouble. It's not something I'm proud of."

"How long ago was this?" I asked.

"When I was twelve, Dad got me into martial arts. To teach me discipline. It worked."

"What made you so mad?" I asked.

He looked away. "Life. Lots of things."

There was more to this story than he was telling me. Was this a description of a confused young male or the first glimpse into the mind of a future killer? I had a feeling it was the former and that was not what I needed to hear.

"You're not angry now?" I asked though the answer was obvious.

He turned to me. "No. What about you? What made you get into martial arts?"

"Me?"

Ben grinned, his eyes crinkling up at the corners. "Yes, you."

"Martial arts makes me who I am," I said. "It's part of

me."

I loved everything about it from the cardio-rush to the achievement from improving and the confidence it gave me. I even got perverse pleasure from the pain. Most of all, I loved the sense of power.

Ben didn't speak right away. He leaned closer, a satisfied gleam in his green eyes as he held my gaze. At that moment, I felt close to him, much closer than I should.

After a while, he said, "I know exactly what you mean."

And he did. I could see it in his eyes and the set of his mouth. Except we weren't supposed to be on the same wavelength. We were on different sides even if Ben didn't know it.

I tucked my legs under myself, ready to leave.

Ben held my gaze as if he didn't want me to go. "This is a great place for someone like me. I can come here and train and be a different person, someone who's aggressive. I can be something I'm not."

But Ben Tanner was going to do something extremely aggressive – fatal, in fact – when he created the killer virus.

I stood to leave. "Time to go."

Ben jumped to his feet. "I'll catch you tomorrow."

On my way to the locker rooms, I walked past the other girls who congratulated me on my performance with Moose. Except I hadn't meant to put on another show. That wasn't why I was here and this wasn't going to plan.

I slumped down on the bench beside my bag. I couldn't get Ben out of my mind. Hardly surprising since he was my target.

My methods were sound. Gathering information was my initial priority. Meanwhile I was ingratiating myself into

Ben's life because that would give me more opportunities to get close and finish him. If he was a friend, no one would be suspicious of my motives or my presence, least of all Ben.

When the time came, I'd have to decide where to complete the job. Not at school because there'd be too many witnesses. It could be at his house or some secluded location. Still, I didn't need to stress about where to do it just yet. I had to work out *how* first and then the location would follow from that.

Yes, I'd have to choose a method to eliminate him. I'd have to focus, like I had before I'd secured the chokehold. Nothing could get in my way.

It was a simple matter of mathematics: the life of one mass murderer versus the lives of billions of innocent people. It shouldn't be a hard decision. Besides, I had my orders and disobeying was not an option.

Ben and I weren't both going to win.

We couldn't.

CHAPTER SEVEN

This wasn't the first time Ben had walked home from school with me. What's more, these opportunities to get to know him better kept falling in my lap. Fine by me. Every interaction was an opportunity to learn more about him, his routines and movements, his capabilities and weak spots.

"No martial arts training this afternoon?" I asked as we ambled along the path in the mottled shade of the gum trees above.

"I only train twice a week after school," Ben said. "Plus Saturday mornings. That's usually a big session."

I screwed up my face. "Is that all?"

How had he reached such a high level of martial arts with so little training? In New Nation, my whole life revolved around training and improving my skills.

He shrugged. "It's hard to fit everything in."

"Really?"

Now I didn't know what he meant at all. He should've had ample time for school, training and study with plenty of spare time thrown in.

"What are you up to this afternoon?" I asked.

Another shrug. "Nothing much. Probably studying."

"So who else is home when you get there?"

"Dad's at work. My little sister, Celia, gets home not long after me. She usually goes to a friend's house on my training afternoons. I don't like to leave her at home alone too long."

"What about your mom?"

"She's not around," he said quickly. "You're asking a lot of questions."

I shrugged, pretended to be nonchalant. "I'm nosy."

When it was closer to the time, the hours immediately after school presented an excellent opportunity to execute my mission. Ben would be at home, easy to locate, unsuspecting – except if the little sister was around. I couldn't be that calculating or cold-blooded even though I was supposed to be.

We reached the corner where he usually turned off to go to his place.

"See you tomorrow, Nicola," Ben said.

"Sure."

We parted ways and I headed home to dump my school bag and change into jeans and a tee shirt. Mother was sitting at the kitchen table, tapping away at her laptop.

"Good news," she said. "The Everills have set a date. They'll be here at the end of next month."

How could I have forgotten about our old 'neighbors'? And what the hell was I supposed to do?

I froze in the doorway. "Great."

Mother looked at me through hooded lids. "There's no need to be sarcastic."

"Why do they want to come here anyway?"

"In her email, Lydia said they want to get away from things, not that that should make any difference to you."

"They could go somewhere further away."

Like Mom's parents who lived in the South of France or Dad's parents who were dead. The further away, the better.

Her brow furrowed, Mother stared at me. "Look, I know they're both 'computer geeks' as you like to say and they can be a little odd. They only email because they don't like talking over the phone but, honestly Nicola, what is with you?"

I turned and left. "I've got to go."

There was no easy fix for this situation.

It was one step at a time and the first thing I had to do was get back to Ben's. His house was similar to the others on the street. A neat, two-story clapboard place, the garden was well kept with a blue station wagon parked out front.

As I ambled along, Ben came out of his front door carrying an armful of books. He nudged a small, blond girl wearing a dance costume down the path ahead of him. Celia, I presumed.

"Can you stay to watch the performance at the end?" she asked in her high-pitched voice. "All the parents will be there."

"Sure," Ben said.

"I like it when you stay and watch."

"I've got to study as well. Hurry up, Celia."

Since Ben hadn't noticed me yet, I stepped closer and called out. Under the circumstances there was no need for me to hide.

He stopped by the car, his face lighting up. "What are you doing here?"

"Going for a walk." I stepped closer. "You know, keeping up a healthy lifestyle. What about you?"

Celia said loudly, "He's taking me to dance."

"You didn't mention that earlier," I said to Ben.

He shook his head. "Nope."

Ben didn't seem to be in such a hurry now he'd seen me either. He introduced me to his little sister.

"How old are you, Celia?" I asked.

"Seven," she said.

"You're big for seven."

The little girl beamed and Ben said, "We're off to the community center. Do you need a lift somewhere?"

I shook my head. "Then I'd miss out on this wonderful walk."

Celia opened the passenger's door and slid inside the car. "We have to go now."

So did I. I felt a pinprick on my hip. My PR device again.

Ben drummed his fingers on the roof of the car as if hesitating. "You can come along if you like."

"Maybe another time."

Ben waved it off. "Nah, I didn't think you'd be interested."

I watched him get into the car. *All the parents would be there*. And Ben. Why would he be there?

As he drove away, I pretended to continue on my way until Ben's car was out of sight, then doubled back and headed for his house.

He'd already given me all the requisite information. His mom wasn't around and his father was at work. At training he'd mentioned an older brother who was away at college. The house was empty. That was all I needed to know.

I walked down a side path and saw an upstairs window that had been left open. Since it was right next to a tree, this couldn't have been easier. I climbed up the trunk and seconds later, I was in a room with pink walls, framed dance posters and a bed covered in a princess bedspread. Not the right bedroom.

Now I was safely out of view, I peeled the PR device from my hip and checked my messages.

A communications problem has been identified but cannot be rectified. We know you are alive, however your messages are not being transmitted. Continue with your mission as planned.

Yes, my superior officers knew I was alive. Thanks to Geopositrons and advanced GPS technology, they knew exactly where I was. They always knew. Something about that bothered me, though I couldn't put my finger on exactly what. Or maybe I was still jumpy from the news about my parents' neighbors visiting.

Still, at least transmissions from New Nation were getting through even if mine weren't and, as my superiors reminded me, I had a job to do.

Stepping out into the hallway, I found Ben's room was the next one along. I headed straight for his desk, grabbed his laptop, sat on the bed and gave a voice command for my PR to collate all information on Ben Tanner.

A few minutes later, the device had infiltrated Ben's computer and I slapped the PR back onto my hip. I went through Ben's files, emails and internet history, looking for anything that might give some hint of the disaster that was to come. It was extremely disappointing to say the least. I'd even go as far as to say his emails were boring.

I pushed the laptop aside. Damn it, I wasn't even sure

what I was hoping to discover. That he'd been researching weapons of mass destruction? Membership to an anarchistic group looking to overthrow the world? At the very least perhaps an interest in a Nazi-inspired organization?

With ample time up my sleeve, I searched his room. Books and papers were arranged in neat piles on an enormous desk. I rummaged around. Nothing. He'd taped a child's picture of a family playing in a park on the wall in front of his desk. By Celia, no doubt.

Ben's closet was huge with neatly hung and folded clothes at one end, and miscellaneous sporting equipment at the other. I rifled through. This was useless.

Then an idea came to me, not something to do with Ben, but an idea nonetheless. I grabbed the laptop and typed in the Everill's names. I found Lydia's professional profile and resume – a software developer.

I hit the jackpot with Angelo Everill. In fact, I couldn't believe what I found. The computing teacher had been accused of sexual abuse by two previous students who'd been 14 and 15 years old at the time of the alleged abuse.

This couldn't have been better. For me, that is. No way would my parents want a pedophile in the house with their daughter. At least one problem was being averted.

After that, climbing out of the window and down the tree was even easier than getting in. At the bottom, I brushed myself off, checked my surroundings and walked away. I could go home but decided on the community center instead since Ben had practically invited me.

When I arrived, parents and children in dance costumes were milling around outside the building on their way to their vehicles. The class must be over. The other parents, mostly mothers, chatted to each other while Ben came out alone. Celia was in front of him with a little friend, the two of them holding hands and skipping.

Ben saw me and waved. "What are you doing here?"

I stepped closer. "How was the dance performance?"

"Fine. I didn't think dancing was your kind of thing. Did you do this as a kid or something?"

I placed a hand on my chest. "Me?"

He nudged me gently as we walked toward his car parked up the street. "I take it that's a 'no'. I can't picture you in a tutu."

"What about Celia? How did she go?"

"She had a ball. She absolutely loves this stuff. That makes it all worthwhile."

"Worthwhile?"

He shrugged. "It's just an expression."

Still, it was an odd thing to say.

Ben stopped near his car, one eye on Celia and her friend by the side of the road. "Do you really want to know?"

"Yes," I said.

"I had to give up football for dance practice, and the other guys on the team gave me a hard time."

I stood beside Ben. "But you're not the one doing dancing."

"Not exactly. Between martial arts and football practice, all my time was taken up and there wasn't anything left for Celia. Something had to go. I didn't want her to miss out. It wasn't a big deal. I loved martial arts too much to give it up, so it had to be football."

I raised my eyebrows. "And that didn't go down well?"

"No, the other guys didn't get it. They said I'd let the

team down." He flicked his hand in the air. "Anyway, it was pretty juvenile dreaming about being a football player."

Technically we were probably both still juveniles. I didn't point this out. I also didn't believe for a minute there'd been no sacrifice on his part.

I looked around. "What happened to Celia and...?"

One playful push and Celia had ended up on the road. In an instant, Ben reached across and pulled her back. Excellent reflexes. A slow-moving car had already stopped, so it wasn't quite a moment of life or death.

Ben crouched by his sister on the sidewalk. "You've got to be more careful, Celia. I absolutely can not lose you too."

"I wasn't lost," she said. "I was on the road."

What was Ben so afraid of? It hadn't even been a particularly close call. Kids wandered off and did silly things all the time.

He wrapped his arms around his sister and pulled her close while she flung her scrawny arms over his neck. His eyes squeezed shut, he put everything he had into that hug, or as much as he could without squashing the little girl.

Though I had a big brother in New Nation, I'd never experienced a moment like this one. I'd never felt loved like that. Never felt much of anything. At least I'd always tried not to.

But I felt it now – a wisp of jealousy for what I'd missed out on, amazement at the scene unfolding in front of me, and a longing I'd never experienced before. I felt it all. And I had to stop feeling. This wasn't supposed to be happening.

Ben cared about Celia.

And *I* shouldn't. I left them to it. His love for her was selfish and had nothing to do with the greater good of humanity. If I'd had any doubts about my mission before, there were none now.

I had bigger things to worry about.

CHAPTER EIGHT

Back to school, back to a routine, back to things I was much more comfortable with. Mr. Rodriguez had organized a science excursion to a chemical laboratory to balance out the theory in our study with a practical example.

"This is so boring," Lauren whispered as we passed through one of the labs.

"Yeah." This time, I had to agree. The only thing I'd learnt so far was that I was never going to be an expert in biochemistry.

The chemical lab looked, well, like a chemical laboratory with lots of white benches, computers and scientific equipment, and walls of testing equipment I couldn't identify.

Contrary to my expectation, the staff didn't have white lab coats. Instead, they wore baggy pants and tops similar to surgical scrubs, mostly in shades of green and blue.

"I'd never take a job where I had to wear one of those terrible hair nets like these dudes," Lauren said.

"Good point." That wouldn't be a problem since I

didn't think they'd have her anyway.

Mr. Rodriguez led us along an elevated walkway that looked down onto another laboratory. Inside, the staff wore what appeared to be white space suits. Covered from head to toe, they looked out through glass bubbles that shielded their heads.

The teacher introduced us to Nick Sheridan, the laboratory manager.

"These scientists are dealing with extremely volatile substances and must exercise the utmost care," he said. "The pharmaceuticals they're investigating may be used for medical cures or treatments or the prevention of disease in the future. The research is time consuming and painstaking."

One student put his hand up. "How come they need to wear all that gear? Is it really that dangerous?"

"Yes, it is," Mr. Sheridan said. "We don't know the exact effects of some of these drugs. That's why they're being investigated. The researchers could be infected with something and that infection could spread. It could be fatal."

My mouth fell open. He had no idea how accurate that was. Neither did the people standing around me.

"There could be an epidemic," I said, rather too loudly. "You wouldn't even see it coming. A virus could wipe most of the population and, that's it, you're all gone."

Silence. Followed by laughter. And even applause.

I shrank on the spot. I'd said the wrong thing again. Lauren put her arm around me and gave me a quick squeeze. She was giggling too.

"You may laugh," Mr. Sheridan said, then waited until the noise subsided. "But the young lady has a point. That's exactly why we have such extreme safeguards."

Somewhere along the line, the safeguards must've slipped. In 2041 a virus would spread across the globe and the population would be obliterated.

As I looked around at the faces around me, I wondered which of the students in my class would survive. They were people and they were alive. For now.

Suddenly the history I'd learnt was much more than dates and facts and statistics. The figures about fatalities were no longer faceless people who'd died long before I was born. They were all around me. One day most of them would perish and all of them would suffer. It was too horrible to think about.

Lauren gave me a gentle nudge while Mr. Sheridan kept talking. "You need to lighten up, Nicola."

I didn't say anything. I wasn't feeling very 'light'.

Ben raised his hand to ask a question. "Surely if the government spent less money on defense and more on medical research, you'd be able to find more cures for diseases."

"Yes," Mr. Sheridan said. "There's a direct correlation between the size of our budget and the results we produce. Unfortunately, the work we do is expensive and it costs a lot to run this place. We're not a pharmaceutical company. This is a government research facility that relies heavily on public funding."

Ben's hand shot up again. "If biochemists want to find treatments for individual diseases, where do they start? How do they go about it?"

"Good question," Mr. Sheridan said. "Generally, it takes years of concerted research. Sometimes, discoveries are made by accident but most of the time nothing happens the easy way."

Ben was about to ask something else when Mr. Rodriguez interjected to say this was the end of our visit.

We headed outside toward the bus, only to find the vehicle was there but the driver had disappeared, so we waited while Mr. Rodriguez headed across the road to find him.

Ben brushed up beside me, by accident, of course. "You made an impression in there."

"I could say the same about you."

He shrugged. "I just think there are better things we could be doing with government funds than inventing wars in foreign countries and killing people."

My eyes wide, I swallowed.

Ben continued. "Wouldn't it be better to spend that money helping people and improving lives? Not everyone is as well off as you and me. There are plenty of kids who don't even get a chance at a good education. With more money, we could give those people something to look forward to, better lives, lives with hope."

"Wow." Perhaps I should've come up with something more intelligent but that was the best I could do.

Ben didn't sound like a future mass murderer, not that I'd met many in the past or had a comparison point. I was fairly sure, however, that psychopaths weren't interested in giving people opportunities or helping them.

"So what would you do with the funding?" I asked.

"That doesn't really matter. I'm never going to be a politician so I'll never be in a position to decide. That's part of the problem. The people with the power to make those decisions don't care enough."

I frowned. "That's so…empathetic."

"You say that like it's a bad thing."

Ben didn't just care about himself and Celia. He cared about a lot of things. I felt something deep inside, surprise at his compassion, a sense of warmth. His humanity touched me.

Or maybe it just touched a nerve. This didn't fit with what I'd been told about Ben Tanner. Nothing fit. I had to focus.

The timing had never been better to bring up the subject of mass annihilation of the human race, not a subject that came up in everyday conversation.

"What did you think about the idea of an infection being released and causing an epidemic?" I asked.

"Mr. Sheridan must've been talking about the possibility of some sort of industrial accident," Ben said. "There's no way someone would release dangerous chemicals into the air and put lives at risk *on purpose*."

"It's a possibility, though."

His eyes narrowed. "What on earth would drive someone to release a killer virus into the air? Who would do something like that?"

It was a very good question. I had some questions of my own.

"Someone like you, maybe?" I said.

He put a hand on his chest. "Me? You've got to be kidding."

I leaned closer. "Haven't you ever harbored a secret desire to kill off part of the population?"

Ben took a small step back. "You know, Nicola, one of the things I like about you is that you don't beat around the bush. I kind of like the wild questions you ask. But there's such a thing as going too far. I'll give it to you straight. The only secret desire I have isn't even a secret. I'd like to become a doctor."

He had it all wrong. I wasn't the one who'd gone too far. I hadn't released a killer virus and killed most of the population.

Ben Tanner had. It was written in our history.

People could change over time. Maybe something would happen in the coming years to transform Ben from an intelligent, well-meaning young man to a hideous mass murderer. Maybe he'd be drawn by money or power or some other force. Maybe he'd do a complete turnaround from the person he was now.

Maybe.

Suddenly the students around us cheered. Up ahead, Mr. Rodriguez waved for us to join him. The driver was ahead of him, stepping onto the bus, his shoulders hunched and head down as if he'd been caught out.

Ben put a hand on my shoulder. "Let's put all evil thoughts of overthrowing the world behind us and get on the bus." He raised his eyebrows. "No hard feelings?"

I nodded. "Sure."

No feelings of any sort. Or at least there shouldn't be.

He placed his hand on the small of my back and ushered me ahead of him. On top of everything else, he was acting like a gentleman. It was more than I could handle. More than I should have to take.

There was some mistake.

There had to be.

CHAPTER NINE

What kind of science class was this? Mr. Rodriguez's strategy for managing the students and lesson was baffling to say the least. He'd left us to it while we supposedly chose groups for our next project. However judging from the noise and disruption in the room, I doubted the students were working on the task at hand. They were enjoying themselves far too much for that.

Unable to concentrate, I covered my ears. Moments later, I felt the warmth of a hand on mine as Ben Tanner crouched by my desk.

"Hello there, Ben," I said, then realized I sounded like a dork.

"Do you want to partner up for the project?" he asked.

"Sure."

He grinned, his eyes crinkling up at the corners. "Excellent, because I want to do well in this assignment."

I already knew Ben worked hard to get good grades. We discussed the project and how we might approach it, deciding we'd get together to work on it tomorrow night.

"Back to your desks everyone," Mr. Rodriguez called

out.

No sooner had the words come out of the teacher's mouth than the students obeyed, and Lauren took her seat beside me. The way he regained control of the class in an instant astounded me. It was as if he had the students' respect but that couldn't possibly be the case when he was so lax with them.

Meanwhile I found it increasingly hard to concentrate and was probably the only person in the room not paying attention to the lesson.

Lauren nudged me and motioned toward Ben. "He's a hottie."

I glanced at her. "A whattie?"

She looked down her nose at me. "I saw the way you looked at him, Nicola. Don't pretend you don't have a thing for him."

"A thing?"

I did have a thing but not the sort of thing to which she was referring. Not the sort of thing she'd be able to understand. I wouldn't even know where to start.

"Hard to believe anyone would do the dirty on a guy like him, isn't it?" she added.

I was about to ask her what she meant when Mr. Rodriguez glared at us. We both stopped talking while he gave the next instruction. I should've been listening. Instead I was thinking about Ben.

*   *   *

Preparing dinner was a menial task. I didn't do menial tasks, but I hadn't been able to get out of this one. Recently Mother had started her new job and I had to help out at home. It was as simple as that. And as complex.

Looking around the kitchen I took deep breaths, trying

to talk myself into it. I could do this. I could cook spaghetti.

I found my two favorite knives in the top drawer: a large chef's knife and a paring blade which was similar to the blade I'd used to slit the throat of a wild boar after shooting and wounding it. Putting a bullet through a moving target had taken skill but it was the knife that had made the experience worthwhile. The slashing sound came back to me, the rush of blood, the satisfaction.

The knife was always my first choice. With a knife, it was always personal.

That was why I'd already bought the perfect five-inch blade from a store in town.

Perfect for my future needs.

Staring at the doorframe, I picked up the paring knife, took aim and threw the blade. It landed smack bang in the middle of the wooden frame. I grabbed the chef's knife, did the same, and practiced for a while, then decided I should get a move on with dinner.

As soon as I started, I could tell this wasn't going well. I was seriously good with a knife but when it came to the world of vegetables, I was out of my league. Then there was the smell when I started cooking. Not good.

Mother walked in, looking very smart in her work clothes while I probably looked very frazzled at the stove. Her eyes on the doorframe I'd been using for target practice, she brushed away some splinters. "I didn't notice that before. We must have woodworm. I'll have to get your dad to look at it."

I lowered my gaze. "Hmm, yes."

She sniffed the air. "That smells…interesting. I think you need to turn the heat down, darling. Can I give you a hand?"

"I really don't like having an audience," I said rather more sharply than intended.

After she left, I put the pasta on, finished cooking and called out that dinner was ready.

"Something smells good," Father said as he sat at the table.

Mother joined him. "Certainly does."

I looked down to admire the meal I'd made, overcome by a wave of pride. Mother had asked me to prepare dinner and I'd risen to the task.

Then I took my first mouthful and knew something was seriously wrong.

"Hmm." Mother made an appreciative sound.

"Delicious," Father said, his head down.

It wasn't. The pasta was an overcooked, soggy mess topped with a sludge-like sauce infused with an acrid smokiness that was clearing my nasal passages. Luckily I'd had some truly terrible army rations while on training exercises near the Badlands, so I could handle this. I only hoped my parents had been hardened the way I was.

"It's okay," I said. "You don't have to finish it."

"This is lovely," Father said. "However, it is very filling."

I kept eating and looked at them both. "Wow, you two are so polite I can't believe it."

"You've gone to so much trouble with the meal," he said.

I nodded. "But it's terrible. You can say it."

The two of them laughed and stared at me with what could only be described as affection. Affection? Where had that come from?

Father kissed me on the cheek. "Thanks for dinner, Nicola."

I couldn't look at him as he left the room. I didn't need this. I had Lucien waiting for me in New Nation. He was more than my superior officer, more than someone who understood me, more than the man who'd helped mold me into the soldier I was.

Lucien had saved my life. It was during a training exercise with live ammunition. He'd seen a recruit taking aim, seen that I was in the way, and had thrown himself in the line of fire to take the bullet himself. His shoulder still ached from the wound.

I had to be the best soldier I could possibly be. For my country. For Lucien. Because he was my hero.

Mother took her plate to the kitchen bench. "I'll do the dishes if you like, honey."

Her shoulders had slumped and make-up failed to cover the dark smudges beneath her eyes. It didn't take a genius to work out she was tired.

I stood and joined her by the sink. "Why would you offer to do the cleaning up? You're exhausted."

"Because I can see you're struggling. Because you tried so hard with dinner. And because I probably pushed you too hard. Cooking takes practice. It's not easy."

This was worse than I thought. The kindness in her voice when she talked to me…The fact the two of them had eaten the sludge I'd cooked…The way they looked at me…

"It's because you love me," I blurted out.

Mother laughed. "You don't have to say that like it's a disease. Of course I love you, silly."

How could she love me when she didn't know me?

My real parents in New Nation didn't love me, not as far as I knew, anyway. They'd visited my schools on many occasions so they were hardly strangers to me, but they'd never expressed anything resembling love. Pride at my success, yes. Satisfaction that I was doing my part for New Nation, yes. But never love.

My biological parents had been brought together for procreation, selected on the grounds of genetic compatibility for the best chances of producing strong offspring. They lived together in government lodgings, along with hundreds of other couples, whose roles for the state had been the same.

Love didn't come into it.

"All parents love their children," Mother said. "It doesn't matter how old you are, you'll still be my baby and I'll always love you."

She put her hand on my shoulder. I felt the warmth of her body beside mine, firm and reassuring. I felt a lot of things, none of which I wanted to face.

I turned to the sink. "I'll finish up on my own."

I'd only been here a month. This was ridiculous. I certainly didn't appreciate the pang of emotion in my gut.

"One more thing," she said. "Just because we love you doesn't change anything about the Everills' visit. I've asked them to stay with us."

"What?"

"You heard."

"Mom, there's something you don't know about Angelo Everill." I cleared my throat. "I don't know how to tell you this, but he's been accused of sexual abuse by two female students."

Horror in her eyes. "What?"

"It's all over the internet."

She covered her mouth, then reached for my hand. "Surely he didn't go near you. He wasn't *your* computing teacher after all."

"I'm fine," I said.

"This isn't...I can't...Honey, I'll leave you to it. I'm going to check the internet and speak with your father."

At least, that part of my life was under control, as I was sure the Everills would not be coming to stay. But my relationship with my so-called parents still bothered me. A lot. Their feelings for me, the way they took care of me, even the way they spoke to me – this was getting out of hand.

As I started cleaning up, it hit me. Suddenly I knew what was so wrong with this picture. Apparently, my parents' love for me was perfectly normal.

And my superior officers knew.

They'd known all along.

They'd planted memories of raising a child in the minds of Jan and Philip Gray, and the concept of love was part and parcel of that. The men who'd sent me on this mission knew that parents loved their children, that they'd do anything for their offspring.

So what else hadn't my superior officers told me about?

CHAPTER TEN

I'd survived another day at school and had got through another dinner with my parents too, though that was much easier when I wasn't doing the cooking.

Mother pulled up outside Ben Tanner's house. "I'll pick you up at nine thirty unless you call first."

"Thanks for the lift." I closed the car door behind me, my laptop bag slung over one shoulder.

Hearing the driver's door open, I glanced back to see her getting out of the car.

Her heels clicked on the front path as she rushed to catch me. "I just want to meet his parents to check everything is okay."

I stopped at the door. "Ben said his dad's home. There's no need for you to come in."

Mother put her hand out as if making a stand. "I know you're embarrassed."

"That's not it. I don't want you to waste your time."

"Looking after your safety is not a waste of my time. I'll feel better if I meet Ben and check everything is okay."

Far from being embarrassed, I found her response

touching. Or I would if I were the sort of person who was touched by emotion, which I wasn't.

I pressed the doorbell. "It's not as if this is a high-danger zone."

She stopped by the front door. "This may be news to you but sometimes terrible things happen in the world. Not everyone is as nice as you."

I wasn't as pleasant as she thought. *Nice* didn't come into it. I'd been sent here to complete a task, part of which involved fitting into this environment which was turning out to be harder than it should be.

Ben opened the door, smiled politely and suggested Mother come in. Ben's father was cleaning up in the kitchen, and seemed very glad to meet us. Deep lines bracketed his mouth, even more so when he smiled, his sandy hair cropped short because it was receding.

"Are we going up to your room, Ben?" I asked.

I'd already seen the enormous desk in his bedroom but stopped myself from myself from mentioning it. Meanwhile Mother glared at me.

"No, I've set us up in the dining room," he said.

"Let's get started then."

Ben reached across to shake Mother's hand. "Lovely to meet you."

She beamed, clearly pleased.

I looked at Ben's father. "Thanks for having me over."

He smiled. Despite the amount of time I'd spent in Altabena, it wasn't always easy picking the right thing to say.

Ben and I headed down the hall to the dining room. Sure enough, Ben's laptop, a pile of books and papers, and a tray with a bottle of water and two glasses sat on the long mahogany table.

"Not my favorite room in the house," Ben said under his breath. "Take a seat."

The walls were painted deep burgundy and a long buffet covered with framed photos lined one wall. A large picture of the whole family took pride of place in the middle. Ben's mother held a blond toddler on her knee while his father had his head close to his wife's, his arms around a much younger Ben and the older brother.

We hadn't been seated long when Ben's dad popped his head inside the door. I couldn't help but notice how much he'd aged in the few years since the portrait was taken.

"Just checking you've got everything you need in here," he said.

I looked up and smiled. "Sure, thanks."

"Yes, *Dad*." Ben sounded annoyed. "We're fine."

"Okay." His father left.

"Is something wrong?" I asked.

"Honestly, I don't know what he thinks we're going to get up to in here." Ben rolled his eyes. "Maybe he thinks we're going to be studying the reproductive system or something."

"Where would he get that idea? That's not what the science project is about."

Ben laughed. "Sometimes you crack me up."

I smiled casually as if that was what I'd intended all along. The way Mother had glared at me when I'd suggested going to Ben's room came back to me, raising even more questions.

"Is that why we're here instead of in your bedroom?" I asked. "So we don't get up to anything unseemly?"

Ben grinned. "Unseemly? Where did you learn to talk that way?" He waved a hand. "But, yes, that's basically it. Dad wants to make sure there's no 'funny business' as he puts it."

Funny business, I'd have to remember that term. There'd certainly be none of that.

"I only came here to study," I said. "For the science project."

He looked at me as if I was weird. Maybe I'd missed something.

"I can see that," he said. "Let's get down to it."

"There's a lot to get through but I've got a plan."

He raised his eyebrows. "A plan?"

I always had a plan of attack. In the longer term, I was thinking about eliminating Ben but it was too early to do the job just yet. Meanwhile I was still a high school student, a competitive one at that.

We set to work, deciding which areas needed further research and what else we'd need to do. Half an hour later, there was a gentle knock at the door.

"Dad, we're fine," Ben said without looking up.

I turned to see Celia standing quietly by the door in pink princess pajamas and a matching bathrobe.

"Ben," she said in a small high-pitched voice.

As soon as he looked across, his shoulders relaxed. "Oh, it's you. Come in, Squirt."

"Hi Celia," I said.

She waved and returned my smile, then turned to her brother. "Dad said I wasn't allowed to disturb him yet. My movie finished and I can't get the next show to start. I didn't know what to do."

He stood and ruffled her hair. "Let's take a look,

then." He motioned for me to join them.

The living area was much more relaxed than the dining room. Cushions were scattered on two sofas and there was a pleasant level of clutter in the room.

Celia sat back and pulled a doll onto her lap while I perched on the arm of the sofa. Ben reached for the remote control on the coffee table, found a program on the system and pressed play. A cartoon popped up on the television.

Strangely it was one I'd seen as a kid. In New Nation, the television industry was very small and few new shows were produced other than news services and government programming. We could watch what we wanted but there wasn't much to choose from. That was why I'd watched so many old TV shows and movies. It helped me escape into a different world, if only for a while.

"Thanks, Ben," the little girl said.

"No problem, Squirt."

Celia looked up at him with big blue eyes, her eyelashes impossibly long as she blinked. With her soft cheeks and smooth skin, it was as if her features were designed to make her appear cute and vulnerable. It was having an effect, even on me.

"Thanks, Ben." She threw her arms around him, then settled back onto the sofa, her eyes glued to the screen in a scene that was so ordinary and yet so heartwarming.

"I don't like using the television as a baby sitter, but sometimes we have to," Ben said as we left.

"What about your mother?" I asked. "Where's she?"

"She's not around," he snapped.

He'd told me that once before. This time, the terseness of his reply took me by surprise.

As we settled at the dining table again, he added quietly, "It's just Dad and us three kids, except Josh has gone to college in Seattle. Not that he ever did much to help."

"Was he supposed to?" I asked.

"Of course he was supposed to. Dad couldn't do everything and Josh always pretended it was all too hard for him so I got lumbered with extra work around the house. Not that Celia's hard work. She's a great kid." He stared at me. "I hope I'm not going on about it. You haven't been through this sort of thing, have you?"

I'd missed out on more than he could imagine and was riveted by what he had to say. My life in New Nation was complicated, only in a different way. There was always an upcoming challenge, training exercises designed to push us to the limits, as well as high academic standards to maintain. Yet somehow the complexities of Ben's life took things to a whole new level.

"You've seen how cute Celia is," Ben said. "I can't just forget about her."

His eyebrows went up in the middle and his green eyes sparkled as he spoke. I'd seen that same sort of expression before, when my parents had given me that loving look last night.

"That makes you feel good, doesn't it?" I asked.

Ben frowned. "You're a strange one. I don't normally talk about this stuff, but I feel like I have to explain it all to you."

Maybe that's because you do.

"We should probably get on with the project," I said.

My head down, I shuffled through the papers on the table while Ben was on the computer.

He slammed the laptop shut and dropped his head in his hands. "I can't believe they ask us this shit."

"Sorry?" I asked, wondering what shit he was referring to.

He leaned back, folded his arms. "This is a load of crap. As part of the assignment, they want to know how much blood you can lose before the onset of death. What kind of question is that?"

"What's so unusual?" I asked. "In class, Mr. Rodriguez asked you about how much blood there was in the human body and you knew all the answers."

"Photographic memory."

"Then what's the answer?"

"Screw the answer."

Where had that come from? Weren't we simply working on a science project?

Ben gritted his teeth. "Generally you can lose up to forty percent of circulating blood volume before hemorrhaging sets in. After that, aggressive resuscitation is required to prevent death."

I pulled the laptop across and opened it. "Forty percent sounds like a lot, a huge loss."

"This is such bullshit. It's all so clinical. It misses the point."

"What point is that?"

"Blood is vital." He jabbed his finger on the table. "Blood is life. But they don't put that in the textbooks. They don't teach us what's important."

Blood is life.

He was looking way beyond the literal question we'd been asked, showing depth, providing an insight into human life. Why? And why this intensity?

I cleared my throat. "So what are you planning on doing with this photographic memory and vast store of knowledge you have? You want to be a doctor, don't you?"

"Yep, it's what I'm most interested in. What about you? What do you think you'll do when you leave school?"

"I might join the military," I said.

Ben covered his mouth to hide a smirk, then burst out laughing. At least it broke the tension.

"That wasn't a joke," I said.

"I know. That's what makes it so funny."

"What does your dad do?" I asked.

"He's an accountant."

"And your mom?"

"She was a lawyer."

Was. So that was it. She was dead.

"I'm sorry, Ben," I said. "When did your mom pass away?"

"Five years ago."

He'd said he'd been angry as a kid. It must've been a lot for a twelve-year-old to cope with. A lot for anybody, for that matter.

"So now your dad looks after you, and you look after your little sister," I said.

"That's pretty much it."

I remembered what he'd said to Celia when she'd slipped onto the road. I cannot lose you *too.* That was why he'd reacted so strongly. Because he was vulnerable. I felt for Ben. I shouldn't but I did.

"I can see why you like Celia," I said. "She's a sweetie."

"You and Celia have something in common. Why do

you think I chose you for this project?"

I held his gaze. "Because I'm smart and hardworking."

"Because you're funny, Nicola."

"No, I'm not."

"And because you're cute. You have the prettiest blue eyes."

He slid his fingers across the table and covered my hand with his. My mouth fell open, my lips parting in surprise.

Surely this didn't mean what I thought it meant. He couldn't be trying to get intimate with me when only minutes ago he'd been so worked up.

I pulled my hand back and motioned to the laptop. "We'd better get on with the assignment."

He leaned closer and I felt the warmth of his body next to mine. *Oh, no.* I suspected we were heading into the field of 'funny business' his father had been so concerned about.

Ben cupped my chin in one hand and tilted my head so I was looking at him. My eyes met his. There was no getting away from this.

My lower lip trembled. I'd never trembled in my life, not when I'd faced fear, not when I'd crept up behind two madmen with guns and supposedly become a hero. So why should this happen when facing Ben Tanner?

He pressed his lips against mine. The downy hair on the back of my neck stood on end and something sizzled inside me. First trembling, then sizzling. This shouldn't be happening.

As he pulled back, I realized that was a kiss. I was screaming on the inside. *THAT WAS A KISS.*

My parents back in New Nation had procreated, I

knew that. Lots of people had sex. If we didn't, the race would die out. It was simple mathematics or science or something.

It had nothing to do with me. As a soldier I had my own important role to play and it had nothing to do with kissing. Kissing was heading in one direction, the direction of procreation, the direction of funny business.

Ben smiled and something told me he'd done this before, probably many times.

"Not so bad, eh?" he said.

"Not...bad, exactly," I mumbled.

He leaned closer again and this time I could see it coming. What's worse, I did nothing to stop it. He covered my mouth with his, wrapped his arms around my waist and pulled me closer. I slid my arms behind his neck and kissed him right back. I encouraged him. I did more than that. I reveled in the experience. This was getting worse by the second.

And I hoped it would never stop.

A gentle knock at the door threw us apart. Celia stood in the doorway rubbing her eyes, her hair messed up, her pajamas rumpled.

"There's a monster in my room," she said.

Ben stood. "There aren't any monsters, Squirt."

Oh, yes, there are. There was a giant monster inside me, one I hadn't even known was there, an emotional monster that was taking over. How could I have veered this far off mission?

By the time Ben got back from Celia's room, I'd packed up my things. He looked surprised but didn't stand in my way.

I'd done my duty for the night.

More than my duty.
I couldn't get in any deeper than I already was.

CHAPTER ELEVEN

I'd only been here six weeks but already it felt like six years. Longer maybe. I knew what would happen – my superiors would give me the go-ahead and then the pressure would be on for me to do the job properly and get the hell out. In the meantime, I was kept in the dark, unable even to contact them. I was killing time when I should've been killing something else. Someone.

Lauren and I walked side by side down the street toward the town center.

"My mother wants me to be more socially responsible." Lauren rolled her eyes. "Honestly, it's a Saturday and that makes no difference to her."

I shrugged. "It doesn't make much difference to me either."

Lauren's mom insisted she go to a rally protesting about the multi-story development planned for the site of the community center and skate park. Lauren had been mortified at the thought of attending with her mother so I'd stepped in.

"Thanks for saving me from a fate worse than death,"

she said.

Closer to the site, the streets had been blocked off and pedestrians had taken over the road, all heading in the same direction. At the top of the hill, we stared down at the development site in awe. The streets were filled with a huge mass of people standing around a podium set up at one end of the square with an enormous banner saying, *No high rise for Altabena.*

My mouth fell open. I'd never seen anything like this. I'd imagined a group of perhaps a hundred radicals might gather to make their point, but this was much bigger than that. Where had these people come from?

"Whoa," Lauren said

She had that right.

Turning to me, she added, "We'll stay ten minutes, then get going. That way I'll sound convincing when I tell my mom about it."

"Okay."

That should be long enough for what I wanted. The main reason I'd agreed to come along was so I could document proceedings and gather information for my mission.

I whipped out my phone and took several photos to capture the size of the crowd, the podium and banner. I could transfer the pictures to my PR device later. Something significant was going on, something bigger than a few individuals, something my superiors might be interested in after all.

Lauren scanned the crowd. "What is there to take photos of?"

"Do you see anyone from school?" I asked, changing the subject.

"No such luck."

These people were protesting. This was unheard of in New Nation. Yet this all seemed perfectly run of the mill to Lauren and everyone else here.

The crowd became quiet as the first speaker, the Mayor of Altabena, gave an impassioned speech. She then introduced the next speaker, the previous mayor, a tall man with striking salt and pepper hair.

Several large police tactical vehicles appeared at the outskirts of the crowd not far from where Lauren and I were standing. Armed officers wearing helmets and body armor poured out of the vehicles, stationing themselves throughout the crowd.

Lauren didn't seem alarmed by the sight of police and neither was I, however I had to wonder if their presence was necessary when there was no sign of violence or aggression.

"Let's go," Lauren said.

I nodded toward the speaker on the podium. "Five more minutes. I just want to see what this guy has to say."

Lauren moaned. "Fine, but you owe me."

I fiddled with my phone, set it to voice record the rest of the proceedings and shoved it back into the pocket of my denim jacket.

The speaker said, "Most of you have come here today to stop developers knocking down our beloved community center for a high rise office block. We live here and we care about this place. State Ruler Harrison Bartley doesn't give a damn about our town."

A rumble went through the crowd at the mention of Bartley. I'd never heard his name mentioned in that tone, never heard it mentioned with anything less than reverence.

"The people of this town deserve better," the speaker continued. "You deserve to have your say. You deserve a government that listens."

Murmurs of agreement filled the air. I glanced around. More police had arrived, more vehicles too.

"The government is running roughshod over the people," he said. "They're going to bulldoze our community center to build a high rise. They'd bulldoze us if they could."

Cheers of agreement from the audience.

Fired up, the speaker jabbed his finger in the air. "This is about more than our community center. Bartley made himself State Ruler. He overrides local decisions in favor of big developers. Why would a legitimate politician do something like that? Because he's colluding with the developers. Accepting money from them. He's corrupt."

Okay, I'd definitely never heard anything like this.

The crowd roared, not because they were shocked by such ridiculous allegations, but because they agreed. Fists were raised in agreement, not in violence.

That was when the police moved in.

In the distance, a dozen officers stepped on the stage, handcuffed the speaker and dragged him off. The roar in the audience increased. Still no aggression. Not from the crowd.

A shot was fired, from where I don't know. Nearby, police officers yelled at people to move. Move where? The streets were packed. There was nowhere to go.

I looked around, seeing panic and fear in the faces of the people around me. Beside Lauren, two young women huddled together, tears in their eyes. Ahead of me, a man wrapped his arms around a small child, trying to push his way out of the crowd.

"Move it," a police officer yelled at the two women near Lauren.

They froze. If they didn't move, it was because they couldn't.

The policeman reached for a canister from his duty belt. "I said, MOVE."

Then he sprayed their faces, oleoresin capsicum spray, no doubt. It was painful and debilitating. And way out of line.

A small spark inside me flared. I had to do something. I couldn't let this happen.

Stay back. There are too many police officers and they're the ones allegedly upholding the law. *You won't win. That's not why you're here.*

Outraged, Lauren gesticulated at the policeman. "Hey, they didn't do anything."

The officer turned, the can of pepper spray pointed at her. I gave Lauren a quick shunt to get her out of the direct line of spray, shoved someone else out of my way, and slipped to the rear of the police officer.

Lauren screamed in pain, brought her hands to her face, and started coughing. The cop still had his eyes on her, not me. He didn't see it coming.

I slammed a kick into the back of his legs so he lost his balance and fell to the ground. Much kinder than he deserved.

Now we had to get the hell out of there. And fast. I put my arm around Lauren and pushed through the crowd like a steamroller.

"I can't see," she yelled.

"Keep moving."

Stumbling ahead, we made it out of the crowd and onto a side street. I glanced around. Hoped we weren't being followed.

I thought about all those people in the crowd left at the mercy of the overly enthusiastic police force, but there was nothing I could do, not on my own. We kept moving until we made it to a small gas station. My arm still around Lauren, I led her around the corner and sat her against a side wall.

"Don't touch or rub your eyes," I said.

She looked up at me, tears still streaming from her eyes. "It's a bit late for that. This hurts like hell."

She was lucky I'd pushed her out of the policeman's way so she wasn't in the direct line of spray. Then she'd know about pain.

"The blindness is temporary." I crouched beside her. "It feels like you've been set alight, like your face is on fire. The pain in your face, nose and throat is incredible."

Her mouth fell open. "How do you know? Was it the police? Did this happen to you before?"

"Something like that."

It all came back to training. We'd had to endure being assaulted with pepper spray but that was only the beginning of the exercise. We had to keep fighting. *That* was the drill.

Guys a lot bigger and meaner than me had fallen, but I'd kept going until the end. I remembered the pain, the feeling that my eyelids were boiling, and I also remembered the intense need to keep fighting through it. I wanted to beat the pain. I wanted to win. There was a reason I was top of my class.

"Don't rub." I pulled Lauren's hands from her face. "I'll be right back."

I left before she could argue, and headed straight to the convenience store attached to the gas station to buy baby shampoo, the one thing that might reduce her symptoms.

As I strode back down the side path toward Lauren, shampoo bottle in hand, the door to the restroom behind her swung open and a woman left. I raced down, just in time to grab the door before it closed.

"Come on," I yelled to Lauren.

"What now?" she mumbled as she rose and joined me in the ladies' room.

Ladies' room was a bit of a misnomer as this was not a room fit for a lady. The floor tiles and walls may once have been white but were now cracked and gray with dirt. It was probably just as well Lauren was temporarily blinded so she couldn't see how filthy the place was.

I helped her wash her face with baby shampoo, then rinse it off.

"That's much better." She dried her face with paper towels. "Nicola, how do you know this stuff?"

"What stuff?"

She stared at me. "Like what to do after a pepper spray attack."

"Science class," I said, thinking quickly. "At my old school."

"Wow, so you actually learnt something useful in science. Who'd have thought?"

"Lauren, what happened back there? I can't believe the things that were said about Harrison Bartley."

"Bartley's a horrible little Nazi. Everyone hates him."

"But the people voted him in, didn't they?"

"And now they're sorry they did."

The bulk of the population *must* approve of Bartley. That was how he'd got into power. Also how he'd stay in power through several elections until his son took over the role. That was history. I knew this much.

I'd assaulted a police officer.

My head dropped into my hands. What had I done? How had that happened? Lauren was the one who acted rashly, who had primal urges, who was impulsive. Not me.

She peeled my fingers from my face. "Are you okay?"

"Fine."

"I thought you were crying."

I shook my head. I didn't cry. Ever.

She screwed up her nose. "You're weird."

"Let's get out of here."

Something was wrong. Very wrong.

CHAPTER TWELVE

"Bye, Mom," I called out from the front door.

Mother came pacing down the hall. "Not so fast, honey. I never get the chance to talk to you. I haven't even told you about what Lydia Everill said. The allegations against Angelo are unfounded."

Why couldn't I just leave the house in peace?

"Charges were laid," I said. "It was all over the internet."

Mother rested her hand against the open door. "He's innocent until proven guilty. Lydia says the claims were made by two disgruntled ex-students who are out to get him."

"They can't come. No way."

"You're not the only one who lives here, you know."

"No, but I'm the only one who's been…"

Mother's mouth dropped open.

I didn't want to say it, didn't want to make up such a filthy lie about someone I'd never even met, but I had no choice.

"He didn't touch me, Mom, but he tried to."

Mother's hand flew to her mouth. "Oh, Nicola."

She threw her arms around me which only made me feel dirtier at the sordid lie I was telling. I didn't know if the allegations against the man were true or not, only that I wouldn't have been able to make up a story like this without them.

Mother held me at arm's length. "Can you tell me about it, honey?"

"I don't want to talk about it."

"But—"

"I just want them to stay away. That's not too much to ask."

She put her hands up. "I'm so sorry. I'm in shock too, honey."

"I want to go and be with my friends now, okay?"

Mother planted a quick kiss on my cheek. "We can talk later. You're the most important thing in the world to us. I'll email the Everills now. Tell them they can't come."

Which was just what I wanted. So why did this feel so disgusting? As I left the house, I hoped the guy really was a pedophile so my accusations weren't completely false. Anyway, this was kinder than eliminating him and his wife to stop them meeting my parents. I consoled myself with the thought.

It was time to switch to teenager mode as I headed for Lauren's place where she was having people over. I was grateful for the diversion even though 'hanging out' was not my specialty.

In the kitchen at the back of the house, Lauren's mother greeted me more rather more enthusiastically than usual, taking my hands into hers. "Nicola, how lovely to see you. Now, I'm sure you'd like pizza, wouldn't you?"

"Um, no thanks," I said, causing her hands to drop from mine immediately.

"See, I told you, Mom," Lauren said. "We're *fine*. There's heaps of food."

Her mother turned to her. "No need to use that tone with me, especially since you should be studying instead of entertaining."

Lauren's eyebrows went up in the middle. "Mom, we've been through this."

The woman put her hand out and turned away. "*Fine*, then."

As soon as she left, Lauren said, "The pizza oven is in the back yard. That's the reason she suggested it. She only wants to listen in and spy on us."

"Really?" I couldn't imagine she'd find our conversation that riveting.

"Yes, really." Lauren nodded. "And she keeps going on about studying because she thinks I should be a lawyer or an accountant. Honestly, can you see me as an accountant?"

It was certainly hard to picture.

A black and white cat wandered into the kitchen, slinking around Lauren's legs.

Lauren bent over to stroke the feline. "I'm so glad I've got you, Minnie. You understand me."

"I understand you too," I said, "though you can be quite complex at times."

Lauren laughed as she stood, taking a tray of drinks from the island bench and ushering me ahead of her. I pulled open the rear sliding door.

"Simone and Taylor are here." She placed the tray on a nearby table. "They think you're cool."

I didn't agree. Perhaps they thought I was a novelty or an amusement, but I didn't have whatever mysterious elements it took to be cool. And I didn't care.

"A few others are here too," I said.

People were lounging around on the outdoor sofas while others played table tennis, and Simone and Taylor sat on the steps leading up to the pool along with another girl, a bowl of orange crunchy-looking snacks between them.

"What are they eating?" I asked.

"Cheetos." Lauren saw the blank look on my face, screwed up her nose. "You've never had Cheetos? Honestly, you need to get out more."

Ben came up behind us while Rex made a beeline for the drinks tray and asked, "Got anything stronger?"

Lauren glared at him, shoved a can of Coke into his hands. "Not while my parents are home. Maybe later."

"Sure," Rex said.

As he stepped closer, Ben's gaze landed on the blond girl with Simone and Taylor, his face clouding over immediately. I'd seen horror in his eyes when he'd thought his little sister was close to being hit by a car, but this was horror of a different sort. He swiped a can from the tray.

"He used to go out with her," Lauren whispered.

"Why is she here?" I asked in a low voice.

"She came with Simone. I didn't invite her." Lauren linked one arm through mine, the other through Ben's, and led us toward the sofas where Ben took a seat opposite us. Lauren leaned forward. "Can you believe Rex is acting like it's the end of the world because there's no booze. That dude is a loser."

I adored Lauren at times like this. Her conversation

was shallow and that was exactly what was needed to distract Ben from the blond girl. Lauren even made Ben laugh, though I wasn't sure how.

After a while, the girl in question sauntered toward us. She must've had a lot of time on her hands because it would've taken considerable effort to blow dry her long locks, apply a thick layer of make-up and purchase the floaty dress and jewelry she was wearing. She walked in front of Ben, presumably so he could admire her, sat on the arm of the sofa next to him, and started chatting. Ben stared at the coffee table, offering one-word answers.

I couldn't make out what they were saying until the girl asked loudly, "Why have you been avoiding me?"

He looked up at her through the corner of his eye without turning his head. Maybe he'd had enough because he stood and faced her, his back to us, his voice low so we couldn't hear what he was saying.

Eventually, the girl stood too, throwing her hair back in a dramatic gesture. "I thought we could be friends," she said, then stormed off.

I went to Ben. "Can I get you something, a soda, chips? Maybe a knife, machete, dueling swords or some other weapon?"

It took a second for my words to sink in, then he laughed. "You're crazy, Nicola. A really good kind of crazy. I just want to get away for a bit. Do you want to head up to the gazebo?"

I followed him as he wove past the kids sitting on the steps and made his way to the top of the garden. He ushered me ahead of him into the gazebo where we sat down.

"That sounded pretty serious," I said.

He looked at me, disappointment in his eyes.

"Shannon's an old girlfriend," he said. "Or she was until she found someone she liked better."

"Ouch. I'm sure you'll find someone better too."

He shook his head. "I made a big mistake. Got too close to her." He threw his hands up. "And look where it got me."

I glanced around. "In a gazebo with the sun on your back."

"That part's not too bad."

His smile didn't reach his eyes. Underneath, he was still hurt. I wondered if he still felt the loss of his mother too. This was what happened when you let yourself get involved like Ben had. You got hurt. The way we did things in New Nation was much better.

"Shannon's an airhead," he said. "I don't know what I ever saw in her. She only cares about herself. You're not like her, though."

"No, while she'd clearly spent the last two hours grooming herself, I was doing my history assignment."

"That's what I like about you. You don't pretend to be something you're not. And you're funny."

"I wasn't making a joke," I said.

"See, that's exactly what I mean. You're a lot of fun. You just don't know it yet. And that makes it all the more endearing."

He grinned. The sparkle in his green eyes felt like it was especially for me. I turned away. It was safer.

Ben believed in me, though why I wasn't sure. It wasn't because I was a good soldier, working hard and doing my job properly. He believed in me because I was *me*. It made me feel special, warm throughout.

No, that must be the effect of the sun. I shouldn't let myself get confused. Ben didn't really know me. I had to remember that.

"No wonder I enjoy your company," he added.

The nasty lie I'd told about Angelo Everill, a man I'd never even met, came back to me. Not to mention which, the weight of my mission was always with me even if sometimes I pushed it to the back of my mind.

"Do you find it all gets too much sometimes?" I asked. "The gossip, the things we say to each other, the focus on appearances, the pressure of school and acting cool."

"I know what you mean. I like it better like this when we can just talk, one on one, and understand each other. That's good."

"Yeah, it is."

He edged his hand closer to mine on the wooden bench. I was enjoying the closeness between us. And the space.

A missile flew through the air in front of us. A gum nut with red flowers. Where had that come from?

Ben cottoned on more quickly than me and turned to look at some kids who were now sitting on the sofa where Lauren had been. The smirks on their faces told us they'd thrown it.

Another object headed our way, then another, so Ben and I dropped to take cover behind the low fencing surrounding the gazebo. This was so juvenile. It was also kind of fun.

A red flip-flop flew behind us so I reached across and grabbed it. Getting to my feet, I aimed at the culprit and threw the flip-flop Frisbee-style, rotating through the air. Rex stood by the sofa, his eyes wide.

He screamed and ducked, just in time. "On my God, you nearly decapitated me."

"He's right," Ben whispered.

That wasn't exactly what I'd intended, so I yelled, "Sorry."

Ben ushered me ahead of him down the steps.

Rex put his hands out. "You win. I've had enough."

"That's okay," I said. "I'm about to get going."

He moved to one side. "Don't let me stand in your way."

"I'm off too." Ben turned to me. "We can walk together."

I said goodbye to Lauren as we left. Ben waved goodbye to everyone including Shannon, which was polite of him. Lauren's parents were in the living room as we passed by so we thanked them and headed off.

"I'm glad you were there for me today," Ben said when we reached the sidewalk.

"Was I?" I kept walking. "I mean, I'm glad too."

Ben grinned and once again, it felt like his smile was meant only for me. It probably was since there was no one else around.

"Don't ever change, I like you just the way you are." After a while, he added, "If you ever need anything, you can always call on me."

"What do you think I might need?"

"Someone to talk to, a shoulder to cry on, whatever."

I already had an idea what I might need. One day, I might want to lure him away from his house, away from safety, away from any witnesses to a secluded place. I might need to complete my mission.

There was no 'might' about it. It was a question of

where and when. A midnight rendezvous would be an easy way of going about it. Ben would be unsuspecting. We'd be away from witnesses in a neutral location. There'd be forensic evidence of course, all of which would take time to process, and soon after I'd be whisked away to New Nation.

Time was running out too. For Ben and me both.

"What if I called you in the middle of the night?" I asked. "Would that be okay?"

"I mean it," Ben said. "Any time, any place. If you need me, I'll be there."

I stopped at the corner, ready to keep going straight ahead while Ben had to turn off to go home.

"I'll hold you to it," I said.

He took my hand into his. "See you at school then. Or sooner."

His hand lingered. Mine did too. It made me feel close to him, not just physically but in a deeper way too. It was a strange sort of intimacy, though. How strange I should feel close to Ben at a time when I was thinking of finishing him off. It didn't make sense.

Ben did the worst thing possible. Leaning forward, he pressed his lips against mine and kissed me. It was beautiful and horrible at the same time.

I stepped back.

"It's okay," he said. "We can get to know each other better first."

I said goodbye and walked off. When I reached the other side of the street, I turned to see Ben was still standing there. As I waved, he headed off around the corner.

I felt a pang inside. This was all wrong. I needed more

control, more self-discipline, more of the soldier inside me.

CHAPTER THIRTEEN

Life in Altabena wasn't so bad. At home, I was with my parents. At school, with my friends, and now I was back to a martial arts session in the afternoon.

I'd tried to get out of training, however Mr. Matthews had been extremely insistent and since I was supposed to be a high school student, I obeyed. Besides, the martial arts arena was the one place where I felt at home.

Trying to look inconspicuous, I'd warmed up with a group of girls. Ben was wrestling on the mat with a couple of other guys. I nodded hello but didn't join him because close proximity would only muddy my brain.

Mr. Matthews approached me. "Are you ready to go another round with Moose?"

The aforesaid Moose stood in the ring, leaning forward with his arms on the ropes. The grin smeared across his face was particularly dopey, and the guy beside him didn't look any more intelligent. Both of them wore the smaller, fingerless mixed martial arts gloves that provided less protection for the hands, and none for the other person's face.

"I'd prefer to concentrate on other aspects of my training," I replied.

"You don't understand, Nicola," the teacher said. "That wasn't a request."

I shrugged. "Then let's do the drill on the mat, not in the ring."

Mr. Matthews motioned for Moose and the other guy to join us. "I'd like to see how good you are against not one, but two opponents. We can simulate a street fighting situation, as if you were walking at night and came across Moose and Bulldog."

The girls to one side of me stood and watched. I glanced back to see the guys who'd been grappling had stopped too and Ben was heading in my direction.

I raised my eyebrows. "His name is Bulldog?"

"Yes."

"Excuse me, sir, I don't think this drill sounds safe and I don't want anyone to get hurt."

"These boys will stop in time. They won't damage you." The teacher looked me up and down. "If you're scared, you don't have to do it."

He'd used the same line before and knew exactly how to get to me. Maybe I should've shown restraint but part of me wanted this too.

"Sure," I said. "What's the game plan?"

The teacher's eyes narrowed. "This is no game."

Ben stepped closer to me and whispered, "I'm ready to jump in if you need me."

He was too close and I needed to focus.

The rip of Velcro filled the air as I pulled open the straps of a pair of fingerless gloves, slipped them on and pressed the bindings back down. *Rip*, such a magnificent sound.

Mr. Matthews stepped back, while Moose and Bulldog stood there. They had size but I had skill and smarts on my side. In New Nation, Lucien had taught me how to fight. Taught me everything I knew, in fact. He'd taught me well.

Moose lunged at me.

"No," I yelled.

I sprawled my legs back so he couldn't get a purchase. My pulse rocketed, my heart banging against my chest walls. He tried to straighten, but I'd already wrapped my hands around the back of his neck in a clinch so he was hunched over.

No escape, not for you. I had him where I wanted him.

Bulldog stepped closer, so I spun Moose around, keeping him between me and my other opponent. That was the secret with two assailants, because you can only fight one guy at a time.

And I *had* to fight. I sent a knee into Moose's chest. *Bam.* Bulldog tried to get closer so I yanked Moose around again. Sent in one more knee. The air left this body. He dropped to the ground.

Hands out, I stepped to the side and said, "We can call it a draw."

Meanwhile, Bulldog wound up his arm and threw a big right hand. I saw it coming a mile away, weaved under, and stepped right around until I had his back. No need to pummel him, only to finish this.

I shoved him in the lower back to bring him down to my height, and got him in a rear naked choke, my arm around his neck. We stumbled to the ground but I didn't let go. I couldn't.

He tapped. The signal for me to let go. I got to my feet and shuffled back. The further away from those two, the better. A hand landed on my shoulder and I turned, ready to strike.

"Hey, it's only me," Ben said.

"Okay."

Instinctively my eyes went back to Moose and Bulldog where Mr. Matthews was helping them up from the ground.

"You guys are done for the day," he said. "Get your bags and leave."

The two of them turned and left without a word. Their heads down, the dull thumps of their footsteps said it all.

The teacher stepped closer to me. "I don't know what I'm going to do with you."

"You don't have to do anything," I said.

He shook his finger. "You really know how to make life hard for yourself."

Deep inside me, a little spark ignited. Normally I didn't disobey a direct order or talk back. That was changing.

"No," I said. "I know how to survive. You're the one making life hard for me. You wouldn't do this to anyone else in the class, certainly not to any of the other girls."

"I didn't force you to do anything," he said. "It's not my fault you insist on pushing it."

My eyes narrowed. "Maybe I *should* push it and we'll see how far you get."

I stepped forward, ready for whatever was to come, but Ben nudged me aside so he was between me and the instructor.

Mr. Matthews backed off. "Threatening a teacher is not a smart move. Your parents are going to hear about this, the principal too."

"Fine," I yelled as he walked away. "They'd love to explain to the principal exactly what you made me do and how dangerous this was."

Mr. Matthews turned and grinned. "It's a dangerous world out there."

He left.

The small spark inside me blew up into a full-blown fire. My face reddened, my heart raced and I felt ready to blow. I told myself to keep my temper in check. *Don't lose control.*

This was anger, something I shouldn't feel. In New Nation we all had mild emotions, but not like this. I was above this, or I was supposed to be.

Emotions were unreliable, something to be fought, and certainly not to be trusted. We couldn't help having some level of emotion but then they were blown out of all proportion. The folk in the Badlands used their telepathic powers to accelerate and intensify our feelings in order to get power over us. That was why we had to control our emotions. Because they were at least partly an illusion.

But what I felt was real. What's more, there were no Badlands in Altabena and therefore no one to impose their will on us here, so what was going on?

Ben grabbed my arm but I jerked it back.

His brow furrowed. "Do you always do what you're told?"

"What?"

"Like with Moose and Bulldog. Do you always do what someone tells you to?"

"Is that a problem?"

He stared at me as if I had a lot to learn, and maybe I

did.

Deep breaths, Nicola. I walked away. It was what I should've done in the first place.

Ben caught up with me in the hallway outside.

"We need to talk." He stood outside the door of the boys' locker rooms. "Wait here."

He charged inside the room and came back moments later, saying the place was empty. Inside, we sat on a wooden bench against some lockers.

The room was plain with a polished concrete floor and white tiles on the walls. Showers and basins were at the back of the room, the same as in the girls' locker room, yet secretly I'd wondered what the boys' area looked like.

Ben leaned forward, his forearms resting on his thighs. "Just because Mr. Matthews tells you to do something doesn't mean you have to do it."

"But he gave the instructions."

"What if the person giving you instructions doesn't know what he's doing? What if he's an idiot?"

"Do you think Mr. Matthews is an idiot?"

"That's not what I meant. There's such a thing as being too obedient."

"Is there?"

"You shouldn't have listened to the teacher," he said. "And I'm glad you pummeled Moose and his stupid friend."

"I thought you were a pacifist."

"Not when it comes to comes to you. *I* don't want to hit anyone but that doesn't mean you shouldn't."

Because he cared. That was why he stuck up for me. That was why he was giving me this advice.

My pulse raced, my heart thumping in my chest. I was

even angrier than before. At Ben for caring. At myself for getting involved. At everything around me.

Damn it, I was supposed to be better than this. If I couldn't control my anger, the least I could do was channel it in the right direction.

This 'thing' with Ben was personal. It couldn't be any other way.

One day soon, I had to finish him. Not with drugs or poison like some quiet ladylike killer. Not with a gun where I could keep my distance, despite the fact I was an excellent shot. I was going to do this my way. The only way.

With a knife.

A midnight meeting with Ben would be easy to arrange. I'd get close to him. The knife would make it extremely intimate. We'd take 'personal' to a new level.

Decision made, I took a deep breath and let it out slowly. *Control.* That's what this was about. No one else needed to know what was going on in my head.

"I don't get it," I said. "What's Mr. Matthews' agenda?"

"You made him look bad and he wants to get his own back."

"But he's a teacher in a position of respect. It's his job to guide and teach us."

"Don't you get it? Not everyone is nice. Not everyone does their job properly. Matthews makes out like he's a good guy because he does all this training out of school hours but he's just a bully. That's why he likes Moose. Because they've got something in common."

And Mr. Matthews had found a position where it was okay for him to be a thug, as long as he got away with it.

He'd found a way of blending his bullying into his surroundings.

Ben turned to face me, his thigh rubbing against mine. "I can't change the whole world but I can take care of my corner of the world. My family, my friends. And that includes you."

"No way," I said. "I don't need your help."

His eyes glimmered with concern and compassion and other emotions I didn't need to know about.

"Can't you see?" he said. "You *make* me want to take care of you."

"What?"

"Because you're so vulnerable."

I screwed up my face. "That's the most ridiculous thing I've ever heard."

"It's true. There's so much you don't pick up on, the little things you miss, maybe some big things too. And that's despite your obvious intelligence. You need someone to look out for you."

I slid away from him on the bench. "I can look after myself. You saw what I did to Moose and Bulldog today. They were the ones in trouble."

Ben raked a hand through his sweaty hair. "This is too much. Don't you ever want to be your own person? Don't you ever want to do your own thing and truly let rip?"

"I already do," I insisted. "At training, for instance, I give it everything I've got."

There must be plenty of times when I 'let rip' as he put it. I thought about the incident that had supposedly made me a hero. I'd followed my instincts more closely than my orders, then seen an opportunity and taken it. The situation had been traumatic in many ways, yet I'd given it everything I had, and I'd succeeded. I was alive.

It made me wonder if following orders was always the right thing to do.

"Don't you long for more freedom?" Ben spread his hands. "Don't you wish you could just do what you want?"

"You already have immense freedom," I said. "You can choose your subjects at school, and where you might go to college or where you might work. You choose your hobbies, where to go on the weekend and which friends you'll go with."

Ben frowned. "Choosing what to study isn't freedom. You've got it all wrong. Sometimes I think we're all trapped at school, just waiting to escape."

I nodded. Suddenly, I felt trapped too, though not in the way he meant.

People here had so much freedom they didn't know what to do with it, whereas the freedom I had here wasn't real. It was an illusion. Because this wasn't my time. This wasn't my home.

And I'd let it go to my head. I didn't have a choice on whether to eliminate Ben or not. I had a job to do.

Two guys who'd been grappling pushed open the door, walked in and whooped when they saw me.

"It's okay." I stood. "I'm leaving."

I got out of there as quickly as I could.

In the hallway, Ben grabbed my shoulder. "I can't work you out, Nicola."

My back to the wall, I said, "There are lots of things I can't work out."

He pressed his hands against the masonry on either side of my head, caging me in. As if that'd work.

Guilt shot through me. I wasn't much better than Mr.

Matthews. He was a bully pretending to be a responsible member of the teaching community, and I was a soldier from the future pretending to be an innocent high school student.

For all I knew, maybe my superior officers were doing the same. I assumed they were honest, upright, loyal citizens of New Nation but maybe they were something completely different. How was I to know?

Something had niggled at me since I'd first been told about the mission by Lucien and two generals. More than niggled. They wanted to prevent the onset of the virus but that'd change the future so drastically that if I succeeded, it would lead to their demise.

How could they want an end to their own lives?

More to the point, how could I even be asking these questions when Lucien was involved. I owed him my life. I owed him everything.

"You're smart and strong and I've never seen any girl fight like you," Ben said. "Hell, I've never seen *anyone* fight like you. Yet sometimes you don't understand the simplest things."

"I don't belong here," I said.

"Sure you do."

He tilted his head as if he might lean closer and kiss me. I felt the sultriness of the moment, the tension between us. I felt a lot of things I'd never felt back in New Nation.

How could I feel this way? Was it this new environment filled with passionate people? Had I absorbed their emotions by osmosis?

What else could account for it? The food was better here. That was another difference. And I wasn't taking the government-issued vitamin supplements any more, not that I felt any need for them. I seemed healthy enough anyway.

None of which gave me any answers.

I ducked under Ben's arm and left.

CHAPTER FOURTEEN

I still hadn't heard back from my superior officers with a time and a date for my return. Also for my mission to be completed. I'd been here so long that I didn't know if that was good or bad. Sometimes I thought I was losing the plot and other times I believed I was the consummate soldier. Maybe I was both.

A few of us had gathered after school at the skate park next to the community center because, apparently, this was what teenagers did.

Lauren and I sat on a bench in our school uniforms while in front of us, boys on skateboards zoomed up and down a concrete 'bowl' designed for that purpose. I was in awe of their skills and the tricks they could do, while Lauren was in awe of the fact they were teenage boys.

A guy with bleached fuzzy hair with dark roots waved as he skated along the path in front of us, heading for the far end of the bowl. I remembered him from my first day at school and it seemed he remembered me too.

Ben walked up and sat beside us, or beside me, to be more accurate. Lately I'd been extremely confused about my mission and about Ben too, so I'd been doing the mature thing and avoiding him.

In front of us, Rex Anderson was going for it on his skateboard. He skated down a half pipe at the other end of the park, flew into the air, grabbed the bottom of his skateboard and landed smoothly, only to do the same thing again on the other side of the pipe.

My mouth fell open.

Ben leaned forward, his eyes on the skaters. "Rex is getting a lot of air."

"Is that what you call it?" I asked.

"He's seriously good. Spends all his spare time skating."

"The dude's a good skater," Lauren said. "Shame about the personality."

Ben shrugged. "Rex is okay." Lauren glared at him so he added, "Most of the time."

A tiny pinprick on my hip sent a huge shiver up my spine. Another message on my PR I had to check it. Right away. I made an excuse and headed for the community center, found the bathroom and ripped the PR device from my hip.

This is advance notice that computations to the time travel program are being finalized with respect to your safe teleportation back to New Nation. Be prepared to eliminate your target soon. Exact time and date to be confirmed. Meanwhile, continue with data collection on society and government. Nicola, be careful. Lucien.

"NOOOO…"

I slammed my open palm against the door. Pain reverberated through my hand so I kicked the damn door, then dropped down onto the toilet seat, my head in one hand, my PR device in the other.

This couldn't be happening. I needed more time. How could they do this to me?

I knew the answer. The only thing that mattered was the mission. I was also sure Lucien had taken a risk in sending this message. This was personal, an advance warning from a friend, not an official message from my superiors.

I stood up and composed myself, then strode out of the community center. I was a soldier. And a teenager. And I had to do this.

Rex skated along the path in front of me, both he and the board jumping into the air at the same time. I stood on one side of the path, Lauren and Ben on the bench on the other side. It might as well have been a hundred miles between us.

I cleared my throat. Got into teenager mode. "Wow, what was that?"

"An Ollie," Ben said. "It's the first trick you learn on a skateboard."

Rex slid past again. This time the board's tail hit the ground, the board spun 360 degrees in the air, and then Rex landed on it.

"Show off!" Ben yelled.

Rex spun around and skated back to stand in front of us. "I'd like to see you do a pop-shove-it."

Ben grinned. "I would too, but I'm not a pro like you."

"Have you ever tried skating?" Rex asked me.

I screwed up my nose. "Me?"

Rex grabbed the board and held it out to me. "Do you want to have a go?"

More than anything, I wanted to be like the people around me. "Sure."

Ben got up too while Lauren stayed where she was. Rex gave me the basics about how you push off on one foot to get going and keep your arms out. Still shaken from the message I'd received, it took all my concentration.

"Bend your knees for balance," Ben added. "It's like surfing."

Yet another thing I'd never done. I mimicked a surfing pose or perhaps it was a skating pose. It was a bit hard to tell.

I stepped onto the board and Rex gave me a gentle push. I lost my balance in less than a second and stumbled off. *You can do this.* I got back on and lasted a few more seconds. After a couple more attempts, I was moving. Sort of. I wouldn't have called it skating exactly.

This was the perfect distraction, exactly what I needed. I had a few more attempts and eventually ended up gliding along the path that ran alongside the bowl. Each time, I got a little faster until I could actually do it. Kind of.

I stopped next to the two boys and forced a smile. I was supposed to be happy.

"You're being very nice to Nicola," Ben said to Rex, a hint of suspicion in his voice.

"It's not because I'm scared of her," Rex said, too quickly.

"No, you just have a healthy respect for her."

Rex nodded. "Absolutely."

I hadn't had enough yet. It was never enough. I asked for one more turn and Rex agreed.

On this last run I finally had the knack of skating. I had that feeling of gliding through the air. A feeling of freedom and lightness.

Followed by the feeling of crashing and tumbling onto the grass by the path. While I sat on my backside, Rex and Ben rushed up to me.

"Are you okay?" they both asked.

"Fine," I said.

"You sure?" Rex leaned over to pick up his board.

I waved at him. "It's all yours now."

He left, and Ben gave me his hand to help me up. He was always so kind and thoughtful. He was everything he wasn't supposed to be.

So I yanked his hand and pulled him down. He rolled over the top, taking me with him, and I squealed like a girl. Honestly, I don't know what came over me.

We sat on the grass, grinning, and this time my smile was real.

"I'll get the grass off your back," Ben said.

I spun around on my butt. "Thanks."

He leaned closer, his breath warm on my neck. "Don't worry. I won't try to kiss you or anything."

"Good," I said.

If only he knew. Kissing had been on my mind a lot lately. Ben brushed the grass from my back, then I did the same for him. We sat facing each other and continued flicking the grass off the front of our uniforms. The sun was warm on my back, the smell of cut grass filling the air.

Ben held my gaze. "You're embarrassed, aren't you?"

"Me?" I placed a hand on my chest. "About what?"

"About the other night when we were studying at my house, about kissing me."

I wasn't so much embarrassed as shit-scared I'd end up in another situation I couldn't handle. Hell, I was already in a situation I couldn't handle.

"We're just hanging out together," he said. "There's nothing wrong with that."

"Not at all."

I let out a long sigh. When I was with Ben, it seemed as if the world was full of promise, as if anything might happen. Most of the time. That wasn't how it felt now, though.

As we sat quietly, I thought how lovely it would be if I could enjoy the silence and the time together. How wonderful if we could always stay like this.

Eventually Ben said, "You're going to Jake's party, aren't you? It's Saturday week."

"I wouldn't miss it," I said.

I damn well hoped I wouldn't miss it – my first and last party – but I didn't know if I'd still be here.

I could get used to living here. Hell, I *was* used to living here. I loved everything about it. I lived in a comfortable house with parents who loved me; I went to school, which wasn't so bad; and I had friends who cared about me. What was not to like?

Ben leaned closer, pulled a blade of grass from my hair. I had that horrible, wonderful, warm feeling I'd felt with him before. He made me feel special, as if I was the only person in the room. And we weren't even in a room. This was wrong in so many ways.

"Sometimes, I wonder if you're thinking about someone else," he said.

Not someone. *Something.* My mission. *I'm thinking about eliminating you.* Or I was supposed to be, except I couldn't face that right now.

"I've got a few things on my mind." I flicked an imaginary blade of grass from my leg. "That's all."

"Everyone does," he said. "It doesn't mean things are that bad."

"What about you, then?"

"I'm always anxious. I'm just good at covering it up."

I shook my head. "No way."

Ben dropped his gaze, his face clouding over. "I'm always trying my hardest. Always trying to be bigger, better, faster, smarter. Trying to make it there on time. Trying to make up for the past."

"What past?"

What was he talking about? Ben had everything going for him. Except for the fact I was going to eliminate him soon, but he didn't know that.

I took a deep breath and stretched my arms.

"You're very good at avoiding me," Ben said.

Leaning forward, I brushed my hand against his knee. "No, I'm right here with you."

"See, that's what I like about you. I never know what to expect."

Ben grinned and I wished he didn't look so darn cute.

I couldn't believe this young man was going to do such terrible things one day. There was simply no sign of it.

I'd been having other doubts too. Even if Ben was going to go on to release the killer virus – and that was a big *if* – could I punish him for something he hadn't done yet? Was that fair and justifiable? And what kind of person would that make me?

I had so many questions and no time.

The only thing I knew for sure was that Ben liked me. I liked him too, yet that didn't matter. Or it shouldn't.

The mission was the only thing that mattered.

That's what I kept telling myself.

CHAPTER FIFTEEN

Lauren looked out through her bedroom window. "This is the perfect afternoon for lounging by the pool."

I could live with that. In fact, switching off for a while might be the best thing for me. I was struggling with so much at the moment. With these emotions I shouldn't be having. With my mission. With a lot of things. I needed to relax and needed an afternoon off.

"It's a hard life," I said. "But someone's got to do it."

I'd heard that saying and it had stuck. I pictured the two of us sunning ourselves on the plastic recliners in Lauren's yard and dipping into the pool when we needed to cool off. It wasn't such a bad mental picture – or it wouldn't have been if my mission wasn't weighing on me.

Lauren turned to me. "On a sunny day like this, I shouldn't be holed up in my room."

I stood and joined her by the window. "Why would you stay in your room?"

She lowered her gaze. "I have a hobby, something I haven't told you about. You won't laugh, will you?"

"No."

"I have a special notebook that I write stories in. I want to be a writer." She smiled shyly. "My mother thinks I'm on PeoplePlace when I'm in my room."

"Why don't you tell her?"

Lauren shook her head. "That's one more thing she can put me down about. And for God's sake, don't mention this to anyone, especially not Simone or Taylor."

"Why not?"

"It'd be so uncool. I'm never going to be popular by telling people I write stories. They'll think I'm a geek or a dreamer."

"You shouldn't be ashamed," I said.

"I'm not. I just don't want anyone to know." I raised my eyebrows so she added, "If no one knows what I'm doing, I can't fail."

I frowned. "So it's better not to even try?"

"See, this is exactly why I haven't told anyone. Because it's so complicated. Now I'm ruining a perfectly good afternoon."

I understood 'complicated', though I wished I didn't. And maybe Lauren's dilemma didn't revolve around life and death but that didn't mean it wasn't important. I wasn't the only one with problems.

Lauren motioned for me to follow her down the stairs toward her kitchen. "We need mocktails."

I scooted along behind her. "I agree."

In the kitchen, she opened the pantry and surveyed the contents. "And junk food. We'll have to swing by the supermarket first."

"Sounds good." Perhaps I could sneak in a bag of Cheetos and find out what they were like. This might be my last chance, after all.

Lauren closed the pantry door. "Then when we come back we can settle by the pool. I've got a great recipe for mock champagne."

"Small problem," I said. "I didn't bring a swimsuit."

"You can borrow one of mine. It's the refreshments situation that's a problem."

Lauren's mom, Marion, wandered into the kitchen, stroking the cat in her arms and mumbling, "Who's my little cutie Minnie Winnie who likes being patted?" Then she stopped and stared at Lauren. "You're not going to the store again, are you?"

This was typical. The cat was a cutie. Meanwhile Lauren was always doing something wrong. At least that was the way it seemed.

"Mom, what difference does it make to you if we go to the supermarket or not?" Lauren said.

"I was just asking," her mother said.

"The store's not far," I added. "We'll be fine."

Minnie wriggled in Marion's arms so she opened the back door and let the cat out. "Lauren, I worry about your wellbeing and I want the best for you. Is that so terrible?"

"Well, you can stop worrying," Lauren said.

Her mother crossed her arms, drumming her fingers on her upper arm. "Weren't you on your way out, girls?"

"We're nearly ready to go," Lauren said.

Marion turned to the door. "So am I."

"Sorry about that," Lauren said to me after her mother left.

I shrugged. "No problem."

Unfortunately this particular problem was all hers. I didn't have to live here, not for much longer and not in this house.

Lauren wrote a shopping list, checked she had enough money, and the two of us headed off.

As we stepped through the front door, the screech of car tires cut through the air followed by a soft thud.

"Someone's in a hurry," Lauren said.

We headed down the front path as the car sped off. A lump of black and white fur lay on the road to my right.

Oh, no.

I touched her arm. "Lauren."

She gasped and ran to the side of the road. Didn't say a word. Tears were running down her face as she dropped to the ground and picked up the bundle of fur. Minnie.

I sat beside Lauren and put my arm around her. I wished there was something I could say to make her feel better. Minnie was limp and mewing softly. She was alive. Just.

"Darling, no…" Lauren's mom crouched on the other side of us, looking down at Minnie. She stroked the pet. As she pulled her hand back, the cat's fur stayed sunken. The bones below were probably shattered.

"I'm so sorry," Marion said.

A horrible, pained mewing escaped the cat.

Lauren looked across at her mother. "Mom, we have to go to the vet. *Now*."

"We will, honey, but I want you to be prepared for the worst."

Looking down at Minnie, I saw her green eyes were staring out at an uneven angle.

"She's in a bad way," Marion said. "She's in a lot of pain. The best thing would be if she could pass away quickly right now. If I could put her out of her misery immediately, I would."

I could do it.

It'd be merciful and quick, at least. If I carried Minnie to the car, I could snap her neck in two while the others weren't looking. I'd killed animals before for food. This wouldn't be so different and it'd be the best thing for Minnie.

Except I didn't have it in me.

I couldn't do it.

No way could I hurt this little kitty even when that was what she needed the most.

We drove in silence to the after-hours veterinarian, the cat's pained cries loud and clear even over the sound of the engine. Each screech sent a pang through my gut. I could only imagine how Lauren must be feeling.

The duty nurse saw the seriousness of the situation and sent Marion straight through while Lauren and I waited. She didn't have the heart to go inside the vet's office.

Not long after, her mom came out. Alone. Minnie had been euthanized.

I didn't want to leave Lauren by herself that afternoon so we lounged around on the floor in her room and watched a movie. It didn't feel right to go down to the pool after what had happened. Sunshine and grief didn't go together and I hadn't been feeling so good to start with.

After the movie finished, I put my hand on Lauren's knee. "I'm really sorry about Minnie."

She shrugged. "It's not your fault. I'm glad she's not in pain any more."

I was too, but I knew what Lauren didn't. I could've ended Minnie's pain sooner.

I was in trouble. Serious trouble.

If I couldn't kill an animal to put it out of its misery what chance did I have of murdering a human being?

I'd killed exactly two people in the past but that had been under a completely different set of circumstances. It had been in self-defense. Kill or be killed. It hadn't been bravery. I'd had no choice. Somehow that had made me a hero.

But I wasn't a hero.

And I wasn't a murderer.

CHAPTER SIXTEEN

It was 2.00am on Saturday and I was asleep in bed. The pinprick on my hip felt more like a sledgehammer. I'd never been more awake as I ripped off my PR, swung my legs over the bed and stared at the small screen in the darkness. This time the message was from my superiors, not Lucien.

The time travel teleportation device has been updated for your return. You have exactly 48 hours.

That was probably what they considered a generous amount of time. I should complete my mission immediately. It'd be easier that way and it wasn't as if I had a choice.

*　　　*　　　*

I pulled the front door closed quietly behind me and breathed in the brisk night air. I'd already snuck through the house past my sleeping parents, already phoned Ben, already set everything up.

Hands in the pockets of my hoodie, I headed down the street for the park that sat half-way between my house and Ben's.

I upped my pace. It wasn't enough to try. I had to succeed. Getting there was only half of the job. The easy half.

When I reached the park, a tall figure was seated on a bench in the dark. Ben, it had to be. He stood and I walked slowly toward him.

I'd brought my preferred weapon. A knife. With each step, the holster chaffed on my calf under my jeans. Making the holster, buying the blade from the martial arts store, strapping the holster to my leg – these things were routine to me. The next step was anything but routine.

I was closer now. Though it was dark, my eyes had adjusted and I could make Ben out quite clearly. He reached out, ready to fold his arms around me. The thought of that was too much for me so I took his hands into mine and held him at arm's length. I couldn't get too close. Not in that way.

"Glad you could make it." I took a seat on the bench.

Ben sat beside me. "Of course I came. You called. I figured you needed me."

"I just…I had to get away."

"It's okay, Nicola. I'm here."

I kept thinking about Lauren's cat. I hadn't been able to kill the animal. I'd been useless. I couldn't be useless now.

"Do you want to talk?" Ben asked. "Is that it?"

"No," I said.

"Come closer. You need a hug."

Even in the dark, his green eyes glimmered with emotion. My mouth dropped open. I wanted him to hold me. I didn't want him to hold me. I didn't want any of this.

Ben put an arm around my shoulder and pulled me

close. A long breath escaped me as I let myself slide against him and down onto the bench. Though we seemed to fit together so well, it was an illusion. Ben made me feel as if anything was possible when I knew full well it was not.

There were other things I knew too.

Such as exactly how to execute him. I could distract Ben and pull the knife from its holster. In fact, I wouldn't even need to distract him. He wouldn't have a clue what was coming. I could plunge the knife through his heart and he'd gasp. He wouldn't have the air to scream. Then I could slice across his neck and step back so I didn't get covered in blood. And I could leave.

One eye on Ben, I reached down and slid my hand along my leg, over the holster, over the knife, down to the hem of my jeans. I inched the denim a little higher, scrunched up the fabric, and stopped.

I couldn't do it.

But I already knew that.

"Everything okay?" Ben asked.

I scratched my leg, then sat back up. "Just an itch."

Ben put his arm around me and I stiffened.

"You're tense." He squeezed my shoulders, gave them a quick rub. "You've got to relax."

I took a deep breath. "I'll try."

It seemed pointless to relax but, then, what was the point of anything? I was here. I might as well fake it. When I got home, I'd hide the knife under the plinth at the base of my closet in the same place I'd hidden my father's gun. One day the weapons might be found or they might not. That was the least of my problems.

His arm around me, I leaned into Ben's body and tried

to focus on the moment because that was what we had. The two of us together. Now.

I don't know how long we sat there in silence, only that it felt good to be close to someone. Not someone. Ben. He wasn't demanding. He didn't want to know why I'd dragged him out in the middle of the night. He was just...Ben.

Eventually, I asked, "Don't you ever feel like it all gets too much for you?"

"Like what?"

"Everything. This world. The things we have to do."

"I know what you mean. Just getting by can be hard work."

"Sometimes I wish I could go away. Or stay. I don't know which. I don't even know what I want."

"When you're with me, you can talk. Or not talk. You know that, don't you?"

My heart sank. "Ben, you're too good to me."

"If you ever think things are getting too hard for you, call me. Right away. Like you did tonight. You're not on your own. I'll be here for you."

But would I be there for him? He didn't even ask.

And that only made me feel worse. Ben filled me with warmth just by being here, yet I felt sick to the stomach at the thought of what was going to happen. In New Nation, failure was viewed as disobedience – not to be tolerated. The punishment was severe. It didn't get any more extreme.

"You've got so much to look forward to," Ben said. "We both do."

"Like school?" I asked, deadpan.

"Like Saturday night's party. And graduation and

college and a hundred other things."

"What if we only had now? What if the world was going to end in five minutes?"

"Then I wouldn't change a thing. I'd stay here with my arm around you. That wouldn't be such a bad way to go, would it?"

He made me smile. After everything I'd done, the mission I'd planned and couldn't complete, after dragging him out here in the early hours of the morning to finish him. After all those things, Ben still made me feel as if there was hope.

"No," I said. "It wouldn't be so bad."

And it wouldn't.

It'd be a hell of a lot better than what was to come.

CHAPTER SEVENTEEN

"You can't possibly wear that to the party," Lauren said as soon as I walked into her bedroom.

I'd done my bit and got dressed up though not into an actual dress as that would've been taking things too far.

"Why not?" I closed the door behind me. "It's nice. My mother chose the blouse."

"Exactly, it's *nice*." She screwed up her nose. "I'll find the right sort of top for you to wear."

Lauren made a beeline for her closet, opened the doors, rifled through one of the shelves and handed me a scrap of deep pink fabric. "Try this on."

I unbuttoned my blouse and peeled it from my shoulders.

"The jeans look fabulous, by the way," she said.

Thank goodness I'd got at least one thing right. She tapped my stomach and added, "The abs are rather fab too."

"Thanks," I replied though I failed to see why she found my muscle tone so remarkable.

"And that bra is really racy." Surprise in her voice.

"Is it? My mother bought it for me."

Lauren laughed. "No wonder she gave you the sensible blouse to cover up."

I pulled Lauren's top on only to find it clung to me like a second skin. There wasn't much to it. The scoop neckline was so revealing it barely covered my bra and the hem didn't quite reach the waistband of my low-slung jeans. And it was pink. Enough said.

"Isn't this a bit tight?" I asked.

"Perfect," she said. "Now all we need to do is take care of your make-up."

"Make-up?"

There was a first time for everything. We had make-up in New Nation of course, but it was expensive and I didn't know anyone who actually wore it.

Half an hour and much giggling later, Lauren had outlined her eyes in black kohl pencil and given herself glossy lips. When combined with the highlights in her hair, it made for a funky look. At least that's how the other kids would describe it.

Meanwhile I felt extremely unfunky and opted for the natural look though I wasn't sure of the point when I looked completely natural without any cosmetics.

The party wasn't far from Lauren's place so we walked. The front door was open, the house empty until we reached the rear living area. The ceiling was covered with helium balloons, their colored ribbons hanging down.

We stepped through a set of French doors into the back garden where a large group had gathered. Everyone was shouting so they could be heard over the music. Fairy lights shone in the trees surrounding the pool and candles lined a paved area.

My first party. I'd been to many gatherings and functions, but they'd been very different from this. They'd been civilized events organized to celebrate some victory. There was no standing around the pool in skimpy clothing, no giggling, no relaxed atmosphere, no fun. *Fun* had definitely not been the purpose of those events.

This would be my last party too. It was Saturday night. Tomorrow would be my last chance to execute my mission – if I could do it – and in the early hours of Monday morning, I'd be leaving.

Lauren dropped her backpack outside the French doors. "Let's get a drink."

She poured punch from a giant bowl on the table into two glasses and handed me one. I took a sip and tasted orange, a hint of pineapple, and more than a hint of something else. A warm glow filled my belly. Curious, I took several more sips, then identified the mystery ingredient. Alcohol.

I leaned closer to Lauren. "The punch is contaminated."

She glanced across at the large bowl. "Contaminated? Did someone spit in it? That happened at Oliver's party. Boys can be so gross."

I put my glass down on the table. "There's alcohol in it."

Her lips curled up at the corners as she took a sip. "Are you shitting me?"

"No, I'm serious."

She spluttered and covered her mouth. "Honestly, Nicola, which planet are you from? You're hilarious."

Clearly, Lauren had known all along that the punch contained alcohol. If anything, she'd been expecting it, whereas *I* hadn't because I was from that other planet she was referring to.

"I'm not laughing," I said.

She put her arm around my shoulder and gave it a squeeze. "Of course I'm going to poke fun at you. I'm your best friend. You can rib me too if you like. It's what friends do."

I had a best friend. How had that happened? I jabbed my finger gently into Lauren's ribs and she let go of me.

"What was that for?" she asked.

I raised my eyebrows. "Ribs, poke. Get it?"

"Very funny. You don't mind about the alcohol, do you? It's not against your religion or anything, is it?"

"No." Looking around, I had to think quickly. "I'm allergic to it. A few sips is okay but more than that and I have a reaction."

"I'm sorry," Lauren said. "I didn't know. I won't offer you anything from my backpack later on, then."

So that was why she'd brought the large bag this evening. She had a stash of alcohol in there. No wonder it was so heavy.

"Let's mingle," she said.

Ben stood at the far end of the pool talking to Simone and Taylor. A small pang of jealousy shot through me, something I shouldn't be feeling. I decided it'd be better to survey the area and get my bearings first before mingling in Ben's direction.

Not surprisingly, Lauren headed straight for Simone and Taylor.

I went the other way, meandering slowly toward the edge of the garden to stay on the periphery for a better view. A girl I recognized from English class stood swaying to one side, her hand over her mouth, her eyes glazed. Even to my inexperienced eye, she appeared drunk. Charlene, no Charlotte. Moose had his arm around her, practically holding her up, yet something about his posture and expression told me he wasn't being helpful.

Suddenly, Charlotte's face went white and she pushed him aside, rushing down a side path. Moose followed.

Still standing up straight, Charlotte opened her mouth and a column of vomit expelled itself from her body, going straight out on the horizontal before falling onto the flowerbed lining the path. Projectile vomit. Truly spectacular.

Moose stepped up from behind, his hands wandering over her body.

Charlotte tried to push him away. "What are you doing?"

Moose nuzzled his face into her neck, whispering something. The huge hands on her waist crept higher.

"G-go away," she said. "I don't feel well."

More whispering from Moose, more nuzzling

I strode down the side path and reached for Charlotte. "Here, let me give you a hand."

Moose straightened. "We don't need your help."

Charlotte looked my way. "Yes, help."

"Nicola, this is nothing to do with you," Moose said.

"M-Moose, get away," Charlotte mumbled.

"You heard her," I said. "She wants you to leave."

His eyes were glued to mine. "What are you going to do about it?"

"Come on, Moose. She just threw up. She's practically comatose."

He grinned. "She's breathing, isn't she?"

"Leave her alone," I said. "I'll take care of her."

He pointed a finger at me. "Maybe I should take care of *you* once and for all."

I put my hands up between us. I didn't want to fight but there was no way I could leave this poor girl alone with Moose, not when he didn't care what state she was in.

Frustration in his eyes, Moose looked ready to explode. Something was coming but I didn't know what. He pushed Charlotte in my direction and stormed away. I'd got off easy this time.

"Bitches," he said under his breath as he left.

Not sure what to do next, I found Lauren, who located Charlotte's friends so they could take care of her. Better them than Moose.

I stayed with Lauren as she wandered closer to the pool. And Ben. I noticed his eyes on me, and looked away.

"Why would Charlotte do something like that?" I asked.

"She does that at every party." Lauren threw her hands up. "Attention-seeking behavior."

"But she didn't want Moose's attention. His hands were all over her."

Lauren shrugged. "Bad choices. Some people never learn."

She looked away, indicating she'd had enough of Charlotte, then grabbed my arm. "Look, Ellie and Harry are going for a swim."

I knew them vaguely from school. Harry had already stripped down to his boxers while Ellie was taking off her tee shirt and then she'd be down to her underwear.

"Why is it okay for them to strip off but it wasn't okay when I was getting changed for PE?" I asked.

"This is different," Lauren said. "What you did was plain weird."

Great, I was weird. It didn't matter how comfortable I felt in Altabena there were still times I didn't quite understand what was going on.

Daniel, a scrawny Chinese kid who'd been described to me as 'a typical Asian nerd' stepped up to us. At least in New Nation, no one made racist remarks like that. All people were equal and grateful to be alive.

A phone in his hand, he was taking photos.

"What are you going to do with the pictures?" I asked.

"Probably post them online," he said. "There are always people who'll be interested if I get good footage."

"Really?"

His friend Lorenzo joined us. "We're linked in. Interlinked, actually."

"What does that mean?" I asked.

"I'm connected. It's all about online networking. People who won't talk to me in real life want to be my best friend in the online world. I'm a desirable commodity."

Though that didn't necessarily sound like a good thing, the two boys seemed pleased.

Taylor pushed her long blond hair back and walked in front of Daniel while he was filming. Simone followed, stopping in front of the phone to raise her long dark arms above her head and undulate in front of him.

"You wish," she snarled before walking off.

Daniel and Lorenzo looked at each other, probably not sure if they should be insulted or not.

The two girls stopped on the other side of Lauren, long enough for Simone to say, "Computer geeks, we don't want them here but at least they're good for something."

As they left, Lauren giggled at their joke and gave the two girls a little wave.

"What do you see in them?" I asked.

"They ooze confidence," she said. "They're popular. People want to hang out with them. People listen to them."

I didn't want to hang out with them. I'd rather stay with Lauren even if she didn't 'ooze' like those two girls.

"They're also mean," I said.

Lauren opened her mouth to argue, looked thoughtful, then nodded. "Yeah, I guess they are."

On the other side of the pool, Ben waved and headed our way.

"Just as well we can have a party and have some fun, you know, while we're still *allowed*." Lauren rolled her eyes. "There'll be no more of this if Ms. Di Giorgio gets her way."

The principal had been involved in talks with government officials about introducing a curfew for teenagers so that anyone out after 7.00pm would get arrested. No wonder Lauren and all the other kids were outraged.

"Just because *she* can't have a good time, she doesn't want anyone else to either." Distracted, Lauren giggled and pointed to Harry and Ellie in the pool. "Taking your clothes off for a dip is a bit racy, a bit naughty."

"So it's okay to be naughty?"

"Like this, yeah," she said.

They had a strange way of doing things here.

Ben came up to us. Before he'd even spoken, I felt the downy hairs on the back of my neck stand on end. He shot me an appreciative look and grinned, his smile reaching his eyes. A sizzle shot up my spine, my response completely out of proportion to his actions.

I glanced across at the pool. I needed to cool down.

Hooking my hands over the hem of the top Lauren had lent me, I pulled the fabric over my head.

Ben's mouth fell open. "Are you going for a swim?"

"You can never tell with Nicola," Lauren muttered. "She might be getting ready for PE class."

I kicked off my sandals, unzipped my jeans and carefully peeled them off.

Lauren leaned closer, a sly smile on her face. "Have fun. That's what this is all about."

Ben's eyes were glued to me, making me wonder if this was such a good idea after all.

And I liked it. I liked his eyes on me and the way it made me feel. I sat on the edge of the pool and slipped into the water, certain he was watching me the whole time and thrilled at the thought.

Ducking my head under, I let the cool water envelope me completely though it did nothing to put out the sizzle I still felt inside. As my head popped up, I saw Ellie and Harry frolicking and laughing at the other end of the pool. Frolicking had never been my thing and I needed some physical exertion to get Ben off my mind so I started doing laps of freestyle.

It wasn't long until half the party had jumped in the pool, or at least that's what it seemed like, and I had no chance of swimming laps. So much for getting some exercise.

A volleyball net was quickly set up across the middle of the pool and it appeared that Ben and I and several others were on the same side of the net. I decided to stay put even though I was dangerously close to Ben.

He sidled up without touching me. "Looks like we're on the same team."

That couldn't have been further from the truth. He didn't have a clue what I was doing here, not an inkling.

My eyes dropped to his chest and I made sure my mouth didn't fall open like his had earlier. His shoulders were broad, his torso lean and ripped all the way down to the navy trunks clinging to his hips under the water.

It was only nudity. A naked human body wasn't cause for commotion where I came from, and Ben wasn't even naked. Just as well. I wouldn't have coped well if he was.

I looked away at exactly the right moment. A ball had been tossed over the net, headed my way. I punched it back.

"Good shot," Ben said.

"Of course," I replied.

He grinned. "Cocky."

"Confident."

I was only pretending to be sure of myself. The longer I stayed in Altabena, the further my mission kept going off track.

As the game went on, Ben sidled up to me several times. Every time I thought I should stop him and every time I didn't. As much as I tried to deny it, it felt good to be close to him.

A ball headed our way over the net, far too high for me to reach. Ben placed his hands on my waist from behind and lifted me into the air. I felt petite in his arms, as if I weighed nothing.

I lobbed the ball, the movement causing me to fall

back onto him so we landed back in the water together, our bodies intertwined. He helped me up, his hands on my waist again. He was so close, his chest against my back, and I felt that damn sizzle again.

I didn't turn to look at him. I couldn't.

Before, I'd experienced many doubts about whether I could do what was required for my mission. I'd been in denial before and now there was no point trying to lie to myself.

I couldn't eliminate Ben.

What's more I didn't want to.

I just wanted to find a way out.

CHAPTER EIGHTEEN

The volleyball game over, two girls by the pool were complaining about putting dry clothes over their wet underwear.

I rolled my eyes. That was the least of my problems. Besides, I was a soldier and had been through much worse. This was nothing compared to wearing wet combat fatigues in a mosquito-infested jungle where you stayed damp all day. These girls didn't know how good they had it.

Someone had brought out towels so I'd already dried my hair as best I could. My clothes were on and they were staying on. Back home we might not have any qualms about nudity but this wasn't New Nation.

Lauren nudged me. "I told you we'd have fun, Nicola."

Not wanting to miss out, she'd jumped in for the volleyball game too and thrived on it, whereas I wasn't cut out for all this *fun*. I may have been trained by the best officers in New Nation but nothing had prepared me for this.

I worked my way toward the fence, thinking I might watch from the sidelines when Ben appeared beside me.

"You don't like crowds?" he asked.

I shook my head. "It's all a bit much for me at the moment."

He took my hand. "I know a quiet spot."

I shouldn't go with Ben. Given my conflicted reactions, I should behave in a professional manner and keep my distance. What the hell, I followed him anyway.

Lauren's words rang through my head. *Bad choices*. I didn't care.

He led me to a small, grassed area wedged between a small outbuilding and the fence behind some trees at the rear of the garden. Though there was no escaping the noise of the party, this spot felt secluded.

I flopped down on the grass on my back. "It's good to get away from all that."

Ben lay down beside me, much more graceful than I'd been. He didn't touch me. Didn't say anything either. Just looked up at the stars. Glancing across, I watched the rise and fall of his chest, grateful he was wearing a shirt, then looked up again.

The night sky didn't look like this in New Nation where permanent pollution created an obstructive haze. Then there were recent volcanic eruptions that created spectacular sunsets but caused other problems with ash clouds.

"Do you believe there's life out there?" I asked.

"On other planets? Sure."

"Do you think about it much?"

"Not a lot, but we'd have to be incredibly vain to think that on all the planets in all the galaxies in the whole universe that there isn't some sort of life."

There was a big world out there, bigger than Ben knew, probably bigger than I could imagine too. I'd discovered so much in Altabena that it made me realize how small I was, nothing more than a tiny cog in an enormous universe. Small but pivotal.

"For me, the question isn't whether there's life on other planets," Ben said. "The question is what sort of life, how intelligent, how advanced. And maybe that life is so far away we'd have no way of contacting them."

"Would you want to contact them?"

"Absolutely," he said. "If we could, that is."

"Maybe it'd be better just to leave them be."

To leave them be.

Was it possible to do that?

Was that what I should do?

"Maybe," Ben said. "But I think man is just too curious."

"Yes, we are."

The smell of freshly cut grass mixed with the dampness of our bodies and the crisp night air. This wasn't real. We were lying on the grass in the back corner of the garden staring at the stars, pretending we were alone, pretending to be free, pretending everything was all right.

"You don't have this sort of conversation with Lauren," Ben said.

"No, she's more interested in clothes and make-up and boys."

"You're interested in boys too."

The gold streaks in his green eyes glimmered in the dim light. He rolled onto his side and kissed me, just like that. I felt warm inside, a little braver too. My past, New

Nation, it all seemed so far away.

"You've had lots of girlfriends, haven't you?" I asked.

He propped himself up on one elbow. "A few, but that doesn't really matter."

It was kind of him not to make reference to my obvious inexperience with the opposite sex, with sex in general for that matter. He wasn't interested in putting other people down to boost his own self-esteem. He wasn't like Moose.

Ben's expression became more serious. "Not all the girls I've gone out with have been as nice as you. Shannon, for instance."

"Why would you go out with someone who wasn't nice?"

"Well, I didn't know that at the start."

"I guess you don't always know people," I said.

Ben probably thought I was a good person. He didn't suspect the truth. It wasn't something he could even imagine in his wildest dreams about life on other planets.

"It's different with you," he said. "You're honest. You come out with weird stuff and strange questions. You don't care if it makes you seem funny. You don't care what people think."

Oh, but I do care. I cared so much that for the first time in my life, it hurt deep inside.

"Can you always remember me like this?" I asked.

His brow furrowed. "Why? Are you going somewhere?"

"No, but I'd like you to remember what you think of me, what you feel on the inside, what might happen. Can you always remember this moment?"

"I can do that, Nicola. I can remember how you look,

how blue your eyes are and how dark your hair is when it's damp. Is that what you want?"

I wasn't sure any more.

His lips curled to a sly smile. "I can also give you something to remember me by."

He leaned closer and I felt the electricity between us, the tension, the sense of the unknown. Then I felt his mouth covering my lips, his chest on mine, his hands on my waist pulling me closer.

I felt something else from deep within me. I'd remember this moment too, the way he smelled and felt, the way he made me feel.

This special moment.

He took his weight off me and ran a hand through his hair, still wet and messed up from the pool, and leaned back onto his elbows. "You sound serious tonight."

"I don't mean to sound morbid. I just think we should savor this moment, what we have, what's between us."

So I can hold it in my heart.

Even though our time together was ephemeral and, like everything else, it would pass.

"We can see each other tomorrow, you know," he said.

"Sure. I mean, I can't. I'm busy. Family commitments, you know how it is."

Another lie. It was better I didn't see him on Sunday. I'd have to go through all this again and it'd be too painful.

I wasn't sure what to make of all these emotions. I felt the rush of attraction, the thrill, the excitement and promise. I also felt pain like a knife in my gut. Surely love wasn't meant to feel this way.

"It's no big deal," he said. "I'll see you at school on

Monday."

"Yeah, Monday."

Monday would never come. Not for me.

At 2.00am that day Altabena time, I'd return to New Nation and face up to my responsibilities. I'd speak to my superior officers and I wouldn't be able to lie to them the way I had to Ben and everyone else in Altabena.

I'd lied to myself too. I was never going to eliminate Ben. I wasn't a murderer.

My superiors were relying on me back in New Nation. The military was extremely strict and I knew the consequences.

The price to pay for not completing my mission would be high.

The death penalty.

My life.

My choice.

CHAPTER NINETEEN

"What do you mean you're going to work today?" I stared across the breakfast table at my mother. "It's Sunday."

She put down her cup, a quizzical look on her face. "Somewhere along the line, our roles got reversed. I'm the parent. You're the teenager. I'm supposed to question where you're going, not the other way around."

I shrugged. "Sorry, I thought we could do something together as a family."

Father spluttered his coffee and reached for a napkin. "As a family?"

Mom laughed.

"What?" I asked.

"You never want to be seen in public with us," he said. "We don't mind. It's all part of being a teenager. And now, for the first time in years, you want to do something together as a family?"

"Sure." I tried to act casual. "Why not?"

Maybe I appeared normal on the outside but on the inside my gut had frozen into a solid block. I couldn't bear to think about returning to New Nation and what would happen when I got there.

There was no escape, no way out, and nothing I could do. As soon as I thought about it, I started to gag.

The secret was not to think. That was the only way I'd get through the day.

"There's a very good reason why not," Mom said. "Because today I'm helping out at the Altabena Fun Run."

Conversation. I could do this. I could have a conversation.

Mom's new job was for a health insurance fund which sponsored a 'fun run' at the outskirts of town to promote health and wellbeing. She'd come in at the tail end of the project and had offered to help with handing out water at checkpoints to passing runners.

"Can't you cancel?" I asked.

"Honey, I'm expected to be there," she explained. "Besides, I promised them."

"Fine, then Dad and I can come along too. We can join in the run. It'll be...fun."

His eyes hooded over as he peered at me over the newspaper he held at arm's length. "Excuse me?"

Mom burst out laughing and covered her mouth. "Your father? Go for a run?"

"What's so funny about that?" I asked.

Father shook his head. "It's not funny at all. Because it's not happening."

I tapped my fingers on the table. "Why not? Are you scared?"

"Absolutely not."

Mom did a lousy job of stifling another giggle.

"Incapable, perhaps?" I suggested.

He didn't lift his eyes from the newspaper. "Nicola,

that's below the belt and it's not true."

"If you don't want to spend time with me, that's fine. You've probably got something better to do. There must be lots of things that are much more important than…" I lowered the newspaper, "…bonding with your daughter."

Silence. I leaned back and waited. Let him stew.

I was determined to do *something* today and it wouldn't kill him to join in.

After a few moments, Mom said, "She has a point. You've been saying we don't spend enough time together. Here's your big chance."

"This is ridiculous," he said. "None of us should go. You shouldn't go either. You should be resting."

"Nonsense," Mom replied. "I've got another appointment tomorrow. I'll rest when the doctor tells me to."

This was the first I'd heard of doctor's appointments.

"Fine," Father said. "You've railroaded me into this silly run, but not until I've finished my coffee and read the paper."

Mom smiled. I did too.

She left well before we did thanks to Father's dithering and procrastination. The two of us arrived at the park in time, registered and paid a small fee. Seconds later, the starting gun went off near the banners at the front while we were at the back of the crowd. Which was where we stayed.

I couldn't believe my superiors had assigned a parent to me who was so unfit. Where had they found this man? In fact, I found it hard to believe that someone who appeared to be in reasonable shape simply couldn't run. So we walked.

We passed a woman with a baby in a stroller, holding the hand of a toddler who stumbled alongside her. At least there was someone slower than us.

"You can go on ahead," Dad said.

"I wouldn't dream of it," I replied.

I'd imagined 'getting into the zone' as I did whenever I exercised, particularly with longer events. I loved the feeling when your body takes over and you keep going, regardless of exhaustion or pain or anything else.

That wasn't the feeling I was getting now.

A skinny white-haired man in running shorts overtook us. I put his age at around a hundred. This was getting embarrassing.

"Don't worry about him." Dad put his arm around me and gave my shoulder a squeeze as we walked. "He's on his own. He's missing out on all this *bonding*."

I upped my pace a little. "I wouldn't miss out on this for the world."

Strangely, I wasn't sure if I meant it or not. Entering the fun run was a walk in the park, literally, compared with the training I'd done under Lucien's guidance in New Nation. He'd put me through grueling endurance exercises that tested me physically and mentally. Discussed military strategies with me. Pushed me further than I thought possible.

Lucien had been like a father to me, or I thought he had. But the relationship hadn't been like this. He'd never spent time with me simply for the sake of it.

Which left me wondering how I could even contemplate letting Lucien down when I owed him everything.

Tomorrow I'd be the loser. Tomorrow didn't bear

thinking about. But today I was part of something.

"You don't have to hang around with your mother and me all day, you know," Dad said. "We won't mind if you want to go out with your friends."

"No, I can do that next weekend."

Or not. Or never, in fact.

What did it matter? Did anything matter?

After a while, Dad said, "Your mom really appreciates the way you're supporting her work today. It means a lot to her."

Was that what I was doing? I hadn't looked at it that way. Hadn't given a thought to how it might appear from her point of view.

We spent the rest of the fun run – or 'walk', as it had become – planning dinner and the movies we'd watch together that evening and, most importantly, the junk food. In New Nation, we had chocolate and snacks and treats, but not the variety.

At home that night, the three of us watched a new action movie that had just come out. I'd seen it before, but couldn't let on so I pretended to be blown away by the fight scenes and impressed by the computer-generated images. To tell the truth, the CGI *was* impressive, though I still found it astounding that someone would put so much time and money into something so frivolous when there were so many other uses for the technology.

I sat at one end of the sofa, my parents at the other. After a huge scene with car chases, explosions, fireballs and buildings blowing up, the movie finished and Mom looked at me.

"I meant to tell you how glad I was that you told me about what happened with the Everills." I didn't say anything so she added, "Do you know when I got in touch with them, that man denied ever even knowing you?"

"Really?" Though it shouldn't matter, it made me bristle.

"He's in complete denial. It's truly bizarre."

I grabbed the remote, dropped it and fumbled around before picking it up. "Forget about them. We've got one more movie to watch."

Dad glanced at his watch. "I don't know if we have time for a second movie. It's getting late and you have school tomorrow, Nicola."

School tomorrow...

Not for me. A pang shot through my gut. I was leaving. For me, there *was* no tomorrow, not in Altabena.

I had to make this moment – these final moments – last. I didn't want to go to sleep, not now, not ever. I wanted things to stay exactly as they were.

And I sure as hell didn't want to wake up. I needed a diversion. Needed to keep myself occupied.

I scrolled through the list of movies on the screen until I found the one I wanted. "We sat through your action thriller. Now you can watch this with us."

"It's not the movie I mind." As he spoke, the soft tones of romantic backing music to the film's opening credits filled the air. Turning to Mom, he added, "It'll be way past her bedtime before the movie finishes."

She laughed. "Bedtime? Come on, she's not nine years old any more."

Had I ever been nine years old?

What had happened to my childhood?

"Two against one." Dad looked at me. "You win."

"What was it like back then?" I asked. "When I was

young."

Mom leaned forward to catch my eye. "In some ways it was easier. You were happy to tag along with us wherever we went. We'd take you to the park or the pool or the movies and everything was still a big adventure. We took pleasure in the little things like pushing you on the swing or throwing a ball around with you. You've grown up since then."

"Was it better before?"

"Not better, just different. Don't get me wrong, you were a gorgeous kid and a lot of fun, but we wouldn't want you to stay that way forever. Life gets more complex. It's just the way it is."

A lump swelled in my throat. I swallowed.

The question I shouldn't ask:

"Would it be easier if I wasn't here?"

"Are you kidding? That'd kill us. I had a lot of trouble getting pregnant, a couple of miscarriages, then various medical treatments, and it was all worth it. If we hadn't had you, our lives would be so boring. I don't want to even think what life would be like without you. You give us so much pleasure just by breathing."

"It might be quieter," Dad said loudly.

"We were having a serious conversation," Mom said.

He pointed to the television. "I thought we were watching this romantic comedy, the one you two insisted on."

"Okay, we can watch the movie."

I stared at the screen while the words rang through my head. *I gave them so much pleasure just by breathing.*

This was terrible, worse than I could ever have imagined.

One thing I knew for sure. The authorities wouldn't bother removing the chips from my parents' brains after I'd gone. It was difficult to bring items back from the past, especially if their return hadn't already been programmed. Besides, my superior officers wouldn't give a shit about Jan and Philip Gray. No way.

So what would happen to my parents tomorrow morning when they woke up and I wasn't here? Would I just go 'missing' and they'd lose their daughter forever? They'd be devastated. Their lives would go on but they'd never recover, not fully, maybe not even partially. They'd hold that grief in their hearts every day of their lives.

What was the quote my English teacher had come up with? *'Tis better to have loved and lost than never to have loved at all.*

No, it wasn't true. It was a lie.

It'd be better for my parents if they'd never met me, never known me, never loved me. Then they wouldn't have to go through the pain of losing me.

I'd come here, infiltrated their lives, and hadn't given them a second thought. They deserved better, much better than I'd given them.

So what kind of person did that make me?

The pain in my gut rose to my chest, and my throat tightened again. I glanced at Mom and Dad, slid across the sofa and threw an arm around each of them.

I'm not going to be here tomorrow.

I swallowed.

Tomorrow, they're going to kill me.

As a soldier, I'd thought about death but it had never been like this. It had never been so close. Never felt so real. I'd never really believed it would happen.

And I'd never had so much to lose.

I held on to my parents. Eventually I let them go. Because I had to.

Dad pretended to look offended. "What was that?"

"A hug break," I said.

He couldn't keep the smile from his face. "It's been a while since we've had one of those. It's nice to know there's a human being there inside our teenager."

Mom motioned to the television. "We'll get into trouble again if we don't watch the movie."

I settled back onto my side of the sofa, staring at the screen mindlessly. That was what the authorities wanted me to be – mindless and obedient. It was what I'd been when I'd landed here.

But I wasn't that person any more.

And I couldn't stay.

There was no way for me to change the time travel program. My time was up and there was nothing I could do.

My superior officers should never have sent me. I should never have found Ben and friends and family. Or this place with freedom and choice and promise greater than anything I'd imagined. It wasn't fair to give this to me then take it all away.

Damn it, I liked it here. And I should never have let myself get so comfortable.

My eyelids were heavy, drooping shut.

Stay awake.

So drowsy. It must be the stress that was doing this to me. My blinks became longer and heavier.

Stay awake.

There was no avoiding it.

INFILTRATION

Sleep…
Tomorrow…

CHAPTER TWENTY

Large hands on my shoulders shook me awake. "The mission...you didn't succeed."

Of course. The mission was the only thing that mattered.

My eyes flickered open and I tried to focus. The face before me was familiar and should have given me comfort. Instead I felt only dread. And that was all right. It was *my* emotion, one I was allowed to have, though not one I would share.

Don't give yourself away.

I leaned forward, my head dropping into my hands.

Get a grip. Get control.

It didn't matter that I was still groggy and dazed from the trip. It made no difference that it felt like I'd been ripped apart limb from limb and put back together. I had to take stock of the situation, get my act together and work out how on earth to handle this.

Earth, that's where I was, a different Earth.

I lowered my hands into my lap. "Lucien."

"It's me," he said. "It's okay. Take your time."

Nothing was okay.

I took it all in: a concrete floor, blackened ceiling, white walls, a large mirror with two-way glass. The only furniture was the leather chair in which I was sitting. The arms bore the imprints of hands having gripped them with small moon-shaped cuts as if from fingernails, mine perhaps, though I couldn't remember. How strange to have traveled through time and have no recollection of the journey.

Captain Lucien Everett rubbed my bare shoulder. I was naked, exposed in a way I'd never been before. An unpleasant shiver went up my spine.

There was nowhere for me to hide, no way out, no alternative except to face the music.

Lucien's touch gave me little reassurance, not with what I had to tell him. His smile didn't quite reach his eyes, though his expression was concerned and fatherly.

Deep lines bracketed his mouth and his brow was furrowed with crevices from worry. It wasn't possible he'd aged that much since I'd last seen him. Had I been brought back to a different time? His skin was olive like his army uniform so he appeared to be a monotone of color. He always kept his head immaculately shaved, except now his scalp was covered with a soft fuzz of brown hair, his chin with a thicker stubble.

"You didn't shave," I said. "That's not like you."

That smile again, the one that didn't reach his eyes. "Don't worry about me."

"Do you have my clothes?"

"Of course."

He bent over, picked up my neatly folded uniform and handed it to me. Lucien offered me his arm but I shook my head and stood on my own. My legs were stronger than I thought, my body in good shape. It was my mind that was letting me down. Where I'd had direction before, now there was only disaster.

I'd let everyone down.

Lucien's eyes were on me as I put on my uniform. Nudity had never been an issue for me yet somehow a fifty-year-old man watching a teenage female get dressed didn't feel right.

There were other eyes on me, too.

I motioned to the mirror. "They're out there, aren't they?"

"Yes."

"We should join them."

There was no point trying to evade my superior officers when they were on the other side of the glass and could see and hear everything. Better to face them.

Lucien opened the door, ushering me out and around the corner to the room where the men waited. I couldn't help but look through the window into the area where I'd just been, now empty except for the chair.

I shook hands with the two men waiting for me. General Willis was tall with red hair and a ruddy complexion while General Tan was of Chinese background and not much bigger than me, except in terms of authority.

It was Lucien who'd first introduced me to them, Lucien who'd said I was the perfect soldier for the mission, Lucien who'd briefed me. These men didn't mean as much to me as he did.

He and I sat on one side of a rectangular table, the two generals on the other.

"Nicola, you didn't succeed," Lucien said.

"Is this still the year 2120?" I asked.

"Yes," he replied.

"And I've been away two and a half months?"

He nodded.

That was the way it worked with the time travel program. While I'd spent two and a half months in Altabena, the same amount of time had also passed in New Nation. If they'd set the program for a ten-year visit, on my return I'd be ten years older and so would everyone here.

General Tan leaned forward, his eyes narrowing. "You failed."

"The mission wasn't straightforward," I said. "I had trouble locating the target. Then, even after I found him, he kept eluding me. I couldn't get to him within the time frame."

How easily the lies rolled off my tongue. What kind of person had I become? What kind of soldier?

"Tell us everything," General Tan instructed.

So I told them about life in Altabena, how the school system worked, how society was structured around families, how people voiced their complaints about the government and how they protested. I stuck to the facts without voicing any opinions.

I was a soldier. I didn't have opinions. I obeyed orders. That was what I wanted them to think.

I cleared my throat. "I have evidence of protests and the political situation back then."

General Willis put his hand out. "Give me your PR device."

Panic ripped through me. The device also contained

data on Ben, information I didn't want them to have, only I hadn't thought of this earlier, and now it'd only look suspicious if I didn't give them what they wanted. I rolled back my sleeve, peeled off the device and slid it onto the table in front of me. I'd have to find some other way of getting the device back later.

I looked at the two faces in front of me. "Generals, if you don't mind my saying so, you don't seem surprised that the people of Altabena acted this way, though it's contrary to our historical records."

The general pointed to my PR device. "You've got evidence?"

"Yes," I said. "Photographs, records, newspaper articles, all the information you need."

He nodded. "Good."

Was it?

I'd been shocked to go back in time and discover the people disapproved of the government, perhaps even despised it, but the generals weren't surprised.

They knew.

They knew everything.

And they hadn't told me. Hadn't even given me an inkling. Just sent me on my merry way despite the risks involved. Meanwhile I'd taken the greatest risk of all in not completing my mission.

So this was what it was like to have nothing left to lose. It made me braver.

"There's something I was wondering," I said. General Willis nodded so I continued. "As soon as I returned, you knew immediately that I'd failed."

"Of course," he said.

"Because if I'd succeeded, the future as we know it

wouldn't have taken place."

It was part-statement, part-question, while I was trying to work out what had happened.

The general nodded.

If society had stayed on the path it was on, mankind would probably have kept abusing the environment and many of the disasters that ensued would probably still have happened. Nothing Ben or I did would've had an effect on the earthquakes, tsunamis and floods that devastated the planet. That side of history would've stayed roughly the same.

That was big picture stuff. Changing history would also change the human details, the way people met and had children.

It would affect births.

I held General Willis's gaze. "Society would have progressed very differently. Your grandparents may never have met, let alone procreated, and your parents may never have been born."

"That's right."

"You may never have been born either," I added.

"That's right too."

If I'd succeeded in my mission, these men wouldn't be here. None of us would. That was how the generals knew I'd failed – because they were still here.

They were willing to give up their lives for the sake of the mission. *Hoping* to lose their lives, in fact, so that billions of others could live. Hoping to die so there'd be a different world.

But there was more to it that that.

According to the generals, Ben was going to create the deadly virus. So if I'd eliminated him, the virus would never have happened, or so these men told me. The billions of people who died would still be here.

I knew my history. It was *after* the virus that the Bartley government took supreme control and re-organized society based on the good of humanity. That was when the government consolidated its hold on the people. That was when they replaced the family unit with the current structure and pigeon-holed individuals into their various roles.

After the virus took hold, choice and human rights had taken a back seat. People had simply needed to survive, and the Bartley government was good at that one thing. Surviving. Then thriving.

The virus was pivotal to the success of the Bartley government. They *needed* that virus.

So how did the role of the generals fit into this?

How could it fit at all?

The generals were part of the government, a government that could never have stayed in power without the virus, a government that would never do anything that'd lead to its own demise.

Yet that was exactly what the generals had been planning – the end of the virus, the end of the Bartley government, the end of New Nation as we knew it. Why would the government have planned its own end? That didn't make sense.

Except it did.

Surprisingly calm, I leaned back in my chair and shifted my gaze from one general to the other. Ben's words about people not always being what they seem came back to me.

And I knew.

"You're not working for the government, are you?" I asked.

Silence.

General Tan turned to the other general and stared at him, a stern expression on his face. The two men whispered something and General Willis nodded.

Eventually, General Tan said, "It's not what you think."

"I think you're some sort of rebels with a plan to overthrow the government. Your plan is so ingenious that no one will even know what happened. The ultimate crime."

The general's eyes narrowed, fire in his dark irises. "It's not a crime to give people back their human rights, to give them some choice in their lives, to give them freedom."

I shrugged. I didn't have all the answers.

General Willis leaned forward. "You're right. We're rebels, dissidents, renegades, whatever you want to call it."

My mouth fell open. They'd spun me a story about helping to save the world when their aim had been to overthrow the Bartley government.

"You're with us now," he said, his voice steady.

"How do you know I won't inform on you?" I asked.

"You can't." He looked me in the eye. "We're traitors. So are you."

"I'm a soldier."

"Not any more. If the government finds out what you've done, where you've been, what you tried to do, they'll kill you. They won't hesitate."

"Will they?"

"Don't be so naïve, Corporal. They'll kill you like they kill everyone else who disagrees with them. This government is clever. They don't make it obvious with public executions. They get rid of people quietly. Individuals who criticize the government have accidents, they disappear, they lose their jobs. But with you, they won't take your job away. There are no two ways about it." He paused and spoke slowly. "They will kill you."

It all fell into place. There were a few reporters who'd criticized the regime and they'd all disappeared, one way or another. I also recalled a rock band whose songs had ridiculed the government. Band members had died when the vehicle they'd been traveling in had a head-on collision. That was what happened to people who disagreed with the government.

The general continued. "Ruler Bartley insists you have rights and choices and that you can have your own opinion. He's very good at giving the *illusion* of democracy, but that's all it is. An illusion."

General Willis was right. I'd seen the other side of the coin with life in Altabena and didn't need convincing, not any more. Before, I'd believed in the New Nation government, believed it was a force of good – because that was what they'd always told me. I knew better now.

But were these men any better?

They'd used me.

Put me in an impossible position.

Taken away my choices.

It was a knife in my gut.

I turned to Lucien who was so much more than my superior officer. I'd been speaking to generals Tan and Willis because they were in charge. And Lucien, what was his role in this?

My heart rose to my throat. No, not Lucien, not the

man who'd saved my life, taken a bullet for me, the generous man who'd always taken care of me. Surely he wasn't in on this deception.

I'd trusted him.

Yet now as I stared at the familiar face lined with worry, I saw his concern was not for me, but for the mission. That was all he cared about.

The knife in my gut twisted deeper. I knew exactly what this was.

The sharp pain of betrayal.

I kept my voice even. "You too, Lucien?"

"It was the only way," he said. "You've got to believe me, Nicola."

"I believe you."

How quickly I'd become proficient at lying. I'd never give away my thoughts and feelings, not to these men.

I pressed my eyes shut and rubbed my temples.

What the hell was going on? Thanks to what my supposedly superior officers had done and the decisions they'd made, I wasn't even a soldier any more. I was a traitor working against the government and it made no difference whether I was a willing participant or not.

I didn't know who I was any more.

"Are you all right?" Lucien asked.

"It must be the trip," I said. "It took it out of me."

He wasn't the man I thought he was.

How long had he been planning this? How long had they all been in on it together? Lucien had probably seen years ago that I was perfect for the role because of my obedience. Also, like all good soldiers, I was expendable.

I couldn't depend on Lucien or the generals or the New Nation government. These things meant nothing to me.

I didn't belong with them. I didn't belong here. I was on my own.

Screw them.

I was going back to Altabena.

The generals were the ones with the power so I shifted my gaze to them. "Send me back. I need more time."

"You failed the first time," General Tan said.

"This time I will succeed. I've located the target and gained access to the community and I can finish this. I'm still the best person for the job."

Tan drummed his fingers on the table.

My eyes narrow, I leaned forward. "I'm more motivated now. I fully understand the importance of the mission. I know exactly where I stand."

He slid something across the table, then leaned back. "We have a new PR device, one that should allow for two-way communication while you're in Altabena. We can't know for sure whether it will work until you use it."

Was that a yes?

It sounded like it.

General Willis' expression was grim. "There's a problem. Sending you back in time isn't something we can do on a whim. It's extremely complex, and requires incredible energy and resources. The technology is still new and it takes time to regenerate the power needed to send someone back."

"It is necessary," Tan said.

Lucien reached for my hand, then pulled back. "You know that if you go back, we can always find you, no matter where you are."

"Yes," I said.

He knew me far better than anyone, far better than the generals. Was it possible he had an inkling of my plan?

There would be no escape. The generals would always be able to trace me through geopositrons and advanced GPS technology. This would be a visit. Temporary.

Lucien's eye twitched. "Make sure you keep taking your vitamin pills."

A strange instruction since he was the one who'd forgotten to transport them to me. He knew I hadn't been taking them. He knew...

That was when it hit me. The so-called vitamins must be some sort of emotion suppressing drugs. That was why I'd changed so much.

I nodded. Didn't give anything away.

General Willis stared at me. "We can try to send you back but the process puts you at risk. You might not make it. If it doesn't work, the atoms in your body will be obliterated on the journey. You could die."

They'd already proven I was expendable. Why should they be so worried about this now?

"It's a risk I'll take," I said.

Willis looked at the other general and nodded slowly. Tan did the same.

"You can have eight days," he said.

The time travel program would be set and there was no way of changing it. The technology simply didn't allow for it.

I kept my eyes riveted to Willis and reached across the table for my PR device – my *old* PR device – and slid it back onto my arm.

"I will succeed," I said.

I was walking a tightrope, but I'd done it. They hadn't

noticed I'd taken the old PR device filled with information about Ben, and left the new one on the table. Now I was going back to Altabena for another week.

I had to find a way to keep Ben safe, even if I had no idea what that would be. It broke my heart to think of Ben dying before his time. He wasn't going to create a deadly virus. The Ben I knew wasn't a killer. I didn't believe it. The men sitting at this table had lied to me and they were lying about that too. They were wrong.

When I returned to New Nation – and I *had* to return – the generals would execute me quickly and efficiently. They wouldn't hand me over to the government. They'd do the job themselves.

I didn't want to die, damn it. I wanted to live.

Though not here. There was nothing left for me in New Nation.

In the meantime, I had just over a week in Altabena with Ben, other friends and family, one week as a normal teenager, one week to do anything I wanted.

One week to live.

One last chance.

CHAPTER TWENTY-ONE

The shrill electronic sound of dogs barking cut through the air. Who on earth had set such an annoying alarm? I stretched out my arm and fumbled blindly for the phone at the side of my bed. My eyes opened into two slits and I switched off the alarm, staring at the phone's dark face and bright pink cover. Pink?

My eyes sprung open.

I was awake. And alive.

My atoms hadn't been obliterated on the journey. How wonderful was that?

Sitting up, the bedding fell to my waist. I was naked, something we couldn't have, not in Altabena where nudity seemed to cause such controversy. So I jumped out of bed, grabbed the pastel-colored toweling robe hanging on the back of my door and slipped it on. Pink again.

I tried to take it all in. My bedroom door, my *pink* robe, my room with the dark pink feature wall. Clearly I loved the color or I wouldn't have so much of it my room.

Hands up in the air, I twirled around on tip-toes.

"MY ROOM," I yelled, then covered my mouth.

Hopefully I hadn't woken my parents, not with what I had planned for the start of the day.

I had the world's quickest shower, put on my school uniform, pulled my wet hair back into a ponytail and headed for the kitchen. I filled the coffee percolator with water and added coffee grounds, then laid out the ingredients and utensils so everything was ready. The trick was to take it one step at a time.

Today's breakfast would be pancakes. Surely I could master pancakes, especially since the process was made easier by the prepared mix you only had to shake up.

Ten minutes later, Mom walked into the room sniffing the air. "Phil, did you make coffee already?" Then, "Nicola?"

"Take a seat." I motioned to the pancakes piled onto a platter in the middle of the table. "Get started while they're still warm."

Dad stepped through the doorway. "Honey, is that pancakes I can smell?" Dropping onto a chair at the table, he looked from the platter, across to Mom, then up to me. "I thought..."

Why should it be so surprising that I'd made breakfast? What was with these people? I served up the last of the pancakes and joined them at the table.

"They won't be the same as Mom's but I'm sure they're still good," I said.

Mom swallowed a mouthful. "They're excellent."

Shock in his eyes, Dad said, "They're..."

"Edible," I finished.

"Better than edible."

That sounded like a compliment.

As we ate, I looked at the two people opposite me.

They weren't Jan and Philip Gray, the strangers I'd been sent to live with. They were much more than that, much more than they could know. They'd given me a place where I was welcome despite my moods and cooking skills. I was wanted here.

I was home.

This was something I'd never had before and I wasn't going to take it for granted.

After finishing breakfast, I sat back. "Dad, I hope you have a good day at work today."

He looked confused. "What? Since when have you been interested in my work?"

Mom reached for his hand. "I think you should make the most of this while it lasts."

I stood and gathered their dirty plates. "I'd better start the cleaning up."

Dad spluttered his coffee. "What's going on here?"

"I'll take care of the dishes," Mom said, taking control of the situation as she always did. "I'm not going to work today."

Dad's face clouded over, his voice low. "You didn't tell her?"

"Later," she said.

"What's going on?" I asked.

Mom glanced at her watch, then back up at me. "You need to get going."

I deposited the dishes on the sink. "If you're sure that's okay." She nodded so I added, "I wouldn't want to be late for school."

"Nicola, don't take this the wrong way." Dad's brow furrowed. "But has an alien taken over your body?"

"No aliens," I said.

Boy, was he way off the mark? Not even close.

I gave each of them a kiss on the cheek, then Dad shook his head and said, "Definitely an alien."

The walk to school reminded me of my first day in Altabena. In a way, it *was* my first day again, the first day of my new life.

It was still early so the sun was low, the air fresh, and though it hadn't warmed up yet, the day held such promise. My heart swelled in my chest. It felt like the sort of day where anything could happen.

Ambling ahead, I heard footsteps behind me. I glanced around but couldn't see anyone. The footsteps quickened. Leaves crunched on the pavement behind me. Someone was following me.

I stepped off and turned to face my opponent, my hands up so I was ready for whatever would come my way.

Lauren screamed and backed off, stumbling off the pavement. "Whoa, take it easy, dude."

I hadn't planned on this. Training was a hard thing to shake.

"I was going to scare you but it didn't quite work," she added.

"Lauren..."

Doe-eyed and disappointed, she looked so innocent, so unaware of what lay ahead, so deserving of a better friendship than the short one I could offer. I threw my arms around her neck and gave her a big hug. She let out a nervous giggle, then returned the embrace, albeit briefly, before holding me at arms' length.

"I'm so glad to see you," I said. "I missed you."

Lauren looked at me like I was an idiot. I was getting used to that.

"You missed me?" she said. "I saw you on Saturday night."

I nudged her so we started walking together. "You have no idea. It has been an eternity. It feels like a hundred years has passed."

"Is something going on?" she asked, curiosity in her voice. "Did you go all the way with Ben at the party and didn't tell me? Is that it?"

"No, I'm just happy to see you."

I was beaming inside and out, and wanted to share my newfound feelings. Was there anything wrong with that?

"Whatever you've been taking," she said, "can I have some?"

Horrified, I said, "Surely you don't think I've been taking drugs?"

"No, I think you've always been a bit weird."

She kept coming back to the subject of Ben and sex, as if it wasn't possible for him and me to simply be friends. In one way, she was right. There was nothing simple about the relationship.

As we neared school, Lauren also gave me the latest about the proposed multi-story development site. Apparently they also wanted to get rid of the skate park next door and that had outraged everyone at school, so much so that they were planning on a sit-in.

There was also the issue of a curfew for teens. Government officials seemed eager to keep teenagers under their thumbs and Principal Di Giorgio was supporting their proposal. I didn't get it and never would.

"What's a sit-in?" I asked.

"We go there and sit around to show they can't introduce a curfew or bowl over our skate park."

"So we sit around to make a stand?"

She nodded. "I guess so."

It made as much sense as anything else in Altabena.

"I'm going to rally together a few of the troops for tomorrow afternoon," she added.

Troops? Was she talking about war? No, she wouldn't have a clue about that.

There was a twinkle in her eye. "Ben might be there. I'll ask him to come along, how about that?"

I felt a little sizzle inside at the thought of spending time with Ben. More like a volcano than a sizzle, really.

I kept my voice even. "The more, the merrier."

"Sometimes I wonder where you get that stuff," Lauren said. "You sound like somebody's parent."

She was wrong. I wasn't going to be somebody's parent. I wasn't going to live that long and, besides, that wasn't my assigned role in New Nation.

I was a soldier.

And I was going to fight.

"I'm behind you all the way," I said. "You've got my full support."

"That's great but there's no need to get so serious on me. By the way, did you finish your English homework?"

I whacked my hand on my forehead. "No, I forgot all about it."

Lauren chuckled. "See, that's more like it."

Unfortunately we had English first period and I had a feeling there'd be no escaping the wrath of Ms. Swann. Near the end of class, the teacher asked us to upload our assignments onto the appropriate section of the school mainframe. It was just my luck that I was the only person in the class who hadn't finished the assignment.

Ms. Swann sauntered toward my desk, her eyes glued to mine. She might've been an English teacher who taught us to enjoy fine literature and poetry but if she was in the army, she'd have been a sergeant major.

She towered over my desk, appearing much taller than she was. "Any reason you haven't done your homework, Nicola?"

"No, Ma'am," I said.

"How did you think you were going to get out of this one?" she asked. "Did you think there'd be no tomorrow?"

How did she know?

"You're extremely perceptive, Ms. Swann," I said. "I apologize for not finishing the assignment but that's because I didn't think tomorrow would come, not for me. I was a lost soul floating in a universe that had no place for me. Imagine my surprise when I awoke this morning to a fresh day with new hope. Now I'm ready for everything this world has to offer, ready to live life to the fullest, ready for a second chance."

The teacher stood in front of me, her eyes wide with surprise. Through the corner of my eye, I saw Lauren's mouth fall open. I was half expecting sniggers around me since that was usually what happened when I spoke the truth, but there was only silence, a resounding silence, the sort that usually precedes a detention. Had I put my foot in it again?

"Poetry," the teacher said. "That was pure poetry and for that, you just earned yourself an extension." A low rumble echoed through the class and Ms. Swann added, "By the way, that's not going to work for anyone else so don't bother trying it."

A buzzer went off, marking the end of the class.

"That was cool," Lauren said in the hallway.

"What was?" I asked.

"That stuff you came out with about 'no tomorrow'." She nodded knowingly. "I've got to hand it to you."

What was she handing to me? I was never going to understand these people.

Ben was heading in our direction. A smile on his face, he looked so normal, so happy and healthy, so alive.

If only he could stay this way. If only he could keep living and breathing. If only I could keep him safe from everything that was to come.

Something inside me melted, just a little. It melted, then swelled like a wave building and gathering power. Damn it, I hated having all these feelings I couldn't quite identify, especially when I didn't know what to do with them.

Still, they were mine and they were real.

I'd always been told that only the weak succumbed to emotions, that we should know better. I'd been lied to about that, just like I'd been lied to about a lot of things so I could concentrate all my energy on serving New Nation.

Well, those days were over.

"I'll leave you to it," Lauren whispered, then walked off.

"Ben," I said. "It's you."

We stopped in the middle of the hallway while the other students milled around us. I wanted to reach out and touch him, to make sure he was truly there, but stayed frozen to the spot instead. Whatever I said or did, it'd be the wrong thing, and I desperately wanted everything to be right.

"Yep," he said. "I'm here."

"It's so good to see you again."

"I had a feeling we'd see each other again. You know, since we go to the same school."

"We don't have a lot of time," I said.

"I know. We have to get to class."

I only had one week and there was no way of knowing how long Ben might have. I reached for his hand and gave it a quick squeeze. He was okay for now. I had to remember that.

"I need to talk to you," I said. "What about this afternoon after school?"

He shook his head. "No can do. I've got training and a ton of homework."

"Tomorrow?"

"We've got the sit-in after school. Lauren's already got me signed up for it. Loads of kids will be there. We have to stick together and get behind the skaters. You're coming too, aren't you, Nicola?"

I nodded. "Sure."

"Good, then there's no problem." He grinned, his green eyes sparkling, and I wished he didn't look so damn gorgeous. "I can see you and remember you all over again."

I saw it in his eyes. He thought the things I'd said on Saturday night were cute. And had no idea it was a miracle I was here.

Leaning across he pressed his lips against my cheek, just like that, in the middle of the hallway. And he was off.

I stayed riveted to the spot while students brushed past me on their way to class. On my own again. But I couldn't do this on my own.

Ben had no idea what was going on, what he was up against, or what I'd planned when I first arrived in Altabena. What's more, there was no reason he should have an inkling. The truth was so extreme he'd never believe me.

So how could I make him understand?

I had less than eight days. Ben had to learn what to look out for if he was going to protect himself, but he was so completely unaware. He was smarter than me, had a sharp mind and intelligence. Those things worked for him. But he didn't have the awareness, that survival instinct or the training, that would keep him alive. I was far superior to him in those fields.

I knew how to stay alive.

Usually.

CHAPTER TWENTY-TWO

At home, I set to work on my English assignment since I was fairly certain tomorrow would come and the excuse I'd used today wouldn't work a second time. I still had to go to school, and that meant I had to do the work.

I was finishing up on the laptop when there was a knock on my bedroom door and Mom walked in. She sat on the bed so I turned from the chair at my desk to face her. Would the novelty of having a mother wear off? Probably at some stage but I wouldn't be here long enough to find out.

Mom sat on the edge of the bed, her face looked drawn, her smile tight. "I wanted to catch you on your own, Nicola."

Something was definitely wrong. I might not know much about emotions but even I could work out that much.

"Sorry if I've been a pain lately," I said. "Things will be much better from now on. I'm turning over a new leaf."

"It's not that, honey." She looked down at her hands. "Remember how I had several doctors' appointments when we were living at our old house?"

I knew nothing about our old house but recalled some recent talk about a doctor's appointment and this morning there'd been something up with her and Dad at the breakfast table.

"Yeah," I said.

"Well, I went to a different specialist today and he confirmed what I already knew." She looked up at me and I saw it in her eyes. Bad news. "It's about the lump I found in my breast."

"You found a lump?"

"It's cancer."

I couldn't work it out. Mom clearly seemed disturbed by this, but a small cancerous lump was easy enough to remedy. Things could've been a lot worse.

Except they couldn't.

Humans didn't have a remedy for cancer yet. Before the cure, the disease had been a scourge on society, everyone's greatest fear, a matter of life and death.

No, it couldn't be.

The air left my body. My throat constricted and words wouldn't come out. I was choking. This couldn't be happening.

No, not my beautiful mother.

I flew across the room and wrapped my arms around her. If I held her tightly enough, perhaps everything would be all right and this would all go away. I wanted to console her, make her feel better, but it wasn't working. I'd never felt so useless. And though I wanted to support her, it was really the other way round. She let me hold her. She squeezed my shoulders. Tried to take as much of the load as she could.

She was my mom and that's what mothers did. That much I knew instinctively.

After a while, she held me at arm's length and stroked my hair. "Don't cry, honey."

"I'm not."

I wiped my cheeks, surprised to find they were wet. How had that happened? I had to be stronger than this.

"The doctors can help you, can't they?" I asked.

"They think so," she said. "But sometimes there's only so much the doctors can do."

My heart rate rose and blood rushed through my veins. Something surged inside me, ready to explode, ready to lash out at this miserable situation that had let me down.

"They *think* so?" I shouted. "That's not good enough. They have to do something."

"Calm down, honey," she said. "Getting angry isn't going to help."

Was I angry now? Was that what was happening? I didn't know how to cope with all these feelings. Life had been easier when I'd been an obedient soldier doing as I was told. I may not have had as many emotional highs, but I sure as hell hadn't had these lows. I hadn't felt like my world was falling apart.

BUT THERE'S A CURE.

My chest constricted. I wanted to speak but the words wouldn't come out. I'd never felt like this before, this pain, this fear of what might happen. I'd never cared about anyone else before, not like this.

I cleared my throat. Found I could speak after all.

"What about Dad?" I asked.

Mom reached for my hands, enveloping them in both of hers. "He's not taking it very well."

"But you're the one who's sick."

"In some ways, I'm stronger than him, honey. They call women the weaker sex but that's not true. It's one of the reasons I wanted to talk to you on my own. Because it'd only be harder if I told you and then Dad fell apart too."

"Like me? Like I'm falling apart?"

"It's perfectly understandable."

Except it wasn't, not from a citizen of New Nation where emotions were suppressed, not from a hardened soldier.

But I was neither of those things any more.

And I wasn't going to fall apart more than I already had.

"Is it treatable?" I asked.

Mom nodded. "It might not even be that bad. They won't know for sure until they remove the lump. The doctor said there's a good chance I might not even need chemo or ray treatment. There's no point getting too upset until we know exactly what's going on, honey."

Mom wasn't as calm underneath as the words that came out on the surface. She couldn't be, but at least the prognosis wasn't fatal.

I'd only just found my mother. I couldn't lose her. Dad couldn't lose her either. What would he do without her? In a week, I'd be gone. The memory chip would still be in his head. He couldn't lose both of us.

The authorities would never let me stay either for my own good or to look after my parents. There was also no way they'd remove the memory chips from my parents. They wouldn't even understand the request, heartless bastards that they were.

Maybe I'd been like that before too.
But not any more.
I'd always had a brain.
Now I had a heart to go with it.

CHAPTER TWENTY-THREE

The sit in wasn't so bad. A large group of us had lined up, several people deep, along the edge of the skate park across the entrance to the community center. Ben stood on one side of me, Lauren on the other.

Some kids sat cross-legged on the ground while the rest of us stood. Home-made signs proclaimed 'No curfew, no way' and 'Our skate park, our right'. Behind us, skaters did what they did best. They skated.

In true teenage style we had Coke, donuts, large packets of chips as well as the Cheetos I'd been longing to try. Though I doubted much actual cheese had gone into the production of the Cheeto, it was delicious.

Lauren pointed to a group of people crossing the road. "What's *she* doing here?"

Principal Di Giorgio never let her lack of height get in her way when it came to standing out. The small mountain of bleached hair piled on top of her head looked like a beacon and she was busting out of a tight red blazer.

"I don't believe it," Lauren said. "That's State Ruler Bartley behind her."

I couldn't believe it either. I'd learnt all about the first Bartley at school. He'd died before his son had taken over the reigns of New Nation and his son after that, and now I was privileged enough to see him in real life.

Maybe 'privileged' wasn't the right word. Either way, this was history in the making even if it was just a small slice of the past.

"You look like you've seen a ghost, Nicola," Ben said. "Are you okay?"

"Fine," I said.

Harrison Bartley was just a man. Sure, he was State Ruler of California and hadn't yet become Supreme Ruler of the country, but he was still a man, albeit a very powerful one.

Behind us, the swish of small wheels on concrete was replaced by silence as the skaters stopped what they were doing. A murmur went through the crowd.

"This is typical of those dudes." Lauren rolled her eyes. "It's the adults on one side, kids on the other."

At that moment, Mr. Rodriguez cut in front of the group, brushed against one of the bodyguards and strode across the road, heading for the students. Was the science teacher joining us?

He shook hands with a couple of kids at the far end and stepped in alongside them. Though he had more facial hair than the average teenage male, he fit in with our group just fine.

"Maybe I spoke too soon," Lauren said.

Ben nodded toward the men gathered around the State Ruler. "Do you think they're expecting trouble?"

"They might be expecting it but I doubt they'll get any," I said.

Bartley was surrounded by four or five bodyguards. There was no mistaking the big men with earpieces, dark glasses and even darker suits. 'Inconspicuous' was not a word I'd use to describe them. Police officers also dotted the surrounding area.

The guy with badly bleached hair I'd met on my first day at school bumped into a policeman, then put his hands up as if apologizing. Funny I should keep seeing him.

While the officer pointed and moved him on, Daniel and his friend Lorenzo slipped past the officials and made their way toward us. The two boys had their phones at the ready and were filming, just as they had at the party on the weekend. It seemed to be their role in life.

Daniel turned to Ben. "If anything happens, we'll make sure there's a record of it."

Ben nodded.

"We're quicker than the media," Lorenzo added. "I can get footage online in seconds. In minutes, hundreds of people can be looking at it. Newspapers take too long. They're out of date."

Ben and I left them to it. Meanwhile, two men who I recognized as the current and previous mayors were speaking to Bartley though they were too far away for me to make out the words. Ms. Di Giorgio was nodding her head earnestly.

Somehow Bartley seemed to command their attention when he responded. He smiled, his shoulders relaxing, and the men around him chuckled as if at a joke. Though I didn't quite understand the concept of charisma, it was obvious Bartley had it in spades.

I'd seen ancient footage of Hitler shaking hands and speaking to individuals who'd lined up for hours to see him and were mesmerized by his presence. The same thing was happening here. As much as I hated to admit it, Bartley was charismatic. People listened to him, only I wasn't sure he listened back.

Glancing across, I saw two women with camera equipment were almost upon us. I'd been so preoccupied with Bartley that I hadn't seen them coming. I had to be more alert than this.

"We're from *The Altabena Times*," one of them said.

Ben leaned closer to me. "We might end up on the front page. That'd be cool."

No, that would absolutely not be cool. If he was going to survive, he'd have to keep a low profile to make it harder for the authorities from the future to track him down. This was all wrong.

I couldn't let Ben get his picture in the paper. No time to think, I cupped my hands around his jaw, pulled him closer and planted my lips on his.

It brought a smile to his face. A distraction, at least.

"What was that for?" he asked.

"For you." I grabbed his hand. "Let's go."

"Where?"

Anywhere but here. I dragged him away from the crowd down a narrow side path. A door along the side of the building was locked so we kept going to the rear of the community center. A miniscule parking lot held two cars parked side by side and a tiny courtyard. Actually, it was just a tree with a bench under it. Good enough.

I slumped down onto the bench, relieved to have escaped the press. Ben sat beside me, so close his thigh rubbed against mine. Somehow I didn't think avoiding photographers was foremost on his mind.

He slipped his arm around me and drew me closer. The citrus aroma of his shampoo wafted across. I hoped I didn't smell like Cheetos. He tilted his head, looking at me through lowered lids, and I felt a delicious sense of anticipation.

Then he kissed me, like I knew he would, and I kissed him right back.

"That's not why I brought you here," I mumbled.

He titled my chin up with one hand. "Still, we might as well make the most of it."

So we did. Hell, I liked being with Ben. It made me feel good. And I was making up for lost time. Time – not much of that left.

After a while, he left his arm around me and pulled me close so my head was nestled on his shoulder. Shaded by the surrounding buildings and the tree, no sunlight could get through so it was surprisingly cold though Ben made me feel warm and safe.

"We got some bad news the other day," I said. "My mom has breast cancer."

I don't know why I blurted it out like that. Earlier I'd wanted to share the news, horrible though it was, with Lauren but I hadn't been able to get the words out.

Ben loosened his hold, then leaned back to look at me.

"Sorry, that kind of ruined the moment," I said.

"That's okay, Nic. You're upset. I can see that."

He gave me a big hug which was exactly the right thing to do, as I told him about the prognosis and how scared I was. He listened and nodded, also the right thing to do.

After a while, he asked, "Your mom's nice, isn't she?"

A strange question. "Of course she's nice."

"My mother wasn't. At least that's not how I

remember her."

People generally spoke respectfully of the dead, not to mention which they usually had a soft spot for their mothers. I might not be an expert on families and relationships but even I'd noticed that much.

"What did she do that was so bad?" I asked.

"She killed herself."

I hadn't seen that coming despite the fact I knew she was dead.

"I'm sorry," I said.

"You don't need to be when you didn't do anything."

Though he was trying to sound casual, bitterness tinged Ben's words. His loss was much bigger than he was willing to admit.

"What happened?" I asked.

"Mom had post-natal depression after Celia was born, and it never got any better. She couldn't shake it, couldn't live with it, couldn't live with us any more. I didn't really understand what was going on. I was only twelve."

"Does Celia remember her?"

"No, she was only two."

"But you remember?"

"I remember everything."

The sadness in his eyes told me that wasn't a good thing.

"Is that why you got so upset when we were studying together?" I asked.

"Yes."

I cast my mind back to that night. The circulatory system...blood loss...a question about how much blood you could lose before the onset of death.

"Is that how she killed herself?" I asked.

He nodded. "She slit her wrists."

I turned my hand over and stared at the blue veins that stood out against my pale skin. Red and white blood cells were being pumped through my body, along with something else. Geopositrons.

Ben's words came back to me. *Blood is life*.

When he'd said that, I hadn't known how deep the words ran, how personal, how cutting.

I reached for his hand and enveloped it between both of mine. "Does it get easier?"

A small smile. "Yeah, it does. I know she was ill and that it wasn't her fault. I understand a little better now."

After a while I asked, "Do you believe in life after death?"

"No. I believe in a lot of things – in science and facts and also in intuition, but not in life after death." He added with a shrug, "My dad says that Mom lives on in me and Celia and Josh."

"What about alternate universes?"

"If the scientific evidence is there, I'm willing to listen. My dad also says that if Mom could've looked into the future, she'd have seen she could've got over the depression eventually and that things would've got better."

I swallowed. "Do you believe we'll be able to travel through time one day?"

"Maybe. Time is relative, not absolute. At least that's what Einstein said and he was a lot smarter than me. Traveling backwards would be easier than traveling into the future. If we could travel faster than the speed of light, we'd be able to see what just happened and look into the past. That's the theory anyway."

My heart raced. It was too soon to tell him where I

was from. Still, there was a chance one day soon he might believe me, a chance I might be able to help him.

"But if you could travel one way, then surely you'd be able to travel in the other direction too," I said.

"That's all academic." Ben smiled slyly, his eyes narrowing. "Nicola, are you trying to get out of kissing me?"

I leaned closer, my lips parted. "Actually, that's something I'd like to do more of."

We kissed but it didn't feel right, not after the news about my mom and not after what he'd told me about his mother.

Ben took my hand and slowly stood. "I was thinking about you and your mom. You know how I'm interested in medicine and research? It's more than that. I'd like to help people. One day I'd like to discover a cure for cancer. I know it sounds incredible but that's what I'd like to do."

My mouth fell open. A light bulb went off in my head.

I jumped to my feet. "Maybe you will one day."

He shrugged it off. "Ah, I'm just dreaming."

"I'm serious. Maybe you'll really do it one day."

"Yep, and if we could look into the future the way my dad suggested, we'd know it was going to happen."

That was it exactly. It was at least half right. I knew a cure for cancer would be discovered one day. But when? And by whom?

I barely dared think it. Ben would definitely have a significant role in scientific or medical research if he was supposedly the one who discovered the killer virus. What if he also discovered the cure for cancer? Could the two be linked?

Holding my hand, Ben ambled toward the side path. "I

like the way you ask stupid questions and say whatever comes into your head."

"Not *all* my questions are stupid." Even as I said the words, I realized how incriminating they sounded.

"With you, what you see is what you get."

"Is that good?"

"It means you're honest. You're not trying to impress anyone. I don't like it when people pretend to be something they're not."

That's *exactly* what I was doing.

I'd lied to everyone. Sure, it had been part of the job, such a small aspect of the mission I hadn't even given it a second thought. I was supposed to pretend to be a regular high school student, something I wasn't. I was supposed to lie to my friends, parents, teachers, everyone, as part of my cover.

I was a liar and a fake and I'd done a damn good job of it.

Now I'd lied to my superior officers too, the deadliest lie of all, because there was no way they'd let me live after this.

Strangely that was the only lie I didn't care about because it was the right thing to do.

Not that I wanted to die, far from it, but I could never be a murderer. My superiors were the killers, not me.

Maybe it was just as well I didn't have much time left in Altabena. I wasn't sure how much longer I could keep this up.

I had to convince Ben I was a liar.

To get him to believe the truth.

CHAPTER TWENTY-FOUR

Only six more days left. Time was slipping through my fingers.

I'd been doing all the right things. I went to school and did my homework, helped around the house, spent time with my parents and a lot more time catching up with my friends. Life was good, except for the part where my mother had cancer and I was about to be booted out of Altabena, never to see any of my friends again. Apart from that, things were going beautifully.

Having woken up before my alarm had gone off, I got out of bed and opened the plantation shutters to let in some light. Another sunny day with a smattering of fluffy white clouds in the sky. Plenty of sunshine here in California. No wonder everyone seemed so happy.

I might as well head for the shower. Since I was in the habit of wearing pajamas, I could head down the hallway *sans* bathrobe without fear of shocking anyone in the house.

Glancing around the room, I saw a slender item sitting on my desk, and froze. How long had that been there? It wasn't there when I went to sleep last night. They must've transferred it while I slept.

I stepped closer to my desk and picked up the PR device, the more advanced one my superior officers had tried to give me before I'd left New Nation. Of course, they could send it to me here in Altabena. I could never get away from them. No point even trying.

In New Nation, the government always knew where we were. They knew everything and had many ways of keeping tabs on people.

A message was waiting for me on the new PR

Reply immediately to confirm receipt of this message. Provide update on mission status and whether you have closed in on the target.

There was no 'please', I noticed, not that I was expecting one. I didn't have to answer them. I didn't have to do anything. I threw the device at the opposite corner of the room behind the door – for all the good it would do.

There was a quick knock and Mom pushed the door open.

"I heard something," she said, concern in her eyes. "Everything okay, Nicola?"

"Fine, Mom," I said.

"Okay."

She glanced around, seemed satisfied with my answer and closed the door behind her as she left.

I stomped to the corner of the room, picked up the damn device and slumped on my bed. Perhaps I could use it to check the New Nation networks and do some snooping of my own. I started looking.

Several sources all confirmed the same information:

Ben Tanner discovered the cure for cancer in 2041. *I knew it.*

So why would the rebel generals send me back in time to kill someone who cures cancer? My pulse racing, I kept searching.

The chemical composition of the cancer cure formed the basis for that of the killer virus, so one thing followed from the other. There appeared to have been some sort of industrial espionage and a person or group of people stole the cancer-curing compound, creating the killer virus as a side effect. The identity of the thieves was never verified.

My superior officers couldn't send me back in time to kill the industrial thieves because they didn't know who they were. Instead they'd sent me back to kill Ben.

They wanted to stop the virus because that was what allowed Bartley to consolidate his power. Without the virus, Bartley's authoritarian regime would never have become all-encompassing. That was what the rebel generals wanted: a democratic future for our country without the Bartley government.

And Ben was in the way. His discoveries led to the creation of the killer virus. The generals didn't care whether Ben was innocent or that he discovered a cure for cancer. That wasn't relevant.

My superior officers were using me. I could use them too. My heart thumped in my chest.

I typed in my reply, advising them that though the target had relocated, I was closing on him.

Two minutes later, they replied.

Message received. L.

Lucien was at the other end. I drummed my fingers on the edge of the bed. Perhaps he still felt a hint of loyalty for me or perhaps he was blindly obedient to the generals. I couldn't be sure.

Still, I had nothing to lose. I typed in a request for a vial of the cancer cure. Generals Willis and Tan would never send it but maybe Lucien would. Only one way to find out.

No response. I stared at my desk, willing a vial to appear among my books. Nothing. Then again, even if Lucien complied, it'd take time for him obtain a sample of the cure.

Next I deleted all the information about Ben from my old PR device. School records, photos, personal details, everything. I wished I could obliterate the information completely however the only way to be certain was to destroy the PR device and that could only be done at a government installation. Still, there might be a way.

Time was running out.

I only wished I could do more.

CHAPTER TWENTY-FIVE

Ambling down the hall at school, I turned to see Ben coming up behind me. It was as if I'd sensed his presence.

He sidled closer. "Looking forward to math today?"

"Not particularly," I said as we walked. I'd learnt long ago that this was the correct answer, regardless of my personal inclination.

"Do you want to ditch class?"

The Ben I knew was a good student so this didn't sound like him at all. What he'd suggested was against the rules, though luckily I stopped myself from saying that and appearing like a complete dork.

"You're not worried about what Ms. Di Giorgio will do when she finds out?" I asked.

He shook his head. "We can go back to my place. We'll have the house to ourselves. There's no one else home."

"Sure," I said. "Did you want to do some extra study?"

Ben put his arm around me. "Yeah, we can do some work on anatomy."

"But we don't have any anatomy homework," I said.

He laughed, gave my shoulder a squeeze. "Sometimes you're really funny."

Hilarious.

Then he got all serious on me and asked, "You're sure you want to come over, Nic?"

"Yes," I said, though I had the distinct feeling I was missing something.

As it turned out, cutting class was easier than I thought. We simply walked off the school grounds. I wasn't going to be here much longer so I didn't need to worry about getting into trouble for truanting and Ben seemed to be doing what everyone else around here did. He'd worry about the consequences later and enjoy himself in the meantime.

Passing through Ben's house, we headed for the backyard to make the most of the sunshine. He swiped a couple of towels from the hall closet on the way. It was eerily quiet inside, reminding me there was no one else home and that we shouldn't be here.

We stepped through the French doors at the back of the house onto a patio bordered by flowerbeds overflowing with greenery. The lawn looked freshly mowed, the smell of clippings hanging in the air.

A pool glimmered at the rear of the yard, drawing me to it. Blue mosaic tiles lined its edges and water trickled into the pool along a rock feature, the sound soothing.

I dumped my bag beside a plastic recliner, sat down and kicked off my sneakers and socks.

Looking up, I saw Ben behind me, his hands on his hips.

"You can go inside and get your swim trunks," I said. "I'll wait."

There was a strange sparkle in his eye. "We don't need swimwear."

"No problem."

It wouldn't be the first time I'd gone swimming in my underwear. I whipped off my school shirt and skirt and stepped closer to dip my toes into the pool. Still fully clothed, Ben sidled up behind me. His hands on my waist made me feel small. Made me feel a little sexy too, if I was going to be honest.

"Can I interest you in a little skinny dipping?" His breath was warm on my neck.

I'd heard the term 'skinny dipping' mentioned in old movies. His question was still an odd one. I thought nudity wasn't acceptable in Altabena, something I'd worked out on my first day.

Since I didn't wish to muck things up again, I said. "Just in our underwear is fine."

Stepping up onto the edge of the pool, I dived in and felt the water caress my body. I was an able swimmer and had trained hard in the past, but I'd never enjoyed the sensation of water more than I did at that moment. My senses were heightened, maybe because of Ben's presence or maybe because I didn't have much time left. Either way, I was making the most of it.

I relaxed when I got to the other end, my back to the pool wall, my arms draped along its edge.

My eyes were fixed on Ben. He stood at the far end wearing only a pair of fitted athletic trunks that clung to the top of his thighs, his waist and everywhere in between. His shoulders were broad, his arms and chest well muscled. I already knew he had the brains. Clearly, he had the brawn too.

Besides, he was a good person who would go on to do wonderful things for humankind. He was going to discover the cure for cancer. He wasn't going to release a killer virus into the air. Someone else was going to do that.

And I was allowed to admire Ben. What else was I supposed to do when he was standing there looking so hunky? There was no law against ogling, or at least I didn't think there was.

He dived in, heading my way underwater, but I ducked out of the way before he reached me. We chased each other in and out of the pool, splashed around wildly and made a whirlpool. At one point, I pushed Ben in and he pretended to be offended.

I enjoyed every moment of it, every touch and shove and giggle.

Panting, I sat on the steps at one end of the pool to rest. Ben joined me, planting his hands on the step on either side of my hips as if caging me in. He was panting too, that strange glimmer back in his eye.

A current shot up my spine, a pleasant one with an edge to it. Something was different.

I backed off up the steps, then grabbed a towel and lay down on the grass on my back. Eyes closed, I enjoyed the sun on my bare skin and breathed in the fresh smell of the grass in summer. Ben lay down on a towel beside me and I wished we could stay like this forever, just the two of us with all the time in the world and no one to bother us.

How odd that doing nothing made me feel so alive. This was such a strange place and such a weird way to live. And I liked it. A lot.

Ben slid his fingers onto my arm, reclining on one arm close to me. I closed my eyes again. He slipped his fingers onto my waist, then higher as if counting the ridges of each rib. My skin tingled. His fingers traveled higher.

I was on fire on the inside. This was wonderful. This was bad. This shouldn't be happening. My eyes sprung open.

He tilted his head toward me, his lips parted, green eyes narrowing. I savored the delicious anticipation though I knew exactly what was coming. He covered my mouth with his, pressing his chest against mine. I had the feeling perhaps I didn't know exactly what was coming after all. His hands wandered.

This wasn't about kissing or making out. This was about sex. Even I could work out that much.

I pushed him away. "I can't do this."

Ben rolled off, holding me at arm's length. "Did I do something wrong?"

"No, it's not you. It's…everything."

He rubbed my arm. "I like you, Nicola. A lot. That's why I asked you to come here today."

That was why he'd asked me here. I had so much to learn. How had I got myself into this situation? Ben, too. I'd got him into this as well.

I'd never even thought about someone experiencing such strong sexual urges and had certainly never contemplated anything like this before. Talk about being out of my depth.

Eyes wide, I said, "So you want to have sex with me?"

"Sorry, I didn't mean to upset you."

"You haven't answered my question."

"Is it so surprising?" He gazed at me longingly. "You have the bluest eyes and lovely light brown hair. You don't even need to try to look gorgeous. You just are."

"Me? Gorgeous?"

He leaned back on his hands. "That's another thing that makes you even more attractive. Girls who are good looking and use it to their advantage annoy me, whereas you're really cute but you act as if you're oblivious."

There was a very good reason for that – because I didn't have a clue. I'd never placed much importance on attractiveness or attraction. Neatness in my appearance and a reasonable level of grooming was expected and it was only respectful, but only in so far as it was practical. Why would I want to spend hours in front of a mirror doing my hair or getting dressed up?

"Besides," Ben held my gaze. "You can feel it too. You like the way it makes you feel when we're together."

"Yes, but…"

He was right. I couldn't deny it, not any more.

"Then you agreed to come here. It's pretty obvious what I thought." Ben shrugged. "Dad's at work. There's no one home. We've got the place to ourselves. I thought you knew what'd happen."

Maybe any other teenager in Altabena could have read between the lines and worked out what was going on, but not me. Things-I-didn't-know was a large group of items.

I sat up and hugged my knees to my chest. "I'm sorry, but this is all too fast for me."

"I'm sorry too." Ben sat up as well. "I don't want to push you into anything. Is it because you're upset about your mom? Is that it?"

"Yes." I was ready to pounce on any excuse. "It's that. It's everything."

Deep as my feelings were for Ben, I knew this wasn't the right time or place, not for me, not for us. I felt it deep in my gut.

I felt a lot of other things too, this distinctly sexual desire that started as a sizzle on the surface and built up to a deep longing inside. I'd read about it in books but had no idea it could be like this, so compelling, so all-consuming, so overpowering.

My body was saying 'yes'. I wanted some pleasure for myself. Was that so bad? I also wanted to please Ben, wanted to make everything right and be everything he wanted me to be.

I wanted it all.

But my head was saying something else, and I couldn't let these other sensations overwhelm me. Our relationship was complex, a lot more complicated than Ben knew.

A little fear niggled inside me.

Maybe it was a big fear.

I had a feeling Ben wouldn't like me quite so much if he knew the truth. Hell, at the moment I wasn't sure *I* liked me. I sure as hell didn't appreciate the situation I was in.

"You've had sex with girls before, haven't you?" I asked.

"Some people would think that a personal question," he said.

"Really?"

"Yes really. Look, I've had girlfriends but that doesn't mean we have to do the same thing. What has happened before doesn't make any difference. That shouldn't come between us."

It made *all* the difference. He was so much more experienced than me it wasn't funny.

"I haven't done this before," I said. "Nowhere near it

and I can't start now."

"Today we'll hold hands and swim." He enveloped one of my hands into both of his, then slipped my hand back on my knee. "That's fine, but you've got to learn to be more careful. There are plenty of people out there who'd take advantage of you."

My mouth fell open.

Ben had no idea of the danger he was in, no inkling what I'd had in mind when I first came to Altabena, and no way of gauging what other threats might come his way.

And he thought *I* had to be more careful?

"There's something I have to tell you," I said.

"It's okay, Nicola," he said. "You don't need to say a thing. We can take it easy from now on, take things down a notch."

This would be easier if he was pushy, but he wasn't, and that made it all the harder.

"That's not what I meant," I said.

"I prefer it this way."

"What way?"

"I'd rather you were picky about who you shared your body with than the other way round."

"You've lost me," I said. "Sharing my body, what are you talking about?"

"I'm not talking about you. It was my old girlfriend, Shannon. You saw her that day at Simone's house. She was seeing another guy behind my back. Cheating on me."

Pain glimmered in his eyes before he dropped his gaze. I saw his disappointment, his anger.

Ben had said his ex had let him down but hadn't given the full story. Now I knew. He was talking about the ultimate betrayal.

I might not know exactly what made people tick, but I'd learnt something about emotions and relationships since I'd landed here. Ben had been devastated by his experience, I was sure of it.

There was a lot he wasn't telling me – about the hurt and the anguish – and perhaps some things were better left unsaid.

"I'm surprised you'd be so willing to find other girlfriends after that," I said. "You, know, once bitten, twice shy."

He shrugged. "I'm a guy. Sometimes I can't help myself."

I cleared my throat. "There are other reasons I couldn't go through with this today."

"It's okay. We haven't known each other for long and you're not ready and that's fine. I trust you."

That only made me feel worse. I didn't deserve his trust when I was only going to let him down.

Ben *couldn't* trust me. I'd been sent here to gather information and get rid of him.

But *he had* to trust me. Because his life depended on it. And I was the only one who could save him.

This was such a mess. Where to start?

"Have you ever wanted to disappear?" I asked.

"You ask some strange questions."

"I've heard that before. Haven't you ever wanted to go far away and leave everything behind? Haven't you ever wondered what it'd be like to go somewhere where no one knew you and you could start from scratch?"

"Yeah, I have, but it's not like you think." Ben's face clouded over. "After my mom died, I wanted to run away and give up because it was all too hard. But I couldn't leave everyone and everything I knew, no matter how much I wanted to. And after a while, things got better. Besides, if I'd run away, we would never have met and we wouldn't be here now sitting in the sun."

It would be so much better for Ben if I'd never come, if we'd never met, and if there was no way of sending anyone else back in time. Not so for me.

'Tis better to have loved and lost than never to have loved at all.

I saw new meaning in the words. Life wasn't about obeying orders. People and relationships were what mattered. Love mattered.

That was why I felt this stabbing in my heart, this weight in my gut dragging me down, this pain. Because of the magnitude of my loss. And it was better to go through this than never to have experienced the depth of feeling I had for Ben.

It was worth it. For the first time in my life, I was living. I had a choice in what I did. I was making my own decisions. There were people I loved and they loved me back.

And while I was here, I could do one good thing.

I could save Ben.

"Wouldn't you like to go overseas or learn French," I suggested. "Wouldn't it be fun to keep moving around? You could take care of yourself and not worry about anyone else."

His brow furrowed. "Nic, are you trying to get rid of me?"

"I just hope you can always take care of yourself."

"Of course I can take care of myself." He gave me a playful nudge on the shoulder. "You might be able to knock me out in a stand-up fight, but I'd beat you hands down in a wrestling match."

My hands were lowered. My guard was down and I didn't know what to do.

"But what if you don't know what's coming?" I asked. "How can you defend yourself if you're not aware what's out there?"

He tilted his head closer and pressed his lips against mine gently and I did absolutely nothing to defend myself. I kissed him right back and felt all my problems melt into the background.

If only we could stay this way. If only we could make everything right.

Ben pulled back, smiling. "That's life. You never know what's around the corner."

But I did know.

That was the problem.

CHAPTER TWENTY-SIX

The three of us stared across the road at the pile of rubble where the community center and skate park had stood. Dust rose in the air from the recent demolition. A dump truck reversed into position while another vehicle scooped up bricks and broken concrete.

The demolition crew had been sent in at midnight last night while the town was sleeping. Lauren, Ben and I wanted to see it ourselves so we'd come straight here after school.

"I can't believe it," Lauren said.

"Neither can I," I said.

Except I could. This was exactly how the Bartley government would handle a situation like this. Lauren's mom had been giving her regular text updates throughout the day. Apparently Bartley had said, "A decision needs to be made" – so he'd made one and it didn't matter that it was contrary to the wishes of the people.

"My mom insists Bartley's corrupt," Lauren said. "That he's taking money from developers. That he's building up his personal coffers and wants to take over the world."

I knew what Lauren didn't: Bartley *would* end up taking over North America. There'd be a few more elections. I wasn't sure how many. And Bartley would remain in power until his son took his place, and then the next son after that.

No more elections. No more democracy. All for the pursuit of ultimate power. That was the drug that drove Bartley.

I had trouble working out what made someone so power-hungry. Why did Mao Tse-tung, Josef Stalin and Idi Amin destroy and crush their own people? There was no reasonable answer because they weren't reasonable people. Neither was Bartley. Megalomaniacs, all of them.

"The election's coming up soon," Ben said. "My dad thinks if we don't give Bartley the boot now, it'll only give him more power and he'll get worse. Problem is the people are afraid of a change, afraid to vote for the other side, so Bartley will end up getting voted in again."

"I think your dad's right," I said.

Lauren motioned to the space where the community center and skate park had stood. "We went to that protest rally. Okay, my mom made me go, but I was still there. You too, Nicola. We were in the thick of it. What was the point if no one was going to listen?"

I didn't have an answer. I only knew that when people voted Bartley in at the next election, he'd take it as approval of his policies and tactics. It would only encourage him to cast his net wider. Ruling California was only the beginning.

"This is an important issue," Lauren said. "It's not just about one building getting knocked down. It's about voicing our opinions and being listened to and democracy."

"Lauren, I've never heard you so serious," I said.

"Well, this is a serious issue." She looked thoughtful, not a characteristic I'd attribute to her very often. "I'm tired of writing stories no one will read. I'm going to write a letter to the paper. No, a full-length article. It'll be impassioned and articulate and personal. I'll send it to the newspaper or a big magazine, maybe *Time*. There has to be a way of making people listen."

"You should definitely do it," I said.

"You're right. I should. Right now, in fact." She placed a hand on my shoulder. "Before I change my mind."

Lauren headed off.

Ben looked stunned. "I'm not quite sure what just happened. I always thought Lauren didn't care about anything except boys and clothes."

I shook my head. "She's just good at acting like she doesn't care."

"I didn't know she wrote stories either."

"Not a lot of people do."

I knew efforts to thwart Bartley would be futile yet somehow that didn't seem reason enough not to try. Maybe the future could be changed if people banded together and refused to re-elect the government. Maybe Lauren could give Bartley more bad press. It wasn't likely but anything was possible.

"Let's go," Ben said. "I'll walk you home."

We ambled away. I was glad we were walking slowly because it gave us more time together. We talked about the demolition and school and the people we knew. We talked about everything except the one thing that mattered.

We weren't far from my house when Ben finally came out with it.

"I've been thinking about what happened between us yesterday."

So had I. I'd been thinking about a lot of things. And worrying too. I'd done a lot of that.

"I'm always fixated on the physical side of things," he said.

"Well, you're a guy."

"And you're a girl. It's not as if one of us is right and the other is wrong. We need to find what works for both of us. It's made me see things in a different way. In the past I've been so shallow."

"No, you haven't."

If Ben had been shallow, what had I been? I wasn't the person he thought I was. I was someone else altogether.

"I was always afraid of getting involved," he said. "Not physically, I mean, I never had a problem with that. But there was always something holding me back from getting emotionally involved."

What a time for him to come to this realization about himself. We stopped across the road from my house. That's what it was now, my home.

"This isn't the right time for this conversation," I said.

Ben took my hand in his. "It's never going to be the right time. Yesterday when I said I liked you, that wasn't the complete truth–"

"It's okay," I said.

I didn't want to hear it. I couldn't bear it, not with everything else I knew.

"I *more* than like you," he said.

We'd gone too far and there was no point trying to

deny it. I was in so much deeper than I'd ever anticipated.

"I like you a lot too," I said. "Can you always remember that?"

Ben smiled. "You're getting weird on me again like you did when we were lying on the grass together at Jake's party."

I gave him a quick kiss on the lips and ran across the road.

Things were only going to get weirder.

He had no idea.

CHAPTER TWENTY-SEVEN

Maybe this would be my big chance. I'd let my mind wander in science class, only to hear the words 'faster than light' and suddenly the science teacher had my full attention. I wasn't sure how we'd got onto the subject, only that this was extremely relevant.

"The Milky Way is enormous," Mr. Rodriguez said. "It takes light thousands of years to reach Earth from the other end of the galaxy. Light travels at over 186,000 miles per second. That's miles *per second*, not per hour."

Though he should have been speaking in metric rather than using miles, I got the picture. Light travels fast and the distances are huge.

"The Milky Way is one galaxy," a kid down the back said. "There are loads of others, aren't there?"

"Billions." Mr. Rodriguez nodded. "We're like a tiny little speck in an enormous universe. We're smaller than a speck."

"If we're such a small speck, maybe it won't matter if I don't do my homework," the kid said.

The whole class laughed, just as the buzzer rang to

mark the end of class, the end of the day. The clatter of chairs scraping the floor and papers being gathered filled the air.

Mr. Rodriguez pointed to the boy at the back of the room and said over the racket, "I will be checking *all* the homework."

While the other kids headed for the door, Ben seemed to be dawdling, which was unusual for him. I still had to speak to him, sooner rather than later, and placed my hand on his arm to attract his attention.

"Are you ready?" I asked.

"Not yet." He motioned toward the teacher at the front of the room. "I just want to have a quick word. You can stay if you want."

Mr. Rodriguez stepped closer. "Ben, what can I do for you?"

"I've been reading up on black holes," he replied.

"Shouldn't you be more interested in issues like the curfew? I hear you kids have organized an anti-curfew party for the weekend."

"Yeah, we have."

With the goatee and fine chinstrap of facial hair, Mr. Rodriguez didn't look like a teacher. He also seemed interested – in our protests against the curfew, in us and what we had to say.

"Instead you want to know about cosmic phenomena?" he asked.

"I was reading about the possibility of traveling through time," Ben said. "Some of the books say we could do it if we were able to travel faster than the speed of light."

The teacher nodded. "That's the theory, all unproven

of course."

He wasn't far off. I hung back a little behind Ben. "I think you were closer when you mentioned black holes and wormholes."

"I think so too," Ben said. "There's a lot we don't fully understand about the universe. These cosmic phenomena, we call them *phenomena* because we don't know exactly what they are."

Mr. Rodriguez smiled. "You've got a point, though wormholes have been widely accepted as a hypothesis."

"Physicists have been formulating theories on this subject for decades," Ben said. "It's got to be more than a hypothesis."

"We were talking about this the other day," I added. "If mankind understood wormholes better, perhaps we could use them as a bridge to allow passage between two times."

"That was the theory Einstein postulated," Mr. Rodriguez said. "Wormholes are also known as the Einstein-Rosen Bridge."

"Bridge doesn't quite encapsulate it," I said. "If mankind could capture, stabilize and enlarge these wormholes, anything could happen. If you could take one end of a wormhole and manipulate or move it, then return it to a different position, surely we'd be able to travel through time."

People much more highly educated than myself couldn't always get a grasp on the concept so I could hardly expect to be an expert. I didn't fully understand the theory, only that it was possible. I was living evidence of that.

"Nicola, you've given this lots of thought," Mr.

Rodriguez said. "You too, Ben, but I thought your main interest was in medicine."

"It is," he said. "This is just something we were talking about, and I wanted your opinion."

A soft hum of noise resonated through the closed door from outside the classroom. It only emphasized how quiet it was in here now the other students had left. Too quiet. I wished Mr. Rodriguez would say something.

Eventually he did. "I think anything is possible, and if you're interested in the subject, I can refer you to some books and other information or even to the appropriate college course."

Ben nodded. "I wouldn't mind some reading material. There's a lot of information and it can be hard to tell what's reliable."

"No problem." Mr. Rodriguez leaned across the desk to gather his books and materials.

"Thanks," Ben and I said in unison, then turned to leave.

I only had four more days. This was the time. I could feel it.

"Ben, I need to talk to you," I said.

The hallway was bustling with people and activity, the noise abrasive after the silence inside the classroom.

"I told you," he said as we walked. "I'm okay with what happened."

"This is important."

"I can't," he insisted. "I've got training."

And I didn't. I'd been avoiding martial arts and Mr. Matthews.

"What about straight after training?" I asked.

He shrugged. "Sure."

I was getting much better at reading people and could tell I was annoying him, but there wasn't much I could do about it. Besides, what I was about to tell him would go beyond 'annoying'.

With a couple of hours to kill, I went home, had something to eat, made a pathetic effort to do my homework, then went back to school. Outside the martial arts arena, the girls I'd trained with previously were leaving.

I stuck my head inside the door of the arena, stepped inside and sat on the floor to one side to take off my shoes and socks. Mr. Matthews stood to one side of Ben who was wrestling with another guy. The sounds were amplified, the grunts, the scrape of clothing on the mat, the thuds as they rolled. Everyone else had gone home.

"Let's call it a day," Mr. Matthews said. He strode across the mat on his way out, and said to me, "I don't have time for you now."

The other guy left too. I stepped onto the mat and made my way over to Ben.

I frowned. "What is with Mr. Matthews?"

Ben stood up. "Don't you get it? He's nobody and he's going nowhere. This is it for him. We're all getting out of here, going to college, moving on. He's not."

"You're right. I should forget about him."

Ben curled his index finger. "Wanna have a roll?"

A wrestle was tempting. There was a lot about Ben that was tempting.

I shook my head. "I'd like to talk, that's all."

His eyes narrowed as he stared, sizing me up. It was understandable if he didn't want to talk to me. I couldn't blame him.

"I need a shower," he said.

He was wearing faded gray martial arts shorts and a dark blue tee shirt with a band motif, both of which were covered in sweat. That was okay. I wasn't afraid of a bit of perspiration.

"This can't wait," I said.

Ben sidled closer, his chest nearly against mine. He smelled steamy. He smelled like Ben. My heart swelled and sank. This was going to be harder than I thought.

He reached to grab me around the waist but I was too quick and shot away. The grin on his face told me he was playing with me. Maybe he knew something serious was coming and wanted to avoid it.

As much as I couldn't blame him, this wasn't a game. I had to make him listen.

I shunted him in the chest, hard. Shock in his eyes, he looked surprised, then laughed. For me, that was the last straw.

I shot in for the takedown. My hands around the back of his thighs, I took him to the ground but wasn't on top for long. I tried to use my flexibility but he was bigger and far more skilled in ground fighting than me. Still, it felt good to use some energy, to wrestle for position, to be close to him. I wanted to get closer, to be more than physical, to be there always.

Ben was on top but I had my legs wrapped around his waist in the guard position.

"Shall we call it a draw?" he asked.

I might have agreed if it wasn't for that grin. He wasn't concentrating and had left his right arm out ready for me to take. I grabbed the arm, levered my foot against his body, spun around and got him in an arm bar.

He tapped. Game over.

Sitting on the mat opposite me, he rested his arms on top of his knees. "Not fair. I can't hit a girl."

"I'll make you want to hit me," I said.

Still grinning. "You're good."

"No, I was ready. There's a difference. I'm not as good a grappler as you, but I was aware. I saw an opening and took it. That's what you have to do. You have to be ready."

"Why so serious, Nic?" he asked.

"Because this is very serious."

"Is this about your mom?"

The cure hadn't arrived from Lucien. He'd let me down. I couldn't think about my mom now, not with what I had to say.

I shook my head. "It's about me and it's about you."

His eyes hooded over and he held my gaze. "Look, the last time a girl said she wanted to talk to me, it was to tell me she was seeing someone else behind my back. So I think you can see why I don't want to do this."

"There's no one else," I said. "There could never be anyone else."

"That's a good start," he said, though he didn't look particularly relieved.

"If I hadn't come to Altabena, I'd never have met you. It's the best thing that has ever happened to me. It has changed me. I used to be a different person before."

"You're still *different*." His expression told me that was a good thing. "It's one of the things I like about you. You're not like everyone else."

I sat back onto my knees opposite him. "You're a very special person, more special than you know. You're going to do amazing things that'll be remembered for decades. You'll discover cures and help people and go down in history."

Eyes down, he looked momentarily embarrassed. "You don't know that."

"I do know. I was sent here."

He held my gaze. "That's a strange way of putting it. You came here for your dad's job, didn't you?"

Where to start? He wasn't my father, not in the sense Ben meant, and he wasn't the reason I was here.

"I'm a soldier, Ben."

He smiled. "You're tough enough to be one."

"I'm different. You said it yourself. I really am a soldier. I was raised far from here in a military installation where the emphasis was purely on training. That's where I learnt my martial arts skills. That's why I'm tough. It's also why I'm so out of place here."

He shrugged. "You can be a soldier if you want to. You'd make a damn good one."

Not exactly the response I wanted, but not that far off. I didn't know how to make him take notice so I just came out with it.

"I was sent here to get rid of you. To eliminate you."

He kept smiling. "Excuse me?"

"I wish it was different but that's the truth. You're going to make some amazing medical discoveries that will change the world. You're really going to be a doctor, and not everyone approves of what you're going to do."

"Back to this again." He sounded annoyed. "How do you know what I'm going to do?"

"There's so much we don't know, so much *you* don't know. Open your mind. The universe is a huge place.

There are alternate universes, various spaces, different times. Space and time are closely related, almost the same thing. There's a future and a past and they're all linked. That talk about wormholes wasn't just a theory. I know a lot about the future."

I told him everything. About New Nation in 2120 and how the world had been devastated by a deadly virus, also how that was connected to the cure for cancer he was going to discover. I told him about being sent back to Altabena to infiltrate the community, about the mission, and how there was no way I could complete it. I told him how I'd returned to New Nation, how my superiors and my mentor Lucien had betrayed me. I tried to explain how changes in society would lead to a strict authoritarian regime that held tight reigns over the people and controlled their lives. I told Ben how I'd come back to try to warn him, to protect him. Also what they would do to me in New Nation on my return.

And he listened. I had to hand it to him.

He listened to every word.

After I finished, he sat there and I gave him a few moments. He didn't look at me. Though that was a bad sign, I sat there hoping for a miracle I knew wouldn't come.

His eyes stayed glued to the floor in front of him. "Why are you telling me all this?"

"Because–"

"Don't answer that. Wouldn't it be easier just to say you don't want to go out with me? That, I could handle. But not this bullshit, this I can't handle."

"I don't *want* to break up with you. That's not what this is about. I don't know how else to get through to you.

You have to keep a low profile and be careful. You have to be prepared."

He lifted his gaze to meet mine, his eyes overflowing with rage and disappointment.

At me.

It was all directed at me and I couldn't blame him.

"Why are you screwing with my mind?" he demanded.

"Because I don't have much time left. Once the time travel program is set, there's no changing it. There's nothing I can do."

"So you're an assassin? Then you must've killed people, *lots* of people."

His sarcasm cut into me. He couldn't know what a sensitive subject that was.

I dropped my gaze. "Not that many."

An image of the school auditorium flashed in my mind, children and teachers shaking, crying, screaming. And at the front of the room two madmen with guns taking pot shots and laughing.

It was only luck I'd been there at all. I'd been on a promotional school visit with my sergeant, who'd frozen. I hadn't.

After I worked out what was going on, I'd shot the locks off the auditorium door, then aimed and fired at one man, crouched to miss a bullet from the second, and shot him too.

Timing and training – both things had worked in my favor.

The way I'd seen it there hadn't been much choice. I wasn't a hero. I just did what I had to do. It helped that I was a damn good shot.

But Ben didn't know any of this. He didn't know that

Nicola.

He kneeled, his hands hanging by his side. "You're telling me you were sent back in time to kill me? Go ahead. Do it. My guard is down. Take a shot. Pull out a knife. Do whatever you want."

"I can't do it," I said. "I won't."

Goading me now. "Go on."

"No."

He sneered. "Maybe I can learn to hit a girl, after all."

"I won't stop you."

"Come on. Hit me. Eliminate me. This is your big chance."

"You have to be vigilant, not just now but always. You have to be careful."

The sneer turned to disbelief. "You're really serious?"

"I've never been more serious in my life."

Silence.

"I'm telling the truth," I said. "The theories about time travel and wormholes are formulated by physicists and scientists and people smarter than me. They might be theories now but one day many of them will be proven."

"Don't give me that shit. This isn't about science. It's about some weird mind-trip you're taking. If you change the future so dramatically, you won't even be born. You won't even exist. None of this can work. One event causes another and creates a chain of events. Have you forgotten about the laws of causality?"

"They're not laws," I said. "It's all relative. We can choose. We can make a difference."

"Then choose to stay here."

"I can't."

"I don't believe you. I don't believe a word you've

said."

"I can prove it."

I peeled the PR device from my arm and explained what it was.

His mouth fell open. "Let's see you do that again. Put it back."

I placed it on a different part of my arm where it melded into my skin. Ben pulled my arm closer and smoothed his fingers over the device and my skin.

He inspected the area more closely. "There's a freckle and hair growing on your arm. What happened to that thing?"

I peeled the device off, waited a second until it went rigid, then tapped the screen.

"Take a look," I said. "It's plithium. This started off as cellular phone technology."

"That's so sci-fi." Surprise in his voice. "How did you do it?"

He still didn't believe me. Maybe he *couldn't* believe me, even though I was telling the truth for the first time.

"I know," I said. "There's a photo of you taken in the future. I'll show you." I located the picture and passed the PR device across. "Information on you is very limited and this is the only picture my superiors could locate."

He stared, a combination of recognition and confusion in his eyes.

"That really looks like me, only older," he said. "It must've taken some seriously good digital manipulation to get a picture like that. I can't even remember the photo being taken. Why would you go to all that trouble?"

"I didn't."

He shook his head. "You're nuts."

I tapped the device. "How else can you explain this?"

Ben's shoulders slumped and his arms hung down. His posture told me what I already knew.

It was over.

And nothing would change that.

"You lied to me," he said.

I had. I'd lied to Ben, my friends, my family. I was a liar and a fake and I was ashamed.

"You can't get out of this," he said. Also true. "You say you came here to kill me, took on a false identity, and lied to everyone you know. If that's not true, then this whole story you've spun to me this afternoon is a lie and you're taking me for a ride. Either way, that makes you a liar."

"Everything I told you this afternoon is the truth. You have to believe me."

He brushed his hand aside as if swatting a fly. "You're no better than my mom or the rest of them."

"The rest of…?"

I saw it in his eyes. He was talking about his mother, the woman he'd trusted more than anyone, the person who was supposed to take care of him, but had instead taken another way out.

"You think your mother lied to you?" I asked.

"Lots of women have lied to me."

There was his ex-girlfriend, Shannon, the one who'd cheated on him. Surely he couldn't be comparing me with her as if I'd betrayed him in such an intimate way.

Ben stood, looking down on me. His arm flinched and I thought he was going to take a swipe. I wished he had, but I wasn't even worth that much to him.

One last chance.

I'd been willing to die for New Nation. Had never even questioned it. Ben was a much better cause. My life in exchange for his. It didn't seem like such a bad deal since I was going to die anyway.

"I'm not getting out of this alive," I said softly. "I've given up my life for you. My superiors will execute me. I have absolutely no doubt about that."

He gritted his teeth. "I trusted you."

And he didn't any more.

CHAPTER TWENTY-EIGHT

Why were hospitals so dreary? Mom and I were sitting upright in padded navy velvet chairs with firm seats and narrow arm rests. We were lucky to have nabbed the good chairs rather than a seat in the row of blue plastic chairs worthy of a bus depot waiting lounge that lay opposite us. Then, this *was* a waiting area.

Everything here looked ancient to me. The glossy magazines on the coffee table had been straightened but that didn't make them any less dog-eared. The walls had probably once been white but were now an indiscriminate shade of pale gray. The blue carpet bore the tracks of a vacuum cleaner. The place was clean, but that was the best you could say about it. No windows, no prints on the walls, no personality, nothing to make you want to stay. Maybe that was the point.

Dad crouched in front of Mom, holding her hands in his. "You sure you don't mind if I go back to the office?"

"Honey, you know I don't like too much fuss." Mom's smile didn't reach her eyes. "There's nothing more you can do here and I've got Nicola for company."

He leaned across, smoothed my hair and whispered in my ear, "Be brave for your mom."

I nodded. "I've got everything under control."

"That's good to hear."

Bending over, he slid his hand along his wife's jaw and kissed her gently on the lips. His kiss said I care for you, and I love you, and I'll always be there for you. But he had to go, and he was leaving her in good hands.

After he left, Mom dropped the magazine she wasn't reading into her lap and turned to me. "You look worried."

"Of course I'm concerned," I said. "I'd be pretty stupid if I wasn't."

"Anything else bothering you?"

"No, right now you're the most important thing."

Though that last part was true, I was such a good liar. *Everything* was worrying me, and there was absolutely no reason for her to know.

"You could always go to school, then come back later," she said, as if that was going to happen.

"Or I could just stay here."

"I guess anything's better than school."

She had it the wrong way around. Anything would be better than *this*, however there were some things we had no control over. A lot of things.

"Besides," I said. "I might be able to offer the doctors some important medical advice from the vast store of knowledge I learned at school."

At least I made Mom snigger. It was the best I could do. I'd tried to obtain the cure for her and failed. Either Lucien hadn't wanted to help or the generals intercepted my message. I'd probably never know which. And Ben wasn't yet in a position to simply whip together a remedy that was going to take years of concerted research.

Ben… How would I keep him safe when I wasn't here any more? Was there any way of getting through to him?

If only I could keep the people I loved alive. What was it my mother had said not long after I first arrived? *You give us so much pleasure just by breathing.* Now I knew exactly what she meant.

I looked up to see Mom take off her wedding ring and watch, and place them both in her purse while a nurse spoke to her. It seemed so final. I reminded myself it wasn't.

"I'll look after that for you, Mom." I took the purse from her.

She slowly stood. "You sure you'll be all right?"

I grabbed the magazine slipping from her lap. "Sure, I have this riveting reading."

And she left. Just like that.

The surgery she was having had come a long way since it had first been developed. No big deal, as my mom had insisted. They were going to make a tiny incision, poke around with a special instrument and cut away the cancerous lump. In fact, the procedure was so simple it didn't even require a general anesthetic, only a local, so she'd be awake throughout the procedure. I still didn't like the sound of it.

The doctors would take care of her. They had to.

At least there was one good thing I could say about the Bartley government. They'd made vast improvements to the health system so people who didn't have much money could still get adequate care. Mom had told me stories of how people were regularly turned away from hospitals because they didn't have health insurance. I found that unthinkable.

Everything had seemed so much more straightforward in New Nation. Die for my country? No problem. Go back in time on a life-threatening mission? Sure. Kill for my country? Absolutely.

How could it be that life was so much more complex here? I'd never felt this way in New Nation. In fact, I'd hardly felt much at all, and now I could see it was because I'd been brainwashed and whipped into line. Then there were the so-called "vitamins". It made me wonder what else the government was doing to control the people, what other measures they were taking, what else I didn't know about.

I'd learnt one thing in the last few months. You had to be strong to handle emotions.

You'd think I should've been too stressed to doze off in the upright chair with the narrow arm rests, but that's exactly what I did.

Mom shook me awake. This was the wrong way around. I should've been taking care of *her*.

I jumped to my feet. Her purse slipped from my lap but I caught it and handed it to her. She looked exactly the same as before. How could that be? Hadn't the surgery saved her life? Hadn't it changed her?

"Don't look so worried, Nicola," she said.

"We went through this before," I said. "Of course I'm worried."

"I already spoke to the doctor on my own."

"And?" I asked.

"So far, so good. They removed the lump and the surgeon is confident he got it all."

"That's promising, isn't it?"

"He's also concerned it might be a certain type of cancer that leaches into the rest of the body. They've sent a sample off for testing. The results won't be back until first thing Monday."

Words weren't going to cut it so I wrapped my arms around Mom and held her close.

Damn it, I hated all this uncertainty. Hated that there was nothing else I could do for her.

But some things were out of my hands.

CHAPTER TWENTY-NINE

I wasn't in a party mood, didn't feel like acting happy, but wasn't in the habit of sulking so I hammed it up for Lauren's sake. Only two more days after this. It didn't bear thinking about.

Lauren reached for my hand as we walked down the hallway toward the thrum of the party. This may once have been a comfortable living room, however it had now been taken over by teenagers and turned into party central.

A few kids were draped over sofas while everyone else was standing around chatting or shouting over the doof-doof music that blared from a stereo. In a corner, two girls lifted their arms over their heads and undulated, performing a sultry dance while a small group of guys pretended not to look. A giant anti-curfew banner was stretched across one wall, the only indication this was a protest rather than a party.

Outside the French doors at the rear of the room, someone was hunched over, vomiting into the garden. No party was complete without it. Then the boy straightened and I recognized Daniel, the computer nerd. I'd only ever seen him with his friend Lorenzo, the two of them talking about technology. I'd certainly never seen him like this. Who'd have thought?

Lauren headed for the dining table covered with half-full bottles, empty beer cans, dirty glasses and several stacks of clean ones. A punch bowl took pride of place in the center.

She pulled a bottle of white wine out from her bag, unscrewed the lid, and poured a generous serving into a clean glass.

"You sure I can't interest you?" she asked. Before I had a chance to answer, she added, "Watch out for the punch. It's most likely contaminated."

"Allergic, remember?" I said.

"Worst luck. You're missing out, Nicola."

I could've had a glass or two, but I didn't want to use alcohol as an escape. I wanted life, wanted to feel, no matter how hard it was.

"You didn't even notice my hair." Lauren tilted her head, her hair a shade blonder, thanks to more foils.

"It looks lovely," I said.

And mine looked the same as always, light brown and pulled back into a ponytail.

At the far end of the room, Ben stepped inside the French doors with another guy, both of them laughing. He glanced around, relaxed and happy, until his eyes locked with mine and the smile got wiped from his face. He stared with a look partway between disgust and indifference. I didn't know which was worse.

My heart sank. The noise in the room disappeared. Only silence in my head. There was nothing else in the room, only me and Ben, and the chasm between us.

Time stood still. It was true. That could happen.

Lauren nudged my shoulder. "Do you want to tell me what's going on?"

I looked around but couldn't see Ben any longer. He'd moved on, outside perhaps, or away. Away from me.

Lauren's eyes were wide. "Did you guys break up?"

"You could say that," I replied.

"You'll have to win him back."

Simone and Taylor walked into the room. With hair and outfits carefully coordinated and styled to perfection, they looked as if they were ready to perform with a backing band. Their make-up was certainly thick enough to be stage make-up. It didn't look so bad against Simone's dark skin but on Taylor it looked like a disease.

Lauren waved to them, then turned to me. "Ben doesn't know what he's missing out on with you. I'm sorry it's not working out."

"I'm not ready to talk about it just yet." I motioned toward Simone and Taylor. "Why don't you go chat with them? I'll join you in a while."

Lauren raised her eyebrows. "Are you sure?"

I ushered her away and wandered around the edge of the room, staying on the outside. That's what I was, an outsider, and somehow it felt strangely comfortable. I was never going to fit with Simone and Taylor and the cool crowd, and didn't want to. I wasn't a nerd either. I was something else.

Yet being in that room filled me with warmth. Everyone around me looked so healthy and happy, if a little drunk, though that was okay too. They had their whole lives ahead of them and they were having fun. They'd go on to college and get jobs and make their own decisions. They'd have relationships and lovers and search for the right person. They'd live their lives to the full. Or not. They could do as they wished.

Life. This was it.

Feeling a little heady, I wandered outside for some fresh air and bumped into Daniel, literally.

"Where's Lorenzo tonight?" I asked.

"He said he knew where he wasn't wanted." Daniel's words were slurred. The smell of vomit mixed with rum as he leaned closer. "*I* know how to fit in. I've got friends here."

A vacant expression on his face, he turned and walked straight into Moose who spilt some of his beer and swore. Daniel bounced straight off Moose's chest and crashed into his friend. What was his name? Bulldog.

I'd seen pinball machines in old movies and that was what this reminded me of as the skinny Asian kid got bounced around from pillar to pillar.

Bounced at first. Then pushed. The kid was out of his league.

Moose's expression changed as he saw me approach. He knew I wouldn't let him push Daniel around so he put his arm around him in a friendly fashion, his lips curling to a smarmy smile. Moose and Bulldog were the only thing holding the poor kid up as the two of them led Daniel inside the house. He'd probably be safe in there.

I should help him. I should leave. I should do something.

It'd only be polite to let Lauren know I was leaving but the thought of bumping into Ben inside was too much for me. Still, I had to do it. Maybe I was like Lorenzo and knew where I wasn't wanted.

Peels of laughter ripped through the air as I stepped inside the French doors into the living area. A crowd had gathered around something, but I couldn't see what. I pushed my way through and took it in at a glance.

Daniel was sprawled face down on the carpet, his scrawny brown ass exposed, his pants pulled down to mid thigh. Moose stood at the kid's feet, pointing in case anyone in the room had missed the scene. Which they hadn't.

A dull, pained moan escaped Daniel, causing Moose to laugh even more and the girls next to me to giggle.

Why didn't someone do something? How could it possibly be funny to degrade a person like this, even if he was inebriated?

Beside me, Simone and Taylor held their glasses to their mouths, smiles on their faces, their eyes glued to the scene in front of them. Lauren stood on the other side, emulating their stance though she looked uncomfortable, her shoulders scrunched.

"He should know he was only allowed here as entertainment," Taylor said to her friend, rolling her eyes with an air of worldliness.

Enough.

I grabbed her arm, squeezed it. "Is this how you get your kicks?"

"What's with you, Nicola?" She shook her arm free. "He got himself drunk. *I'm* not the one who did that to him."

Absolving herself of all responsibility. Fine. Still, she had the second part right. I could work out who'd humiliated the unfortunate nerdy kid.

Moose was bending over Daniel, his hands on the

guy's pants, about to yank them lower.

I pushed Moose in the shoulder. "No."

There was a secret to giving a good shunt and that was to do it with the force of a punch. His shocked expression told me he'd felt it.

"Leave him alone," I said.

Moose straightened, screwing up his face. "What's it to you?"

He was truly the master of the witty retort.

I was aware of his size, so much bigger than me. Also aware no one in the room would do anything to help me, just like no one had done anything to help Daniel.

I was in a room full of people. Alone.

My hands were up. I was ready. Leaning closer, I repeated my request for him to leave the kid alone.

"What's up your ass?" Moose replied. Another witty retort.

My gaze was riveted to his. "Do you really want to do this?"

Lips parted, he returned my stare. His face flushed pink and I saw it in his eyes. He didn't want a repeat of what had happened at the martial arts arena, not now and certainly not with an audience.

Shaking with rage, he stepped back, spat on the floor beside me and stormed out of the room toward the front door, taking Bulldog with him.

I turned to help Daniel but Ben was already there, along with another guy who was pulling the kid's pants up and trying to get him sorted. It was better they did it than me, less embarrassing for the victim. Ben didn't look up.

As I glanced around, the party was buzzing again as if nothing had happened but I could guarantee that for

Daniel this wasn't nothing. He'd never live this down. I hadn't got to him soon enough.

Not sure what to do, I wandered across to Lauren.

She nodded slowly. "Whoa."

I'd never heard her use so few words.

Taylor scowled at Lauren. "You can't possibly be sticking up for her. She caused a scene, ruined the fun."

Lauren's eyes narrowed as she stared at the other girl but I couldn't read her, couldn't tell what was on her mind.

"What?" Taylor asked. "What's wrong?"

"You have no idea how wrong you are," Lauren said.

"What are you talking about?"

"Your mouth." Lauren leaned across, touched the girl's lips and smeared deep red color across her pale cheek. "Your lipstick's smudged."

Go Lauren!

Taylor was outraged. Simone comforted her. Lauren took my arm, stepping into the back garden with me.

We bumped into Rex Anderson outside, literally. I seemed to be bumping into a lot of people tonight.

"You did a nice job back there saving Daniel from Moose," he said.

For a moment I thought he might've matured since the first day at school when he'd groped me, but his words were slurred and he was swaying. It'd be a long time until he grew up.

I shrugged. "Thanks."

He nodded, his blond hair bobbing over his eyes. "I'm just glad it wasn't me at the receiving end that time."

"You're drunk, dude," Lauren said.

Rex raised his eyebrows. "Not too drunk to get more beer."

"Oh, yes you are," Lauren said. "You'll crash your mother's nice silver convertible."

"Then she'll spank me."

He slipped past her to leave, a wicked grin on his face. If I had the energy, I'd have stopped him.

Lauren sat beside me on a chaise lounge at the back of the garden. "I wish I'd had the guts to stand up to Moose like that."

"That was nothing compared with the way you handled Taylor," I said.

Lauren shrugged. "I've had enough of her and Simone. You were right when you said they were mean. Sometimes there's a fine line between 'cool' and 'stupid bitch'."

I laughed, feeling closer to Lauren than ever before.

Her eyes lit up. "I wrote that story about how the community center and skate park were knocked down, and emailed it to a couple of magazines. I told my mom and dad what I was doing too."

"Good for you," I said.

"My mom thought I was drawing too much attention to myself." Lauren giggled. Maybe she didn't care too much for her mother's opinion.

We chatted until it was time for me to leave and Lauren to continue partying. We each had our roles to play.

I nudged past the people lining the hallway and made my way to the front porch. Signs outside the house proclaimed 'No curfew, no way', reminding me of the supposed reason for the party.

Ben was sitting on the front lawn with his arm around poor drunk Daniel, probably holding him up. A Volvo station wagon pulled up nearby and a skinny Asian man, presumably Daniel's father, rushed out and shook hands with Ben before helping his son up. Ben stood with his back to me as the car pulled away.

People were scattered on the front lawn, a couple lying down as if it were all too much for them, others standing around. Shoulders hunched, Ben's body language said it was all too much for him too. He kicked a rock on the pavement and watched it roll down the street.

In the direction of Moose and Bulldog.

I didn't know where they'd been, only that they were storming toward Ben, scowls on their faces as they passed under a streetlight. Probably pissed because Ben had helped the drunk kid, angry because of what I'd started. That was how they'd think of it.

Instinct. My eyes glued to the trouble ahead, I stepped off the porch and down the front path.

Moose and Bulldog stood in front of Ben on the pavement, two gunslingers ready for a showdown. Ben stepped back to let them pass. Moose shoved him in the chest.

I wanted to step in and pummel that bully. I wanted to teach him a lesson. I wanted to keep Ben safe.

But it wasn't the right time and this wasn't my fight.

Moose stabbed Ben's chest with his finger. "What is it with you and that bitch girlfriend of yours?"

"She's not my girlfriend," Ben muttered.

The kids standing on the lawn gathered closer. There was nothing like the prospect of a fight to get them interested. I pushed to the front, ready.

Moose slapped Ben gently on the face, teasing rather than hurting him. "Are you scared, is that it?"

He swatted Moose's hand away. "I don't want to fight,

that's all. I've got better things to do."

Ben was too kind, much more generous than me. I could see where this was headed. Moose *wanted* to fight.

He put one hand on Ben's face, then held his other fist high as if preparing to hit him in the face. Ben put his hands up in a defensive position. Still trying to talk his way out of it, trying to avoid a fight.

I stepped forward, ready to belt the crap out of anyone who laid a hand on Ben, and felt a hand on my arm, someone holding me back. *I should leave this to Ben.* He wasn't defenseless and if he didn't want to fight, that was his decision. I'd only make things worse.

Ben's eyes were on Moose. He didn't see what was coming as Bulldog came at him from the side with a big body shot. Ben doubled over, the air knocked out of him.

Moose and Bulldog stood there grinning and admiring their handiwork while Ben straightened and collected himself.

Bam! Ben sent a big right hand into the middle of Bulldog's face. The strike came out of nowhere. Hit Bulldog smack on the button. Blood sprayed from his nose. His hands flew to his face as he fell back onto a garden bed.

A couple of guys near me clapped. A car screeched around the corner, a silver convertible, a flash of blond hair in the driver's seat.

"Hey, that'll be Rex with the beer," someone yelled.

"On with the show," said another.

Moose shunted Ben causing him to lose his balance, then pushed him again. Onto the road this time.

And all I could think was that Ben should have got in first and hit him sooner. Time for me to step in.

I saw it as if in slow motion. The silver convertible speeding up, Moose winding up for a big punch, Ben without his balance.

Ben who'd been too nice.

Ben who should've hit him sooner.

Moose's fist landed on Ben's jaw. The punch sent him staggering back into the middle of the road, stunned. He didn't know where he was or what he was doing.

I stepped forward.

The rumble of the car engine filled the air.

Behind me, a girl shrieked.

In front of me, Ben stumbled back.

Straight into the path of the car.

CHAPTER THIRTY

No thought, only action.

I leapt across the pavement and shunted Moose out of the way. Ben seemed so far away.

"*NOOO.*" A primal cry.

I launched myself into the air.

Threw myself at him.

Tires screeched.

Thud. My shoulder landed on Ben's waist. *Whoosh.* We flew through the air. *Thwack.* My foot smashed against something. The car?

I landed on Ben. The air left my body. Then he was on top of me. We'd rolled.

I was sitting up. Didn't know how I'd got that way. Ben was splayed beside me, on his back on the asphalt.

Was he okay? Please let him be all right.

My mouth open, I wanted to speak but I was choking and the words wouldn't come out.

Ben moaned, such a wonderful sound. He was alive.

In the background, I heard a car engine being switched off, voices shouting, car doors slamming. What were all these people doing? Where had they come from?

Two big guys helped Ben sit up. He slapped them away, insisted he was fine.

A hand on my shoulder. "Are you okay, Nicola?" someone asked.

I nodded.

Adrenaline pumped through my veins, so thick I could feel it. I didn't feel pain now. Didn't feel anything. Give it another hour and I would.

Ben lifted his gaze to meet mine. He'd never looked as good as he did at that moment. Dark hair hung over green eyes that glimmered with gratitude, eyes that were only for me. Lips parted, he was breathing heavily.

Breathing…

It was as much as I could've asked for.

He stood, held both my hands in his and helped me up, staring into my eyes as though I were the most magical thing he'd ever seen. He made me feel special, wanted, desired. He made me feel a lot of things.

Ben slipped his hands onto my waist and wrapped his arms around me. He covered my mouth with his and spun me around, twirling me through the air as if I weighed nothing.

A huge cheer erupted from the crowd.

He kissed me harder. Eventually, he put me down, still gazing into my eyes. No words. We didn't need them, not yet.

This was why I lived.

For moments like these.

Ben took my hand and I became increasingly aware of the people around me.

"I tried to stop. I'm so sorry." Rex's voice.

Ben waved to him as if all was forgiven.

A girl shoved Rex in the shoulder. "You're a freaking idiot."

Maybe he was. We didn't care.

"It's all your fault, Rex." Moose's voice stopped me in my tracks. "You were too drunk to drive. You didn't see what was right in front of you."

Still buzzing from the excitement, I slipped my hand out of Ben's and turned. A few people stood between me and Moose. They stepped out of the way, parting like the Red Sea. Fury rose in my stomach.

Moose was so close.

And I wanted to hit him so bad.

"I'm sorry," Moose said, panic in his voice.

Suddenly, my fist landed on the middle of his face. Moose staggered back. Two guys behind caught him. He winced, panting with short breaths, his hand covering one eye.

"Okay, okay," he said. "I deserved that."

"*Now* you're sorry," I said.

Another cheer from the friends surrounding us. These people sure liked a show.

Ben took my hand. It felt right. *This* felt right. I'd found a place where I fit, people who made me happy, a guy who wanted me again. What more could I ask for? Okay, my life wasn't perfect but it was mine. For now. For as long as it lasted.

A murmur went through the crowd. It sent a shiver up my spine. Something was up. I could feel it in the air.

"Who are those people coming up the street?" A voice from around me. "Where'd they come from?"

"They're coming from the other way, too." Another

voice.

I looked up the street. Gatecrashers. A gang of about fifty kids was swaggering toward us on foot down the middle of the road. The boys in the front pointed and gesticulated as they walked. The sound of breaking glass shattered the air as someone smashed a bottle on the pavement. A couple of them laughed. One made a monkey sound. They were boozed up and ready.

It was easy to work out what would happen. These guys had heard about the party one way or another and were here to join in, regardless of the fact they weren't invited or wanted. We were in for a fight, a scuffle at the very least.

Behind them, I saw the short haircuts and dark uniforms of local police officers. Lots of them.

I turned the other way to see a mirror image. It was the same thing, a gang of kids about our age with a gang of police officers behind them.

Caging us in from both sides.

What were the police doing here? How could they know there was going to be trouble before anything happened?

A feeling of dread weighed in my stomach. The officers weren't here to help. They were herding the gatecrashers toward us, giving them nowhere to go, leading cattle to slaughter.

I pulled Ben back from the crowd so we were on the front lawn. I had to do something, and fast.

Lauren was beside me. "What's going on?"

In front of us, there was a scuffle and some pushing and shoving with the Altabena High boys refusing to let the newcomers pass. Nothing major yet. On the outskirts of the crowd, the police loomed.

One thing I knew from my training was that people would do nothing unless you singled them out and gave them specific instructions.

Someone had to take control.

"Listen to me," I said to Lauren. "Get Simone and Taylor. Your job is to record everything that's going on. Use your phones. If the police hurt anybody, film it, and send it to Lorenzo. Tell him to get it out there, post it online, put it on PeoplePlace, VideoTube, whatever. He'll know what to do."

We might not be able to stop the gatecrashers and definitely wouldn't be able to fight the police, but we could let the rest of the world know what was going on. The media and the internet were our only defense regardless of whether it was too little too late.

Even on a Saturday night, people checked their phones and PeoplePlace regularly. If there was police brutality, serious drama and things got out of hand, word would get out in minutes. Lorenzo knew how this stuff worked. He'd be dying to help.

In an hour, the news would be everywhere, going viral. It might be another twelve hours before it hit the newspapers, television broadcasts and traditional media but when it hit, it'd be big-time. What would happen after that, I didn't know.

Lauren nodded and turned to talk to the other two girls standing on the porch behind us.

I looked at Ben. "Get the guys from martial arts. Tell them not to let the gatecrashers into the house or down the side path."

"Okay." He acted quickly.

I grabbed two boys I knew vaguely from English class. "Get everyone inside the house. After that, lock the back doors."

They looked at me blankly.

"Just do it," I said.

Startled, they jumped and did as they were told.

They had their work cut out for them. The girls who were out here would doubtless head inside but the boys were pumped full of testosterone and itching for some action. They didn't know what they were in for.

At the edge of the crowd, the cops were shoving the gatecrashers forward. The kids at the back were complaining. The ones at the front were raising their fists.

The first punch was thrown. That was it, a free-for-all. In front of me, two gatecrashers tackled two Altabena High boys, fists flying.

At the rear, the police yelled and swung their batons, smashing their way through the crowd. I looked to my right. One of the gatecrashers tried to get out of the way of the police. A cop lashed out at him with his baton, across the leg, the ribs, then his shoulders as the boy crumpled to the ground. The cop next to him did the same.

Were Lauren and the other girls capturing this on video? Would it make any difference? I didn't know. I only knew this was out of control.

How could this be happening? These men were police. They were supposed to uphold the law, not beat unarmed people.

A gunshot rang through the air. Then another. How could I keep these people safe?

A fist came out of nowhere. It brushed against the side of my head, the boy who'd thrown it lunging forward. I slammed my elbow into his face. He staggered back. His hand over one eye, blood dripped through his fingers.

I looked in the other direction. Saw the same thing. The cops were beating up anyone in their way. Getting closer.

Suddenly, a police officer was on the other side of me. An Altabena boy had his hands out, backing away from the man. The cop slammed his baton against the boy's legs. He screamed. Dropped to the ground.

The cop raised his baton again. I jumped between the two of them, a human shield.

"Enough," I yelled.

The cop's mouth twitched and he sneered, his arm held high before he lowered it to his side.

"Bitch," he muttered.

Out of nowhere, I saw a blur of fuzzy bleached hair and a fist slamming into the policeman's face. The guy with the bad regrowth was grinning, the cop on the ground. Where the hell had he come from?

Lauren was on the porch with the other girls, phones in hand, all of them filming, for all the good it would do.

Not far from me, an officer whacked a defenseless girl with his baton. She screamed and cowered.

Enough.

Fury burned in my gut and surged through my body. I slammed my fists into the policeman's face. *Smash.* He didn't know what had hit him. I grabbed him around the back of the neck, yanked his head down and sent my knees into his gut. He retched.

I let go and staggered back, looking around, trying to work out what to do. I got punched in the face again so I hit back, well aware I was lucky because the boys were copping it a lot worse than the girls. Then I pushed my way through the crowd though I had no idea where I was going.

Suddenly Ben grabbed my arm. "I've got you. I'm so glad you're safe."

We were on the street at the edge of the crowd. The fighting had died down. Beside us, two girls were hunched over, crying. Other kids had dropped to the ground, beaten. The police were hauling others off into vans further down the street.

"Let's go," Ben said.

"No."

He yanked me along. "We've got two choices, Nic. We run, or we stay and get arrested."

When he put it that way, running didn't sound like such a bad idea. I followed him as we skirted around the front of a police van while officers at the other end threw people into the back. I couldn't tell if they were Altabena boys or gatecrashers.

Clear space ahead of us.

We ran.

I didn't know what was right or wrong any more, only that we wouldn't achieve anything by staying.

We'd done our best.

And I didn't have much time left.

CHAPTER THIRTY-ONE

Was this life? Was this what it was supposed to be like?

Because it didn't seem real. The seconds when I'd thrown myself in front a car flashed before my eyes, then the moment Ben kissed me, the moment I'd won him back. Then the riot afterwards.

Ben held my hand, leading me forward toward Lake Altabena. I'd have followed him anywhere.

We slowed down as we walked across a grassed area dotted with trees. A playground lay between us and the lake shimmering in the distance. It was so quiet here that the party and the events of this evening seemed a world away.

This *was* another world. It wasn't the place where I'd grown up. To the people who lived here, these surroundings probably didn't seem special but for me, they held everything I wanted.

As we neared the playground, a smile lit up my face and I slipped my hand out of Ben's. I'd seen pictures and footage in old movies but had never had the chance to play on one. A swing.

In New Nation only very small children were allowed to use play equipment for their physical development, then they quickly progressed to obstacle courses and more serious training. If I'd been on a swing as a toddler, it wasn't something I could remember.

I could be a kid again, or maybe for the first time.

My hands on the metal chain, I sat back on the swing, pushed my legs ahead and swung through the crisp night air. I felt free, the cool air swishing past my body as I flew through the air.

How high could I go? How far until the laws of physics let me down and allowed me to fall? Higher, higher.

"Slow down, Nic," Ben said.

He was sitting on the swing next to mine. Maybe I'd never have the chance to use a swing again. That was okay. I'd done it once. I scraped my feet on the ground to slow the swing and came to a halt.

Ben stood, his phone in his hand. "You'll want to see this."

He crouched down to show me a video on the small screen of a police officer beating a scrawny guy with a baton, the footage clearly from tonight. Lauren and her friends had filmed it and sent it to Lorenzo who'd loaded it onto VideoTube.

A groan left my body. I hoped the guy was okay, that he was at least getting medical attention. By now, surely many of the people involved would've been taken either to the police station or hospital and parents would have been called.

"The worst thing is he's not on his own," I said. "He's one of many."

"I know." Ben pointed to the screen on his phone. "Look at this."

Five hundred hits. Already.

"This is only the beginning," I said.

He nodded. "That's right."

This had been part of my plan all along, but I still couldn't believe it was working.

"Tonight didn't happen by accident," I said.

"No, the cops were in on it from the start. What I can't work out is why they should care. What's in it for them?"

"They're doing what they're told."

The government – and maybe even State Ruler Bartley himself – wanted to enforce a curfew, to erode our rights, to get control of us any way they could.

And we wouldn't let them.

Ben's phone went off several times and he gave me updates: more videos had been loaded, some were going viral; parents had been called to the police station; lawyers were getting involved.

"Let's forget about this for a few minutes." He switched his phone to silent, shoved it into his pocket and took my hand, leading me to the lake.

The water shimmered in the moonlight in front of us as we dropped down onto the grass. The fresh smell of mulch and vegetation wafted across. The night was too still for waves to lap against the edge of the lake. Only the soft croak of a frog in the distance cut through the night air.

I could have stayed like that forever.

I wished I could.

After a while Ben said, "Earlier, when the car was

coming at me…you saved my life."

Eyes down, I said, "No, I didn't."

"You threw yourself in front of a moving car and pushed me out of the way. You could've died. You risked your life."

I've already given up my life for you.

Couldn't he see that?

My decision had been made well before I jumped in front of that car. I couldn't kill him so I had to die. It was that simple and that complicated.

I lifted my gaze to meet his. "You weren't going to die then."

Ben looked away.

Back to this. Sure, he was speaking to me again, which was something. But he didn't believe a word I said. He was never going to believe me.

Silence. I wasn't sure if I should be the first to speak, but then I had nothing to lose.

"I don't know exactly what would've happened if I wasn't there," I said. "I only know you weren't going to die tonight. Maybe you'd have been injured, rushed to hospital, I don't know. I only know that you don't die now."

He hugged his knees to his chest and looked out onto the lake. "Maybe I *was* going to die–"

"No."

"Hear me out. Maybe if you weren't here things would've gone very differently. For one thing, maybe more kids would've got hurt tonight and maybe that footage would never have made it onto the internet so then there'd be no way of proving what the police did."

"Actually, I don't think that part went very well."

"Your presence here changes things, Nic," Ben said. "You saved me. Earlier, you helped Daniel. You had an effect, created a chain of events."

I shrugged. "I probably do have an effect in small ways. I can't explain it, not exactly. I just don't think I saved your life. I feel it in my gut. I don't believe you were going to die."

Ben reached for my hand and enveloped it between his. "I'm trying to say thank you."

I sat forward on my knees and let my hand drop from his to rest on my lap. He wouldn't want to hold my hand, not with what I had to say.

"Let me help you," I said. "That's a better way of saying thank you. Look after yourself. Keep a low profile. Cover your tracks. Be more vigilant. Be a hard-ass if you have to. If you need to be the one to throw the first punch, then do it. You can't expect others to be as nice as you."

"You want me to be ruthless. You want me to be something I'm not."

"They'll send someone else. Next time it won't be me. Next time it'll be someone who follows orders."

I was being too vague. *They* – I meant my superiors. *Following orders* – they'd kill him.

That was what I meant but I couldn't bring myself to say it, not after the response I'd had from Ben last time I'd tried to explain the situation to him.

He leaned back on his hands. "So I'll have to be careful if I want to get by, is that it?"

Was I finally getting through? Did I dare believe it?
"Yes."

"I've been taking care of myself for a while," he said.

"Celia and my family too for that matter. I'll do my best to look after myself and those around me. I can be quicker. Next time, I'll get in before you and *I'll* be the one to thump Moose. I can lift my game." He added with a shrug, "But that might take some of the fun out of life. I enjoyed watching you punch Moose. It made me proud."

His words brought a smile to my lips.

Ben tilted my chin up with one hand and leaned closer. He pressed his lips against mine, gently this time, and for those few moments we were the only two people in the world. It was only me and Ben surrounded by the night air. No houses, no people, no one else.

A breeze came out of nowhere, waves lapping gently on the shore before settling back into silence.

Ben broke off the kiss, his expression contented. "We can make this work."

No, we can't.

My heart sank. How I wished he was right. How I wished we could be together and stay here in Altabena like two normal teenagers, but nothing about my situation was normal.

I had no way of altering the time travel program. What's more, the system could locate me through advanced GPS technology, something I couldn't escape, and it would send me back, no matter what. My superiors would punish me with death.

There was no avoiding it.

I shuffled back, then stood while Ben looked at me. Somehow I'd got used to the idea of death, in theory anyway, though I might not be so stoic when the time came. But losing Ben was different. I couldn't bear the thought. Couldn't face him. I had to get away.

I turned and ran.

"Hey," Ben yelled.

I didn't know where I was going, toward the road, home perhaps, I had no idea.

Panting, Ben grabbed me and spun me around.

"What's with you?" he asked, his grip firm on my shoulders. "Why did you run away?"

"I *can't* run away," I said. "That's the whole point."

He screwed up his face. "What are you talking about?"

"They'll find me. Whatever I do, wherever I go, my superior officers will always find me."

"We can leave, Nic." His eyes glimmered with promise. "We can run away together."

My mouth fell open but I couldn't get the words out.

"We can go to LA or San Francisco and start afresh," he said. "I can find a job and study at night school."

I shook my head.

"There's always a way. You said I should keep a low profile and cover my tracks. We can do that together."

"You don't understand," I said.

He grabbed my shoulders. "Then make me."

"Where I come from, the GPS technology is very advanced," I said. "Everyone's movements can be traced. In New Nation, my superior officers can check my exact location at any time. It's the same for everyone. We can all be located at any time. There's no hiding. No lying."

"Is the GPS unit in your PR device? We can ditch that, destroy it."

"There's a locator in the device but that's not how they track me."

"Then, how? Tell me and we'll work it out."

"The GPS locators are minuscule. They're called

geopositrons."

Excited now. "Is it some sort of computer chip under your skin? Is that it? We'll find a way to get rid of it."

"You can't see the geopositrons," I said calmly. "They're microscopic and they work in conjunction with each other, hundreds of thousands of them."

"Are you saying they can't be removed?'

"The geopositrons are in my blood, Ben."

"In your...?"

"They're in my blood. They're part of me. The only way to get rid of them is for me to lose all my blood. In which case I'll die."

That was my point. Whether my superiors got to me or I tried some other method, either way I'd be dead.

Blood is life.

Blood is death.

And I didn't have a way out.

CHAPTER THIRTY-TWO

I looked up from my cereal bowl to see Ben Tanner standing in the kitchen doorway in his school uniform, his keys in one hand. It was the stuff of dreams – handsome guy swings by my house unexpectedly on his way to school. And it was the stuff of nightmares.

Still, it seemed perfectly natural seeing him in my house though he'd never been here before. He was the sort of person who fit nearly anywhere.

Mom swept past him and took her seat at the table. "You didn't mention Ben was giving you a lift to school."

Ben stepped forward. "I wanted to surprise Nicola."

I glanced up at him from my plate. "You're full of surprises."

"No, actually that would be you."

Mom and Dad shared a glance across the table as if they both knew what was going on. If only things were that simple.

"I'm sure Nicola won't be long." Dad smiled, though clearly sizing Ben up. "I take it you've seen the papers?"

Ben nodded. "And the television news last night as

well. Phones have been going wild across the neighborhood too."

Not ours. We hadn't been here long enough, but I'd kept up with the news on the internet and talked to Lauren and Ben yesterday.

The headlines read, *Police Start Riot and Blame Students*. A neat summary. The news services confirmed what I'd thought from the start, that police provided transportation for a group of young people from out of town, encouraged them to crash the anti-curfew party and had then beaten innocent, unarmed teenagers. They'd also used their firearms unnecessarily though luckily no one had been shot.

Dad pointed to the newspaper. "People are outraged that a group of kids was attacked. The Commissioner of Police has made a public apology and the government has decided against a curfew. They crossed a line and now they're backing off."

For now. I knew they wouldn't let up, that they'd try again, that they wanted to control the people any way they could.

Excited, Lauren had phoned me this morning because *Today Magazine* had accepted the article she'd written and was already promoting it on the internet as an impassioned, personal tribute. It was never too late for some bad press for the government.

Maybe we did have control over our future. Maybe we didn't have to accept the way things were headed if we didn't like it. We had choices. We could change things.

I knew the direction the world was headed. Maybe things didn't have to be that way if we didn't let them.

Or maybe we deserved what we were going to get. I

didn't have all the answers.

A phone buzzed in the background and my mother jumped in her seat. Mom, I'd almost forgotten about her. She went straight to the cupboard bench top where she'd left her phone and picked it up. His eyes glued to her, Dad slid his coffee mug onto the table. Ben knew better than to speak.

Her back to us, her shoulders relaxed and the tension left her body. As she turned, her pale eyes were wide, her lips curling to a smile of disbelief.

"The test results have come back," she said. "Doctor Simmons said he'd text me as soon as he got them. I've got the all clear."

I felt the tension leave my body as if I was having an instant replay of what Mom had just been through. The cancer hadn't spread. She was going to be okay.

"That's wonderful," I said.

Dad stood, put his arms around her, spun her around and kissed her on the mouth, then held her at arm's length, beaming. Somehow the scene seemed strangely familiar.

"We have to celebrate," he said. "I'll take you to that fancy restaurant on Carson Lane. We can have a bottle of champagne. Tonight. Let's not wait."

"Sure." Mom threw her hands up, then her face clouded over. "What about Nicola? We can't leave her behind."

"Yes, you can." I stood from the table. "In fact, you should. You deserve it after everything you've been through."

I gave her a big hug, held her tight. Pressing my eyes shut, I wished for a long and happy life for her. For Dad too. Maybe wishing could make it true.

A pang of guilt shot through me because I had something on my mind and it'd be easier if they were out of the house. There was always something else. I was never going to get used to having all these emotions coursing through me.

Mom put her hand on my shoulder. "You don't look excited about the idea."

"I'm...calmly excited. And happy for you."

The pang of guilt in my gut twisted like a knife. What would happen to them after I'd gone? How would they cope?

If only there was more I could do for them. If only I had more time.

I looked across at Ben waiting patiently by the table and made my way toward him.

"Congratulations on your good news," he said to my mom.

"I'm sorry, Ben," she said. "I forgot you were there. We were just..."

"It's okay, Mom," I said. "He knows."

He knows a lot more than you do. That damn guilt shot through me again. I didn't want to let them down.

Ben asked a few questions about my mother in the car on the way to school. He didn't say much about anything else.

Student parking was off campus on a vacant lot separated from the school by a small area of bush. It probably would've been just as easy to walk the whole distance to school but the car still ruled supreme in this country. Everyone wanted to drive and sometimes Ben did too.

He closed the door behind him and slung his school

backpack over one shoulder. I was already waiting for him at the front of the car, my bag on the ground beside me.

"I was thinking," he began.

"That's all I've been doing," I said.

"We should make the most of our time together. Maybe things won't be as bad as you suspect. Like with your mom. You thought she was going to be seriously ill but that didn't turn out so bad. Maybe we're worried about nothing and things will sort themselves out. In the meantime, we should enjoy every moment."

"I've only got tonight," I said. "This is my last day."

In the early hours of Tuesday morning, I'd be transported away.

"No, it can't be." Ben's face fell. The bag slipped from his shoulders and he grabbed my arms, gripped them tight. "We've got to find a solution. There has to be a way."

I held his gaze, my eyes telling him there was no easy way out. He got the message and dropped his hands.

Calm now, I said, "I have no way of altering the time travel program. There's no escape."

Ben's brow furrowed, anger in his eyes. "You told me that before."

I understood his frustration, his anger too. I felt it deep in my bones, my veins, my life blood.

"There might be a way," I said.

"What is it?" A flash of hope in his eyes. "You've been telling me I should let you help me. It works both ways. Let *me* help you too. There must be something I can do."

"If I drain the right amount of blood from my body, the geopositrons will be flushed out with it," I said.

Silence.

"You'll die, Nicola."

"It's the only way I can live," I said. "The geopositrons work in conjunction with each other. They're too small to work autonomously. Together, hundreds of thousands of them send tiny electric messages to each other to form a mass, but it has to reach a critical size to function."

"What's the minimum size?"

"I don't know."

"How many of the damn things are there in your blood?"

"I wish I knew."

"That's a lot of things you don't know."

It didn't make any difference. I had to do this. I had to try. If it came down to it, I'd rather die trying.

"It's risky," I said. "A risk I have to take."

A muscle in Ben's jaw flinched. "You can't do it."

"You might be the one with the photographic memory but I was paying attention in science class. I weigh just over fifty kilos. That's 3.3 liters of blood in my body."

He shook his head. "No, not that stupid fucking science assignment."

I remembered the details. I could lose up to forty percent of my blood and survive. The problem was picking the exact cut off point. Another not-so-minor problem was being conscious at the time so I could call for help.

"What about a blood transfusion?" Ben asked.

"It won't work."

Ben grabbed me by the shoulders. "I can steal some blood. From the hospital. The casualty department is bound to have some. What blood type are you?"

"A Rh negative." I shook my head. "Forget it, Ben. I have to get rid of the geopositrons *first*. I have to get rid of those suckers or I'll get transported back. A blood transfusion would only dilute the concentration of the blood I was losing. Besides, no doctor is going to help me drain the blood from my body, no matter what story we concoct. That's why I need your help."

Shaking, Ben dropped his hands. "I can't help you. This is beyond me. There are so many issues with accepting blood. It's a foreign substance. Your body will reject the proteins in the blood. I can't give you a transfusion. I don't even know where to start."

I stared up at him through lowered lids. "That's not what I need your help for."

He covered his face with his hands. "This is fucked up."

I peeled his fingers away but he shook my hands off.

"I can't do this again, Nic," he said.

"Again?"

"You don't know what it was like. My mother…I was the one who found her."

Maybe I should've guessed but I'd had no idea. My heart sank for poor Ben. He'd been so young.

"I saw her and she was gone," he said. "For years I had flashbacks, heart palpitations, panic attacks. I kept thinking if only I'd got home sooner, if only I hadn't gone to football practice that afternoon, if only I'd been quicker, she'd still be alive."

"It wasn't your fault."

"I know that now."

What had I asked him to do? Was there anything that could've caused him more pain?

"I'm so sorry, Ben. I don't expect you to help, not after that."

Realization in his eyes. "That's why you wanted your

parents to go out tonight."

"Yes."

"I can't let you do this." He stepped back. "I'll tell them. I'll tell your parents everything."

I shook my head. What would he tell them? That I was from the future. That I needed to drain the geopositrons from my blood. As if they'd believe him.

"I have to do this," I said.

A strange inner calm overcame me. This must be how it felt when you knew you were making the right decision.

He staggered back. "I can't help you."

"It's okay."

I reached for his hand but he pulled it away.

That was okay too.

If I was on my own, that was the way it had to be.

CHAPTER THIRTY-THREE

I'm sorry.

I looked down at the words I'd written on a piece of paper on my desk.

It wasn't enough, not nearly enough, but I couldn't explain my situation. Didn't know where to start.

I'd spent the afternoon in tears holed up in my room, hoping for another way out, wishing for a miracle, trying to be strong. I was done crying.

I took off my school uniform, tossed the shirt into the hamper in the corner of my room and folded my skirt before laying it on the bed. I reached under the pillow and found my pajamas, pink and white checked long pants with a matching pink tank top. *Pink.* When had I become a girl who likes pink?

Still I didn't want to be found naked in Altabena. If I was going to be found. I might end up back in New Nation if this didn't work.

The note on my desk didn't seem adequate but I couldn't think what to add, so I left it. And headed for the bathroom.

I stood in the doorway. Everything was ready. I'd run a warm bath, the water glistening with a blue tinge in the immaculate white tub. The whole bathroom was pristine, in fact, from the enormous dark brown tiles on the floor to pale ones lining the walls.

I didn't want to get the place dirty. Didn't want to muck things up for everyone more than I already had.

A bolt of guilt shot through me. If I failed, someone would find me and that was too horrible to think about. I didn't want anyone to go through what Ben had.

My cell phone lay beside the basin, the emergency number set to speed dial so I'd only have a few buttons to press when the time came. Earlier I'd placed a razor beside it.

A large clear plastic measuring pitcher from the kitchen sat on the white tiles that lined the edge of the bath on one side. Empty. It'd be full soon.

This item had been a problem because I needed to measure 1.3 liters, but the largest pitcher I could find was a liter. My plan was to measure out the first liter, tip the contents into the bath, then gauge the remaining amount.

How could I be so cool? So calculating?

My phone rang. *Let it ring.* It doesn't matter.

My stomach clenched, my throat constricted and I dry retched over the basin. I was trying to be calm but my body was telling me otherwise.

If I lost too much blood, I'd die. Not enough, and the geopositrons would remain; I'd get transported back to New Nation; and be executed. It was a fine line.

The mirror was in front of me but I couldn't bear to look at myself and turned to the bath instead. Sliding in, I closed my eyes, held my breath, tipped my head back and let the warm water engulf me.

I'd heard stories about people who'd killed themselves or tried to. Even in New Nation it happened from time to time. I couldn't imagine being driven to suicide, how desperate you'd have to be, or how you could think things would never get better.

But I knew this wasn't the way.

Life was too precious, too short, too valuable. There was always a better way, a different choice, and it wasn't *this*.

I was desperate too, only in a different way.

Desperate to live.

I thought about Ben. He couldn't be here. I understood.

And I longed for him.

Spluttering for air, I lifted my head out of the water, smoothed my hair back from my face.

Somewhere in the house a door swished open or perhaps closed. No, surely my parents couldn't be home, not yet.

Then footsteps. Someone calling my name.

Go away.

Ben stood in the doorway just as he had this morning. What was he doing here?

He dropped a bag he was holding, crouched by the bath and cupped my face with his hands.

"Nicola, no." Urgency in his voice. And despair.

"It's okay," I mumbled.

"I can't let you do this."

"You have to."

He stood and turned away. Slammed his fist on the bathroom cabinet and paced the small room.

"Fuck," he yelled.

He had that right.

Ben kicked the half-open door. It slammed against the wall, bounced off with an enormous shudder, then ended up ajar. I couldn't blame him. Better for him to take it out on the fittings than me.

He dropped to my side. "Please, no."

I reached for him and slid one hand along his jaw, his light stubble rough against my wet hand. He covered my hand with his. Though dry, his eyes overflowed with pain, his expression tortured. I hated doing this to him.

"You can leave," I whispered. "No one has to know you were here."

I saw something in the set of his jaw and the way his eyes hooded over that I hadn't seen before, not like this.

"Get out of the bath," he said.

"No."

"We can do this together." He pointed to the bag he'd left on the floor. "A blood transfusion. I can take care of it. I stole a few things."

I didn't get it. "You stole a bag of blood?"

He shook his head. "Couldn't get hold of any. I got some other stuff though, cannulas and tubing."

"How's that going to work?"

"Get out of the bath, Nicola."

I held his gaze. "Tell me how."

"We're both A neg. Same type. We'll replace your blood with mine." He gritted his teeth. "Pull the plug and get out."

"No," I said.

"An auto-transfusion. It's what they used to do in warzones when they couldn't get sterile blood. I'll stick one cannula in my arm and another in yours, joined by some short tubing. It's got to be short so the blood doesn't clot. If I'm higher up my blood will flow into your body. That's what gravity does."

We'd been through this. How could he do this? Didn't he understand?

Firm. I had to be firm. "A blood transfusion won't work. I have to drain my blood *first*. A lot of it."

He rummaged around in the bag behind him. "That's what the other cannula is for. This'll hurt."

That thing looked more like a small pipe than a needle, not that I cared about pain. I cared about living.

I stared. "We drain my blood and then try…"

He nodded.

I reached for the plug, stood in the bath and watched the water swirling down. Ben took my hands as I stepped out of the bath but it hadn't quite sunk in.

I let him wrap a towel around me as I sat on the edge, my back to the wall. He held me close. Pressed a kiss to my temple.

"We still have to measure it," I said. "I have to lose the right amount."

"We can do that. That's what the pitcher is for."

Ben tapped my inner arm looking for a vein, then stabbed the cannula into my right arm. I flinched when I shouldn't have, then reclined back so my arm was hanging down while Ben placed the pitcher inside the bath.

My blood flowed.

So red, such a vibrant color. I'd seen blood before, but never noticed how glossy it was, how rich, how bright.

I pictured the geopositrons in my blood streaming out of me, my body evicting the microscopic invaders. I wanted to be rid of them. I wanted to live. My life, my way.

It occurred to me there should've been more pain. Maybe there was and I hadn't noticed yet. Maybe the adrenaline and my body's natural chemicals were taking over.

I looked down at the pitcher.

Seven hundred milliliters.

Ben was at my side, holding the other two cannulas joined by tubing, exactly as he'd said.

I looked up at him. "Not yet."

His lips thinned. He waited.

One liter.

He reached over and tipped the contents into the bath. It looked like a huge red stain on the white porcelain. I'd lost close to a third of my blood. I had to last longer. Had to time this just right.

I was dozing. Sinking. "Just a little more."

"It's time, Nic."

"Too soon."

Ben crouched down, slid a cannula into his arm. Blood streamed through the tubing and out of the cannula at the other end, dripped onto the floor in big red splotches. He lifted the other end, fingers pressed against the tubing.

"Not yet," I said.

Ben stared at me. "Do you trust me?"

"I trust you."

Lips parted, he held my gaze, deliberating. He took short sharp breaths like a weight lifter ready for an Olympic jerk and clean. One more deep breath and his face transformed with determination.

He picked the free cannula up and stabbed it into my

left arm, then stood up so the blood was flowing from his body down through the cannula, through the tubing, down into my body.

Cold and damp on the outside, I started to feel warmed from the inside out. A pleasant feeling. It made me realize how weak I'd become so soon. How hazy. How weak.

"This is my blood, Nic," Ben said. "My life."

He was giving me part of himself.

A heated wave surged through me – an emotion, a bodily reaction, I wasn't sure. Ben and I were joined together, his blood pumping through my veins, part of him inside part of me.

And it felt right.

Two lives intermingling. The ultimate gift. We'd be together forever, no matter what happened. And anything could happen.

The skin of my inner arms where the two cannulas had been inserted throbbed, the pain intensifying. My blood felt heated, my whole body simmering, nausea rising in my stomach.

"It burns," I said. "It burns."

"Hang on, Nic. You can do it. Getting rid of blood is easy. Accepting new blood isn't."

Was this supposed to happen? Was my body rejecting his blood?

I scratched the skin around the cannula in my right arm, gouged gashes in the flesh. More blood. More pain.

The cannula had to stay. I had to do this.

My insides were boiling, my internal organs melting, my skin heated from underneath. My whole body was burning.

Even if this failed, at least I'd saved Ben's life. At least I'd done one good thing.

But I couldn't fail. I wanted to live. I wanted to stay.

Ben slid his hand onto my face, his fingers scorching. "Stay with me, Nic."

Then nothing…

CHAPTER THIRTY-FOUR

My eyes flicked open. Like a switch, from off to on.

Where was I? What was going on?

One breath in, one breath out. I was breathing. Not so much breathing as suffocating. Panic rose inside me, swelled inside my chest. My throat constricted, my mouth dry.

But I was aware. That meant I was alive.

I heard a small sob. Had that come from me? Did I have the energy?

Focus.

A ceiling hovered above me, a fluorescent light fitting pinned to it. I was in a room. But where?

More panic. Don't tell me I was back in New Nation. Please, anything but that. Surely I hadn't gone through so much only to be back where I started.

I shook my head. The pillow beneath smelled like detergent with a hint of antiseptic. I looked around. Saw pale gray walls that may once have been white.

I was lying on a bed or a mattress. I felt light, as if I weighed nothing. Except for my hand. I felt warmth and a gentle squeezing.

Looking across at my fingers, I saw a hand covering mine. I lifted my gaze higher. It was Mom. She was shaking, her face tearstained, her grip firm. Behind her, Dad had his hands on her shoulders as if holding her up.

Another sob. From Mom. What had I done to them?

She reached across and soothed my hair with her other hand. "It's okay, honey. Just try to relax."

"Where am I?"

"In a hospital."

"What time is it?"

"Take it easy, Nicola," Dad said. "Mom's right. You need to relax."

Relax? How could I relax?

Maybe there was another way of working this out. I glanced around. No windows, no clock, no idea what time it might be. It could still be late evening, or the sun might be up, or days may have passed for all I knew.

I pressed my eyes shut. No, it couldn't be midnight or one in the morning. I couldn't have failed. I had to have made it. Surely I couldn't have put my parents through all this, only for me to vanish from the face of the earth in a few hours. That'd be too cruel. That wasn't what I wanted.

Eyes wide open, I stared at my mother. "What time is it?"

"We're so glad to have you back. Just take it easy."

She must've seen the fear in my face, in my expression, in the tendons straining in my neck. This was anything but easy.

I jerked my head up. "Just tell me what time it is and I'll calm down."

Dad put his hand on my forehead, pressing my head

back onto the pillow. "It's six in the morning. You got through the night."

I'd got through much more than that.

It had worked.

I couldn't believe it, except I could. The relief was too much for me. The air left my body and a low groan escaped my body.

"Are you okay?" Mom asked.

I nodded. I'd never been better in my life. My new life, starting today.

Mom swayed on the spot. Her lips tight, she tried to hold it in but clearly that wasn't going to work. Her body shook and sobs overtook her.

"We thought we'd lost you," she said between whimpers.

Guilt washed over me. I had done this to her, caused this pain.

Behind her, Dad stood up straight. Though his expression was even, a muscle in his jaw flinched. He was being strong, for his wife, for his daughter, but there was no hiding what I'd done to him, to them, my family.

A hundred emotions rolled over me. Never before had I felt so good and bad at the same time. My heart raced. My heart was beating, here in Altabena. I'd made it. I hadn't meant to hurt them.

"We know what you tried to do," Dad said. "And we're sorry."

They were sorry? Poor Dad couldn't even say the word, couldn't admit out loud that he thought I'd attempted suicide, though there was no other rational explanation for what had happened.

No, I wanted to say. That wasn't it at all. I wanted to

live so desperately. I wanted life and this was the only way I could have it.

"It's hard being a teenager," Mom said. "I remember now, but I'd forgotten. There was so much pressure on you with moving to a new town, and changing schools and making new friends and trying to fit in. We should've kept more of an eye on you. Then we could've been there for you."

"Don't blame yourself." I shifted my gaze from her to my father. "You guys are wonderful."

"Things got too much for you." She'd stopped sobbing, at least. "There's a huge world and everything looks scary when you're a teenager."

She had no idea how vast the universe was, no idea how serious my adversaries, no idea what I'd been fighting.

"You got that right," I said.

Now she'd started it seemed there was no stopping her. "You don't have the life experience that we do. I'm not saying we're better than you, just older. We know you can ride through the hard parts of life and that you'll make it. You're such a bright girl and you've got your whole life ahead of you, so much to look forward to. College, career, family, travel. There's a lifetime of fun and excitement coming your way. It'll be hard work at times too but that's just the way it is. Anything can happen. There are so many possibilities."

"There are," I said.

It was all ahead of me. *Now.*

"However bad things seem, they always get better," she added.

My parents were too kind and my guilt ran deep. Mom was so grateful to have me back that she couldn't say a bad word. Dad too.

I cleared my throat. "One more thing. What about Ben?"

Dad raised his eyebrows. "You know he saved your life by calling an ambulance?"

I nodded. He had saved me.

He must've got rid of the cannulas and tubing before the paramedics arrived, must've come up with a convincing story and taken care of the details.

"He's outside in the hallway," Dad said. "He wouldn't leave."

Ben...

My reason for being here.

He was the future.

CHAPTER THIRTY-FIVE

Ben and I kept to the back of the room. I'd been to military funerals before, but never a civilian one and this was my first visit to a funeral parlor, also my first big outing since getting out of hospital. I'd been to school, of course, but that didn't count.

The chapel by the crematorium wasn't such a bad place. Padded benches and chairs were laid out in rows in front of a small podium. The walls were mushroom colored, the carpet a rich burgundy, the tones soothing. Maybe I did like shades of pink after all.

Earlier the guests had been milling around, a healthy buzz in the air. The room was silent now except for the sound of heavy breathing and the occasional sob. Every seat was taken so Ben and I remained standing. A crowded room meant we wouldn't be noticed, exactly as we wanted.

At the front, the funeral director took over and the first of the speeches began. I couldn't help but notice how personal this was, how intimate, despite the number of people here. It wasn't like a military funeral where some general talked about the values of the armed forces and the virtues of New Nation. Here the speakers spoke heartfelt words about the ninety-year-old man who'd died, a brother, father, grandfather; a man who'd lived a good life and had people who loved him.

I looked around at the mourners. Death and loss were hard to handle no matter the person's age. Maybe it was his time, I don't know. I only knew it wasn't my time or Ben's.

Coming here had been Ben's idea. I didn't want my superiors to trace me so I'd disabled my two PR devices as best I could, however the only way to dispose of them thoroughly was to burn them. A regular fire didn't burn at the right intensity. It took a fire of about nine hundred degrees centigrade to incinerate the devices. A cremation fire.

So here we were, the only two people at the funeral who weren't experiencing a huge loss.

Last night I'd taken a look at the only photo remaining in New Nation of Ben Tanner. It was imprinted in my mind. I'd never forget it.

Maybe this was how it was going to happen all along. Maybe I was always going to be sent back in time at which point I'd decide to help Ben. Maybe we were both always going to live through this. Maybe I was always going to meet Ben and be with him.

Who knows? We still had choices, plenty of chances to stuff things up or make them right, depending on our decisions.

I wondered about Lucien. How much did he know? I'd thought he was as bad as the generals who'd sent me to my death – worse, in fact, because he'd been like a father to me.

Perhaps that picture had told him something the generals didn't know. Perhaps it had told him I had a chance. Perhaps he hadn't betrayed me after all and had instead given me life and a future.

I'd never know the truth.

I still found the picture slightly freaky. More than slightly if I was to be honest. I didn't want to think about it. Luckily Ben hadn't cottoned on and I was happy to leave it that way. How could I explain it to him when there was so much I didn't understand?

Ben nudged me. "Nicola, people are paying their respects now."

At the front of the room, a middle-aged man had his arm around a weeping woman who leaned over the open casket. He led her away to make way for the other guests who were queuing up to place their hand on the edge of the casket or throw rose petals in from a basket.

Ben ushered me ahead of him to join them. I hoped this wasn't disrespectful because we meant no harm to the man who'd passed away or his family. Ben had the two slender PR devices in his hand and slid them into the casket along its satin lining.

I tossed a handful of petals in the casket and said goodbye. To the man whose name I didn't know, to the two PR devices, to my old life.

One thing was for sure. I was never going back to New Nation, no matter what.

We didn't stay longer than we needed to. The casket and its contents would be cremated regardless. We watched the casket as it was transported along a conveyor belt into the crematorium, and left.

Outside it was glary with a few small gray clouds in the

sky. A light drizzle fell on us as we walked, more like a wet haze than a proper shower. I didn't think it was anything to worry about but the few people who were around took shelter in the surrounding buildings. The wide red brick path we walked along was lined on either side with attractive garden beds, the smell of mulch rising from the damp soil.

Ben turned right at the end of the path but I tapped him on the shoulder and pointed the other way. "Look."

He stopped and smiled. A rainbow, albeit a weak one that was fading.

Returning his smile, I joined him and we ambled up the sidewalk. This was what life was about – friends, family and relationships. And the occasional rainbow. It was about enjoying every moment, no matter how small.

Still, I had to be aware. I couldn't let my guard down for a moment. Neither could Ben.

"It's not over yet," I said as we walked.

Ben squeezed my hand. "I know."

My superior officers wouldn't stop. They'd send someone else. And next time it'd be harder.

In the meantime, I had now.

I had a future.

REGENERATION (BOOK 2)

Nicola Gray is a typical, slightly awkward high school student. Or so she appears. In reality Nicola is a hyper-fit, elite soldier from the brutal New Nation of the future. Her superior officers have given soldier Gray strict orders to eliminate their greatest threat, Ben Tanner. Her boyfriend.

And New Nation will not give up.

Nicola fights as only she knows how to keep Ben and those around her safe. Pushed beyond limits, she grapples with questions of love and loyalty, right and wrong, life and death. Nicola has a line she will not cross. But that's exactly what she must do...

VALIDATION (BOOK 3)

School's out for Nicola Grey but just as the party is about to begin, she is hauled back to the future to brutal New Nation. Suddenly she's hailed as a hero of the people when that's the last thing she wants and this is the last place she wants to be. *How did things go so wrong?*

Nicola is desperate to get back where she belongs – with boyfriend Ben, in the past. But that isn't going to happen, not when millions will die in a world decimated by a deadly virus, her country ruled by a despotic regime. Unless she can stop it.

It's Nicola versus New Nation. She has to change the future and save the world.

ABOUT THE AUTHOR

Susanna Rogers is the author of kick butt books for young adults. She also writes romance and at one point moved to a life of crime – you might be seeing more of that. She loves writing young adult, partly because she's an overgrown teenager and partly because she can write the kick butt heroines she adores. She's also a kickboxer and dreams of empowering girls and guys around the globe to believe in themselves, to take care and follow their own dreams.

Susanna believes in love and kicking ass and a little bit of murder here and there.

She would love to hear from you – susannarogers.com.

If you like her books, please post a review on Amazon or Goodreads. She'd like that a lot!